HOUSE OF INTRIGUE

HOUSE OF INTRIGUE

Yvonne Strickland

This book is a work of fiction.
In real life, make sure you practise safe sex.

First published in 1995 by
Nexus
332 Ladbroke Grove
London W10 5AH

Copyright © Yvonne Strickland 1995

Typeset by TW Typesetting, Plymouth, Devon
Printed and bound by
BPC Paperbacks Ltd, Aylesbury, Bucks

ISBN 0 352 33055 4

1

The Wheel Turns

He ran his hand across her warm cheek, pushing the hair aside from her ear.

'So I can't get you to change your mind? It's your final decision?'

'Yes,' she replied quietly, the candlelight gleaming in her hazel-brown eyes, 'my final decision.' She looked down at her hands and bit her lip. 'It isn't that I'm not very fond of you Richard, believe me, but I couldn't think of settling down. There are too many other things – things you cannot understand. Anyway, I booked the flight last week, you know I did.'

'OK,' he said, laying down his knife and fork and pushing aside the empty plate. 'But can't we keep in touch – won't you give me a post box address or even a phone number?'

'Richard . . . please, I've told you I can't. Look, you have my mother's address; if you still want to keep in touch, she will forward your letters on to me.'

He remained silent for almost a minute, lifting his glass and drinking a little red wine as he watched her eyes. His gaze took in her soft, light brown hair, which tumbled about her naked shoulders, the silver locket she always wore but was so secretive about, her firm breasts confined by the thin material of the white dress. He thought of how intimately each had come to know the other and how very sensual she could be when she was aroused.

'You can't blame me, can you though?' he said at length. 'You're young and very beautiful, and I feel as if I've known you for a great deal longer than I really have.'

1

'Yes.' She smiled, reaching over the table to place her hand over his. 'And nobody has ever been sweeter to me than you. I've thought a few times that if I –'

'Excuse me, sir, madam,' cut in a voice at their side, 'will you be requiring desserts?'

He glanced from the waiter to Karen, his head tilted questioningly to one side.

'Er . . . no, I think I've had enough,' she said. 'Just a coffee perhaps.'

They stepped from the warm intimacy of the dimly lit restaurant and out into the side street. The night air was chilling and damp and the dark pavements glistened wet in the impersonal glow of the street lamps. Karen pulled her fawn raincoat around her.

They reached the car in its parking bay, a short distance from the main road. Opening the doors, he was about to speak, when even his thoughts were drowned by the shrieking hee-haw, hee-haw, hee-haw of two police cars and an ambulance, careering by among the chaos of moving vehicles, their glaring blue lights flashing out a new discord within the seething madness of the traffic. They fell into the car and slammed the doors.

He took her hand and said, 'You know I'm up in Birmingham tomorrow afternoon. I won't even be able to drive you to the airport because I can't get back in time.' He switched on the engine without taking his eyes from her. 'Look, what I'm saying is, why not come back to my hotel for another hour or two and we can drive around to your flat later. I don't want to say goodbye until we absolutely have to. What do you say?'

She smiled in the dim light, the illumination from the instrument panel glinting in her eyes.

'I've got a better idea if you feel like it.'

'What's that?'

'Well, it's no more bother for me to cook breakfast for two instead of one.' They leaned towards each other and kissed. 'We can still have a drink or two at your hotel first though, if you want to collect a few things from your room.'

2

'D'you know,' he responded with a broad smile as he put the engine into gear, 'I might just go along with that idea!'

They moved slowly through the city streets, through the glaring lights and rearing dark forms of sleeping office blocks with windows blank and anonymous against the darker night sky. The traffic moved, then slowed, then stopped for a time and began to move again in a hesitant, growling stream of glaring and blinking lights.

'Here comes more rain,' he breathed.

The wipers began to hum and squeak away the crawling minutes.

'I'm lost,' said Karen, wiping the condensation from her side window and peering into the semi-frozen river of lights.

'Next main junction and we turn on to Bayswater Road – not too far after that.'

She looked through the window again but there was not the churning of lights in the rain, nor the shifting back and forth of nameless people across the wet streets and pavements. Instead, she closed her eyes and saw the calm blue sky, open and smiling across the vineyards. There was the white villa with its terracotta roof, its portico and its windows, letting in the sunlight through open green shutters. There were the gardens and the pine woods, and across the valley, the distant sea. There were her friends and there was Sonia, head of the little empire whose tentacles of licentious indulgence reached, through her girls, into the highest levels of European government and finance. Sonia, whose house in Languedoc, the house where Karen had taken up employment the previous year, was used for the commercial recording of diverse and bizarre acts of sexuality. This was the Sonia who Karen had resisted for a time but within whose web of sensual darkness she had become so hopelessly entangled.

'You've gone very quiet,' he said, smiling across at her.

'Oh, have I?' She smiled back at him. 'I was just wondering when this awful traffic jam would end.'

'Not long now.' The traffic lights changed to green and they began to edge forward.

'You don't really want to swap all this for an uneventful life out in the sticks, do you?' he continued.

'You must be joking,' she breathed.

Once on the main thoroughfare and heading away from London, their progress improved. Soon, over to their right, a large, modern hotel proclaimed itself in a rising slab of light against the sky.

'Are you going to wait in the bar?' he asked, as they pulled up a little distance from the main entrance.

'Oh . . . er, no,' she hesitated, 'I've changed my mind about coming inside. I'll stay here and listen to the radio. You won't be long, will you?'

'Is it as posh as it looks?' she asked, glancing back at the glittering hotel as he negotiated their way back out into the traffic.

'I've stayed in a lot worse, I can tell you.'

The wipers hissing to and fro with hypnotic rhythm reminded her of that day, which now seemed a lifetime ago, when the cab had collected her from the shop doorway and taken her on that uncertain journey to the interview with Sonia.

The trees and iron railings of Kensington Gardens drifted by on their left in the dark rain and Karen mused, 'It must be very pleasant here in the summer.'

'Steady on,' he laughed, 'we're halfway through May already. It isn't the Mediterranean, you know!'

'No,' she answered, 'it isn't.'

'Oh well,' he went on, 'wherever you end up later this week, next stop is Notting Hill.'

'You have a nice little place here,' he remarked, watching her draw the red velvet curtains across the lounge windows. 'And only a few minutes walk from the underground.'

'Mmm, it's not bad, is it,' she agreed, turning to meet his gaze. She picked up her fawn raincoat from the back of the chair and walked over to the bedroom. 'Bring your coat in here if you like,' came her voice. 'There's plenty of hanging room – I've already packed a lot of my things.'

4

He pulled off his jacket and followed her through, noting as he did so the two small suitcases resting on the floor by the end of the double bed.

'My travel bag – will it be OK in here too?'

'Of course,' she said, smiling at him. 'Unless you've changed your mind about staying.'

'Er . . . no, I hadn't actually,' he answered, watching her slim body in her short white dress as she pushed the two cases back against the wall.

She turned and moved back over to him.

'Thank you for a lovely evening, Richard. I really have enjoyed myself.'

He put his arms about her waist and kissed her. 'I'm sorry about all the hold-ups.'

She returned his kiss, enveloping him with her perfumed warmth. He pulled her closer still and his lips moved from her mouth to her soft neck and down over her bare shoulder.

'Look, I'm going to take a quick shower and get changed.' She stepped back and pushed her hair over her shoulders. 'If you want to get us both a drink, there's some Scotch in the kitchen cupboard. It's all the booze I've got, I'm afraid.'

He watched her walk slowly towards the bathroom, her hands above her neck, seeking the zip fastener at the back of her collar. She hesitated at the doorway, pulling down the zipper as far as her reach would allow. An arm passed around her waist and she closed her eyes. His lips brushed about the back of her neck, making her body tingle. The zip fastener continued downwards until it reached her waist. The dress fell away from her shoulders. The insistent lips moved to the side of her neck and to her cheek while the hands moved about her and firmly cupped her naked breasts, fingers and thumbs gently squeezing the hardening nipples. She could feel his arousal against her behind.

'Is there room for two in there?' he whispered.

She twisted her head and smiled. 'Only just.'

A minute later, he was in the shower with her.

'You're right about it being cramped,' he laughed, holding

5

her close to him under the hot, cascading water. 'It certainly wasn't built for two!'

They lathered each other liberally with pink shower gel, the thick foam building up and swirling about their feet. His penis, hard and inflamed, slid sometimes around the base of her warm stomach, sometimes between her legs, the head slipping easily, but only so far, between the lubricated folds of her sex. Their hands played a voluptuous game with each other's bodies. He splashed the foam away from her breasts and let his mouth close upon her nipples, sucking and teasing them in turn with his tongue until they were reddened and hard. Their fingers played the game of lust, his stroking deeply into her, feeling her relaxed and unresisting, hers closing about his erection and working it slowly back and forth so that his fingers dug into her flesh and he groaned softly.

'We'll never do it in here!' she laughed. 'There's not enough room.'

'Never mind,' he breathed into her ear. 'There are other ways.'

Slowly he eased himself downwards, his lips brushing past her breasts and down her soft stomach, glistening and running with water, until he reached the firmer and silk smooth flesh above her vulva. He liked the absence of hair about her sex and had been curious enough to want to ask her about it, but never considered the time appropriate. Now he was on his knees, his hands running down the curves of her body, his mouth pressed against the lips of her sex, his tongue darting about the core of her sensuality. She was pushed hard back against the cubicle wall, her hands resting on his head, and he moved his knees to either side of her feet in the restricting yet intimate little world of warmth and water. He began to move her legs apart and she responded by placing a foot either side of him so that he could bring his knees together, all the better to gain access to that which he most desired. His tongue rioted within her sex and he was aware of the tension rising within her body as her fingers clawed in ecstasy against his scalp. With his left hand, he reached under her behind and,

6

finding the area between the cheeks slippery with undissolved shower gel, he moved his finger down until he found the little rosebud of her anus. Her body stiffened abruptly as his finger entered there, and meeting little resistance he moved ever further into her. She slid a little down the cubicle wall, pressing down harder on his head and further parting her legs. He knew it would be wrong of him to stop now, even though his own organ of lust had not yet entered the stage, but still waited, fretting and eager in the wings. Her pelvis thrust harder against his face, and while his tongue played its exquisite game, his finger probed deeper into her rear, making her push down harder still. He felt and tasted her climax approaching; heard her breath coming in hoarse gasps; felt her wet body quivering. Then she cried out as if falling from a precipice, her thighs writhing against him until her orgasm was done.

They stood facing each other once more in the crystal torrent and kissed. She felt the head of his penis, hot and eager, butting and chafing against her sex like a thoroughbred at the starting gate, impatient to lunge forward. He caught his breath as her fingers closed and caressed about it and their lips met again for a few moments. She lowered herself down to her knees before him, one hand still about the swollen shaft, the other, with fingernails extended, coursing down his spine. He let out a soft 'Aaah' as her lips closed over the head and her hand slipped under his scrotum. Leaning forward above her, he rested his hands against the back of the cubicle, closing his eyes and feeling her tongue tease and circle maddeningly about him. She moved down further, taking over half of his erection into her until she could accept no more. He, almost involuntarily, moved his pelvis back and forth and felt the flames begin to rise and take control of him, oblivious now to the hissing cascade upon his shoulders and back and aware only of his aching desire within the urgent caress of her mouth. The tide was rising within him and he knew he was about to lose all control. He expected that any moment she would stop and allow her hand to take over for the final act but she did not. As the inevitable approached, he threw back his head.

'Christ! I'm going to . . . I'm going to . . !'

She held him more tightly as he ejaculated, drinking fully the milk of his passion as his pelvis jerked before her in blissful release.

She eyed him from the bedroom as she pulled the deep pink housecoat about her and fastened the belt around her waist. With a bath towel wound round the lower half of his body and a tumbler part filled with Scotch in one hand, he sat relaxing in one of the easy chairs. On the low table before him stood another glass waiting for her. As she entered the room, he rose and smiled, picking up the tumbler and holding it out to her.

'I think we both need this.'

'I suppose so,' she said, smiling, and sat down in the chair next to his.

The radio played soft, cool jazz and they both sat and listened, neither of them feeling inclined to speak for the moment. Karen looked into her glass and swirled its amber contents gently about, reflecting upon what had so recently transpired in the shower. Whether he realised it or not, it was the first time she had done that for a man; the first time she had let it go to the ultimate in that way.

She thought of the others, at the house in Languedoc. To most of them, including those considerably younger than her 23 years, such an act would be a part of their sexual repertoire. To her, a few months ago, it would have been unthinkable. Had her stay in France and her experiences at the house changed her outlook so very much? She had been brought up to believe in the sanctity of marriage and to honour the chastity which, it was said, should prevail outside that institution. She did not regard her relationship with an old school friend, a relationship which had been expressed physically as well as emotionally, as unusual. In the all-girl environment of the school, where she first became aware of her physical needs, such relationships were regarded as normal and, indeed, often

8

encouraged by the very people whose role it was to further the moral well-being of those in their charge. The fact that she had not married but had continued her relationship with Sandra was part of a life which had moved beyond the narrow horizon of her tutors. And so her life had continued, until that final traumatic break; the break which had in the end sent her out into the wider world and, ultimately, to the house in France. Outwardly, she had for so long affected a reluctance when it came to sexual expression with others but her time in employment at the house had forced her to admit, if only to herself, that her desires could not forever be treated as a burdensome inconvenience.

And there was Sonia. With Sonia she had identified and established a relationship which now seemed even more significant than when they were together at the house. There were many doors yet to be unlocked, many dark and secret places to explore and experience. They were not to be found here.

She felt a hand on her knee.

'What are you thinking about?' he asked.

'Oh, I . . . nothing much. Well, I suppose I was wondering when, or if, I would see London again.'

'And what about me?' he asked, running his fingers slowly up the front of her thigh.

She looked into his eyes and placed her hand over his.

'Perhaps if you came to France – I can always take time off. It wouldn't be a problem.'

'Yes, I'd like that. A week in Paris in the summer – how does that sound?'

She smiled. 'It sounds OK to me.'

'Is that a promise?'

'Yes, it's a promise, but you must give me plenty of warning – a couple of weeks at least.'

'I'll do my best,' he said, his hand tightening on her leg. He leaned over the side of the chair to kiss her and she leaned across the arm towards him. 'It's awkward on these chairs, isn't it?' He grinned, patting the two upholstered arms separating them.

9

'It depends on what you are trying to do,' she responded coyly.

But it was obvious what he was hoping to do from the bulge at the front of the towel which he was attempting, with little success, to conceal. Karen smiled to herself, aware of the currents stirring again within her own body.

He stood up and moved around in front of her, then leaned forward and rested his hands upon the arms of the chair at either side so that their faces were a short distance apart. She pretended not to notice his arousal, obvious though it was through the towel. He leaned further forward still and their lips met as she placed her arms around his shoulders. Their lips remained together, burning and inflaming. His hand lifted from the chair and moved down to her waist, pulling at the belt of her gown until it loosened and came free. Their lips were still together when he parted the gown and when her hand reached beneath the towel to quickly find and close upon the engorged and eager shaft. She parted her legs to allow him closer, feeling his penis lying hot and pulsing against her stomach. Their kisses continued more fervently, she taking his organ in her cool hand once more and working him back and forth as she had in the shower cubicle.

After a few moments he pulled away, causing her to release her hold on him, while his mouth closed upon her breasts, circling the erect nipples with his tongue and sucking hard at them in turn. She could see his head moving further down and over her stomach and feeling his lips and hot breath over the firm smooth skin above her sex. She closed her eyes, impatient and ready for him to strike. As his tongue began its wicked game around and within her sex, he placed a hand under each of her knees and lifted her legs up and further apart, bringing them to rest so that they hung over each side of the chair arms, causing her to slip downward and forward in the seat. The tides of lust running through her body were becoming ever stronger and soon she began to lose control of herself. Her breath became shorter and a soft moan passed through her open mouth.

10

'He must, now!' she heard herself saying. 'He must, now!'

But still he did not. Instead, he again seized her legs and rose from the floor as he pushed them up and back until they were hard against the head-rest of her chair and she was doubled up and pinned beneath, sinking down into the seat until she was looking up at him through her wide-spread thighs. With her behind lifted clear of the chair and pointed almost upwards, she was spread with her most intimate parts open to his gaze and to anything he desired to do. Keeping a firm grip on her knees, he arched his body over her and she watched through half-closed eyes as the glistening head of his shaft slid with tantalising slowness to and fro between the inflamed lips of her sex. She closed her eyes tightly, the word 'please' forming repeatedly but inaudibly on her mouth, her mind and body desperate for relief he would not allow her. He tormented her for endless mental pleadings until she was on the verge of begging loudly. At last he struck, entering her hard and deep, making her cry out with ecstasy now the final surge through the gates of fulfilment had begun. She wanted to pull him deeper into her and engulf him as each stroke brought them both sweeping and spinning, abandoned and plunging, into the whirlpool of orgasm.

It was morning, and a cold, grey light filtered weakly through a chink in the heavy green curtains. At the bedside, the radio alarm blinked to 7.30 and music began to play. Karen had been awake for almost an hour. She glanced at him. He had not responded to the sound of the radio but remained with his face half buried in the pillow, fast asleep. Slowly and quietly she arose from the bed and in the dim light, made her way to the bathroom.

When she emerged, he was awake and seated on the edge of the dishevelled bed.

'Breakfast?' she asked.

'Yes please,' he answered, reaching down for his travel bag. 'God, I don't usually sleep so late.'

She moved towards the doorway and then turned. 'I

hope you have a good appetite. We need to use everything up.'

'Yes, of course, you're off today.'

She sensed the disappointment in his voice. As she pulled open the lounge curtains, letting in the grey light, she said to herself, 'He's a nice guy; I could do a lot worse.'

She was well aware that they had the foundations of a strong relationship and just as aware of the deeper and darker one which was calling her back to the house in France. She placed her hand on the locket above her breasts and saw in her mind those dark eyes searching into her and waiting for her to return. She had phoned Sonia five days ago, in the afternoon, to say she was coming back. Kim had answered the office phone to say that Sonia was away, and so Kim was the first to know. Sonia had contacted her the next morning. She had not sounded over-joyed, but Karen had expected that, for it was not in her character to express her emotions too much. Instead, she had spoken softly, as though she was whispering very closely to the phone. 'I'm very glad, my dear.' She had said little more than that. There was no need. Somehow, that voice and those dark eyes filled so much of her mind that there was no room left for anyone else.

A few minutes later they sat at the table; plates empty, coffee half finished, the odour of bacon and eggs still hanging in the air. Outside, a car alarm warbled its electronic message to no avail.

On the radio, a voice announced the nine o'clock news. Karen listened with only moderate attention. Her interest awakened as the voice continued: '. . . is alleged to have spent three evenings at the apartment of a high-class prostitute while in Brussels helping to negotiate Britain's share of farm subsidies.'

'Oh well,' said Karen, wondering if any of Sonia's girls were involved. 'As long as someone gets something out of it in the end.'

'Wouldn't be so bad if they didn't preach to the rest of us,' he commented. 'I see you find it all amusing.'

'Yes, I do,' she replied, smiling, the images of Annette,

12

Cheryl and the others passing vividly through her mind. 'I find it very amusing indeed.'

He looked at her intently. 'Here, you're not involved in . . . I mean, you're not . . . is that why you won't say where you work or what you do?'

Karen lifted her hand to the side of her face and laughed. 'Do I strike you as being that well off? The work I do is very ordinary, it really is. And don't think I'm being awkward with you if I can't say where it is. I promised not to for good reasons – you have to believe me.'

'Yes, I know, and we've been through it several times before. I thought it might be worth a last try.'

'Yes, I can understand,' she said. She glanced at her watch. 'We have to make a move soon whether we like it or not. You have to be in Birmingham by three and I have a bit of packing and clearing up before the landlord shows up for the keys.'

As they left the table he put his hand gently on her shoulder.

'I wish I had time to drive you to the airport but if we were quick, maybe I could at least get you to the terminal. You'd have to wait around there a while I know, but . . .'

'Sweetheart,' she said, kissing him, 'don't worry. We both know you don't have time and even if you did, it's all arranged now. I'm going straight from here to Gatwick by minicab.'

'God! That must be costing you a fortune.'

'It's er . . . well it's all paid for by the people I work for.'

'They must want you back very badly,' he continued, helping her to clear the dishes.

'Yes, I suppose they do,' she answered quietly.

He carried her two small suitcases down to the ground floor and placed them in the dim hallway behind the oak front door, with its Victorian stained glass filtering the outside light through in red and green.

They stepped out into the small redbrick porch. A fine drizzle filtered through the cool air. They held each other for a few moments. Her eyes were brimming with hot tears.

'I'm sorry it's like this,' she whispered. 'You're a lovely man.'

'Never mind,' he said, kissing her lips, 'next time I see you it will be warm and sunny, and in the evening I'll take you out for the best dinner you ever had – I promise.'

She watched and waved as his car disappeared around the street corner and on to the main road. She glanced across the street to the dry area of tarmac where his car had stood. Someone else had already pulled up there and was preparing to back in and take the space.

Glancing at her watch, she saw it was now 10.15. She had 45 minutes to wait before the minicab was due – time enough to pay a visit to the nearby shops to buy a few items she had persuaded herself she ought to have before she left.

It was on her way back, as she passed a small row of shops, that a voice called out from a doorway, 'Got any change to spare, love?'

She turned, startled, to see a youth with greasy, bedraggled hair and old, soiled leather jacket approaching and staring hard at her with his hand outstretched. Behind him, sprawled in the doorway, were two others of similar demeanour and attire, one of them evidently asleep, the other clutching at a small black dog and staring with glazed eyes past her as though he did not comprehend her presence. She clutched her bag and hurried on.

On turning the corner of the street she slowed and breathed a sigh of relief. Outside the house stood the taxi. Inside it sat the driver, who having arrived earlier than the appointed time, sat quietly reading his newspaper.

'Not a very good spring so far, is it?' he mused, as they pulled away from the kerb. Karen took a final look at the flat where she had spent the last few weeks. Parting from almost anywhere was sad, she thought. The comfortable little flat was no exception.

'Yes, it's not very inspiring,' she agreed, looking at the people outside with their black umbrellas and expressionless faces.

14

'Whatever happened to global warming eh, miss?' he asked, grinning broadly.

She smiled back at his creased and worldly-wise face with its bushy moustache and bristled jaw. At least she was travelling to the airport with the prospect of agreeable companionship. This cab company, she thought, must have some arrangement with Sonia. They must carry her girls, perhaps some of her clients here in town. Karen wondered who, and where. She wondered too, if the ice-cool Cheryl who ran part of the operation in London or the wily Annette who spent much of her time at the house, had sat in this very cab and perhaps chatted to this same man.

'You going somewhere nice, miss?' he asked, cutting into her thoughts.

'Oh, yes, the south of France.'

'It'll be warm and sunny there if I'm not mistaken,' he continued.

'Yes,' she mused, 'I daresay it will.'

Thanks to the good-humoured conversation of the driver, the journey to the airport had been pleasant. Nevertheless, she was glad to be among the bright lights and semi-chaotic bustle of the terminal building. Unlike some people she had known, who found airports a daunting prospect, she regarded most airports, and this airport in particular, as a gateway to freedom.

With her cases checked in, Karen had an hour to pass, alone among the throng. At least the flight from Gatwick to Montpellier was running on time. She touched the silver locket with her fingers. Not so very long now.

'There we are,' announced Pauline coolly, tightening the last strap at the girl's waist so that the cocoon of black leather enclosed her body tightly from neck to just above her hips. Jackie's arms, located within the internal sleeve of the restraining garment, were held immobile and folded across her middle. Her blouse and skirt lay across a nearby chair, though she still wore her small, black lace briefs, her stay-up stockings with their elasticated lace tops, and her black high-heel sandals with their thin ankle straps keeping them in place.

Pauline, exercising her dominant role in looks as well as behaviour, wore an open neck, long-sleeved blouse of heavy black satin which offered a stark contrast to her silver-blonde pageboy hairstyle. It contrasted too with the fawn jodhpurs and complemented her tight, knee-length riding boots in immaculately cleaned and polished black leather.

She moved away and around to her desk, saying nothing, watched by the anxious and equally silent Jackie, who stood in the middle of the room. Jackie was often subject to restraint. Sometimes it was in the 'line of duty'; in her role as the damsel in distress or as the victim of evil machinations in the dramas played out and recorded in designated parts of the house. She knew it might be so here as well, for ever alert Pauline, always quick to catch her out for some trivial misdemeanour, had recorded her supposedly private punishments in this room several times before.

Apprehension would not beset her unless she knew she was guilty of serious transgression, but on this occasion she could recall no reason why she should be standing here wearing the straitjacket unless, perhaps, she had overlooked some minor task in her duties. If that was the case, she could expect to be kept like this for the rest of the afternoon to prevent her from going down to the pool or joining the others for a game of tennis.

'Now,' said Pauline, leaning back in her green leather chair, her hands placed in front of her on the desk top, 'how long have you known she was coming back?'

The word 'she' was emphasised with more than a hint of spite.

'Known . . . who?'

'Now don't be stupid,' answered Pauline, regarding her with the fixed gaze of her cold blue eyes, 'you know perfectly well who I'm referring to. Miss Prim and Proper, that's who.'

Jackie shook her long, light brown hair nervously and it spilled down over the black leather.

'Well, speak!' shouted Pauline, rising from the chair. 'And don't dare tell me any of your silly lies!'

'I . . . I can't remember exactly; just the other day. That's all, honestly!'

Pauline reached down to the desk and pulled open a drawer. When she moved away from the desk and into full view, Jackie saw what she held and moved a step backward. She looked not at Pauline's stern expression, but at the small, black, braided leather whip curled up in her right hand.

'No! No, please! Don't use that on me!'

'I want to know who told you and when, and I want to know right now!' She grasped Jackie's shoulder and pulled her around. 'Now!' she repeated, bringing the whip down sharply across the girl's thinly-veiled behind.

Jackie let out a shriek and twisted her body from side to side against the restraint, knowing as she did so that such effort was quite futile.

'All right! I found out a week ago. I heard somebody say in the bar.'

'Who?' demanded Pauline.

'I don't know, I don't know, you must believe me!' The whip descended with a crack, making the girl jerk and cry out once more. She looked at Pauline with tears welling in her eyes. 'Please! I don't want to get anyone into trouble. Please!' The whip raised again and Jackie flinched. 'I think . . . I think it might have been Kim.'

'Good! We're getting there. Now, why didn't you come and tell me?'

Jackie hesitated, fearful of saying the wrong thing.

'I thought you'd know. I was sure you did.'

'And what have I told you in the past?'

'What . . . what do you mean?'

'You silly little bitch!' shouted Pauline, bringing the whip down for a third time with greater force than before. Jackie shrieked, then began to cry. 'Now! What have I told you to do when you see and hear things?'

She looked at Pauline with warm tears streaming down her face. 'You've told me to come and tell you, just to make sure.'

17

'Right! And as so often, you take not a bit of bloody notice until you get a damn good hiding!'

'But you're making me tell tales on people,' Jackie moaned. 'It's not fair! You know it's not fair!'

'I'll tell you what's fair!' growled Pauline. 'What's fair is that I do my job – the job Sonia pays me to do – and that is making sure you all keep to the rules. Her rules, not mine! What you think about it doesn't matter but I need to know at all times what is going on! Do you understand?'

'Yes! All right! Yes!'

'Yes! All the animals in the zoo might be lovely to look at but we still need a keeper whether you and the rest of them agree with it or not.' She walked slowly around the trembling Jackie, curling the black whip around her hand then straightening it out again. 'I don't know why Sonia's having her back. Anyone could do her job, even you. Your problem is your mouth. When you ought to keep it shut you open it and when you should speak out you don't. It seems to me keeping you under more control and out of mischief would be better for both of us.' Jackie looked at her and opened her mouth slightly as if to speak, but no words came out. 'If you want your freedom, you'll have to earn it, especially when she's back. Keep me informed about what everyone is up to and you can keep on enjoying the pool and the tennis, as well as the bar in the evenings. Carry on as you are and you'll find things very different, just the way they are going to be for the rest of this afternoon.'

'What? What do you mean?' She glanced down at her arms, encased in the tight leather restraint. 'I can't do anything like this, can I?'

'You ought to know better than that by now,' remarked Pauline, eyeing her from head to toe.

Jackie waited as Pauline disappeared into the sinister darkened room, opposite to the side where her desk stood, a room with which Jackie had previous acquaintance. When she reappeared, she carried a black plastic bag which she placed down on a small circular table.

'Sit down on there,' she ordered, indicating one of the

low, green leather stools which stood by the table. Jackie obeyed in silence.

'You'll wear this until six o'clock,' said Pauline, moving behind her. But Jackie, trembling in apprehension again, did not see what Pauline held in her hands. Moments later she knew, for the leather harness was placed over her head and the room vanished into darkness as the two triangular leather pads were fitted over her eyes. No sooner were the straps of the harness partially adjusted than the rubber ball was pushed into her mouth. The buckles swished and rattled as the straps were tightened about her head and under her chin, pressing the soft pads more firmly over her eyes and holding the ball securely in her open mouth.

It was when Pauline knelt down to place the short leather straps around her legs that she noticed the small area of moisture at the front of Jackie's briefs. She had expected that. She knew how easily aroused Jackie was and how the restraints and punishments would at once excite her and at the same time prevent her from achieving her desires.

'You'll sit here quietly and without moving,' she said, fastening up the leg straps. 'If you make a fuss or move around, you know what to expect, don't you?'

The sky over Montpellier was a clear, dusty blue and the sun low in the afternoon sky. The sound of the jet engines diminished as the aircraft banked around, preparing for its final descent. Shafts of bright sunlight sped along the cabin as they turned into the main runway approach. Karen peered out over the fields, vineyards and the lazy countryside, watching the ground swing about and rise towards her. She clutched at the edges of the in-flight magazine on her knee. Landings always made her nervous, regardless of the destination.

Once through the minor formalities, she emerged into the main concourse with her two cases perched on a baggage trolley. She looked about at the waiting crowd but of the soft face, light brown hair and welcoming smile she expected to see, there was no sign. She began walking across the concourse towards an area where there were fewer people, a place where she might be seen more easily.

'Karen! Wrong way!' came a voice from close behind her. She stopped and turned.

'Oh Val! Oh, it's great to see you!'

The Latin eyes and vivacious smile framed with long, crinkly black hair thrown about her shoulders greeted Karen.

'And you, love! I waved like mad back there but you didn't see me.'

Valerie took her by the shoulders and kissed her warmly on both cheeks. Karen kissed her in turn.

'I expected Kim . . . I thought that she was supposed to be –'

'I'll explain that later,' cut in Valerie. 'Let's get out to the taxi with your things.'

'Where are we going first?' asked Karen. 'Where's your car?'

'It's near the railway station,' said Valerie as they left the building. 'I thought you might want a bite to eat in the town before we head back.'

'Yes, OK, I didn't feel like eating on the plane but I could polish something off now. Have you anywhere in mind?'

'I certainly have,' replied Valerie, smiling, as they reached the taxi. 'Somewhere for a good nosh and a good old chinwag!'

During her previous stay at the house it was Valerie, in charge of the beauty parlour, and her assistant, Kim, who had given Karen her first orgasm there. True, it had been arranged by Pauline as a trick to embarrass her, but Karen, Valerie and Kim had understood this afterwards and it had not spoiled their friendship as Pauline had intended. Indeed, it had helped to open up within her the need to express her sexuality in ways she had never before imagined and to begin to understand the secret world of the dominant and the submissive. It had gone further still when she found her relationship with Sonia developing and it was the uncertainty of this which had decided her to return to England for a time.

That time was over, for gone was the uncertainty. And what of Richard now she was back in France? She thought of him now as a part of her past. A past never to be repeated.

2

Homecoming

The sound of a door, opening and closing softly, reached her ears. Her hearing was all that Jackie could rely on for the time being for she remained seated where Pauline had placed her. Why was the room so quiet? What was Pauline doing? She sighed, the air whistling faintly around the red rubber ball.

Was it just a trick? Was Pauline waiting for her to move about on the stool so as to find an excuse to use the whip again? But she could hardly move anything, only twist about a little. She decided that Pauline had left the room and that she was now quite alone to contemplate.

They both knew what punishment did to her. The whip hurt her and inflamed her sexually at the same time. Even the thought of its angry sting made the currents stir uncontrollably in her belly. The restraints too could provoke her arousal. She imagined herself helpless and on display in front of strangers, though the imagery in her mind was a product of memory rather than of fancy.

She squirmed her legs against the straps and worked her behind against the leather stool, feeling the stirring in her sex. After a time her breathing became louder and shorter. She began to twist about on the stool, gently at first, but then more vigorously. It was too late for her to stop. She couldn't stop even if a thousand doors opened, even if a thousand Paulines screamed at her. She rocked back and forth on the stool, moaning and gripping the rubber ball with her teeth.

Afterwards, she let out a long, deep sigh.

Only a few minutes seemed to have passed before the

sound of the opening door caused her to turn her head. She wanted to ask who it was but the quiet murmur she emitted was of no more use than the turning of her head in the darkness. She sensed someone approaching and at once sat rigid and upright.

'Hold still!' came the voice close to her ear.

Unseen fingers tugged at the head harness and the straps began to loosen. Light appeared at the sides of her eyes and Pauline, positioning a paper tissue under the rubber ball, withdrew it, glistening wet from Jackie's mouth, and lifted away the harness. Jackie blinked against the brightness and swallowed. The straps had left pink indents about her forehead, cheeks and chin and her jaw ached from the prolonged intrusion of the ball.

She looked directly ahead as the buckles lower down were loosened and her legs freed.

'Stand up while I undo this,' ordered Pauline, tugging at the back of the straitjacket. 'You can run off out and play in a minute,' she continued, 'and let's hope you remember what we agreed. I don't want to find that –' She hesitated and regarded the seat which Jackie had occupied until that moment. A streak of wet glistened on the padded green leather. Jackie saw the expression on her face and turned to see what had attracted her attention. At the same time a hand struck her across the mouth. 'You dirty little bitch! How did you . . ?'

'I couldn't help it!' moaned Jackie, cringing from the blow. 'It just happened!'

'Oh, just happened did it, madam?' responded Pauline sarcastically, her hands on her hips. 'Well, something else can "just happen" now. You'll wear the straitjacket for a while longer, in case you get up to more mischief!' Jackie backed away, almost stumbling, as she saw the whip picked up from the table. But the currents of fear and anticipation in her stomach calmed when Pauline coiled it around and held it in her fist. 'It won't do you any harm to be out of the way for an hour or so and I've got work to do.'

Pauline moved her towards the main door. Jackie

23

thought it better at this point not to question her intentions, let alone to resist, and soon found herself in the first floor corridor. The door clicked shut behind her and she was shepherded directly across to the door opposite, the coiled whip pressed against her back.

'I suppose it's a little unfortunate for some that I now hold keys to a couple of the guest rooms.'

Pauline opened the door and gestured for Jackie to enter first. The room was dimly lit, the only illumination coming from the rose pink cornice lights.

The door closed and the voice behind her said, 'There's somebody in here who might well be glad of your company.'

Jackie looked about her. There was the chrome and black leather furniture, the table and the cupboards, but no one else to be seen. She glanced in apprehension at Pauline as she was propelled across the room towards the far side, where the large archway with its ominous black velvet curtain stood. She moved on, feeling that Pauline was only waiting for her to hesitate, and that should she do so it would be more than sufficient reason for her to inflict further punishments.

Pauline lifted the curtain aside and guided her through. Jackie was, of course, familiar with this, as well as the other 'games' rooms, as were they all. But the events which took place in them and in front of the cameras had a pre-determined sequence; a well-defined beginning and end. Outside 'working' hours, Pauline had long used the facilities in her own suite to restrain and humiliate the girls directly under her control, particularly young Jackie. Everyone knew that Jackie provoked Pauline and they all knew why. Everyone knew as well that she often regretted her actions afterwards.

But why was she being brought into this place? Surely Pauline was not going to be too extreme with her. She had done nothing to elicit real punishment, and that was the unspoken rule between them. There had to be a reason, though Jackie was not always made aware of that reason until Pauline had her under her control.

24

This room was also lit by the subdued cornice lights. Jackie looked about her at the chrome and leather equipment and fittings with their straps and manacles. Then she saw. At the far end of the room stood a figure, quite naked. Jackie was propelled towards her. The figure was stretched out, her arms pulled up above her head and attached by steel cuffs to a chain which hung from a ring set into the ceiling. Her legs were pulled apart and held by steel cuffs, each attached to a short chain and a bolt set into the carpeted floor. She looked at the long fair hair, the soft round face and the mouth sealed tightly shut by the strip of white plastic tape. It was Kim.

'The conversation is going to be a bit one-sided,' remarked Pauline, 'but I'm sure you have a good idea why she is here.'

Standing before the chained figure, Jackie observed the pink weals about her thighs and saw the three-tailed strap laying on a nearby bench. Kim's eyes still glistened with residual tears. She looked from one to the other in enforced silence.

The coiled whip pushed into Jackie's back.

'Come on!' ordered the voice, and she was guided forcibly over to an elegant chair with slim, padded back. 'Sit!' commanded Pauline.

Unable to use her arms, Jackie leaned forward to maintain her equilibrium before falling slowly down on to the seat. Pauline moved around her and took hold of one of the straps hanging from the chair, then passing it around the girl's waist, buckled it securely at the rear of the seat.

'That should do,' she breathed. 'We don't want you walking about, do we?'

Moments later, with a swish of the black curtain, Pauline was gone. Kim flexed her limbs, trying to adjust herself in the creaking chains.

'I'm sorry,' said Jackie, looking up at her eyes. 'She made me tell about Karen coming back and where I got it from. She started to whip me . . . I didn't want to say anything but I . . . but she just kept on . . . I'm sorry I got you into this mess. Honest I am.'

* * *

They alighted from the taxi at the station car park and transferred the cases to Valerie's Peugeot.

'Right, that's that out of the way,' said Valerie. 'Fancy a little walk to the main square?'

'I'd fancy a walk anywhere at the moment. God, the air's so warm and pleasant – I'd almost forgotten.'

When they left the Rue Maguelone and entered the Place de la Comedie, the first stars had pierced the dome of the darkening sky and early evening strollers were scattered about the great marble square. Before them were grouped clusters of small round tables and wickerwork chairs. Valerie gestured towards them and said, 'How about here? We can sit and watch the world go by.'

'Right now,' said Karen, smiling, 'I couldn't think of anywhere better.'

'Good, let's organise some grub and a drop of wine. I'm starving!'

'So, your trip to the UK wasn't all light and happiness,' said Valerie over the empty plates. 'Apart from this bloke you teamed up with, that is.'

'You could say that,' answered Karen.

'Sonia hasn't said a lot,' continued Valerie, 'but she did mention you were keeping in touch.'

'Yes . . . I phoned a few times, except when I was out in the wilds. Then when I rang to say I was coming back, she was away in Amsterdam, closer to London than she was to here.'

'And you left the message with Kim.'

'Yes, she was in my old office, helping out, but Sonia rang me back the day after and said she'd help arrange everything. I was so glad, Val, I really was, but I want you to promise something.'

'Go on, deary.'

'Well, I-I don't know the best way to put this, but I'd rather you didn't say anything to anybody about Richard. It's important.'

Valerie looked into her eyes with mild concern.

'Look love, I'll not say anything, you know you can rely

on that, but if you talk in front of Jackie, or even Lorna, everyone will find out. There's nothing you say or do that will go beyond the older girls. Discretion is part of our work and that goes for Kim as well.'

'Oh yes, I know,' said Karen. 'It's just a bit awkward for me, I mean . . . well, I don't want –'

'You don't want Sonia to know,' cut in Valerie.

Karen looked up at her and opened her mouth to speak but no words came. Then she looked down at her hands, resting on the table, and said quietly. 'Has it been that obvious?'

Valerie continued to watch her for a few moments.

'You are wearing her locket, lovey. No one else ever has.'

'Of course,' said Karen, looking up once more. 'A bit stupid of me, isn't it?'

'No, not to me it isn't. I wouldn't let Pauline see it though.'

'No, I'm going to give it back to Sonia as soon as we return.'

'You can't. She won't be there until tomorrow afternoon – she's at Strasbourg organising a few girls and other things for the next EC conference. It was rather sudden but very important. She'll probably tell you something about it when you see her. Kim probably knows a bit about it too. She was originally going to collect you from the airport.'

'Oh, what happened?' asked Karen. 'Is she all right?'

'I suppose she is, but Pauline's got hold of her.'

'Pauline? Why?'

'Well,' continued Valerie, 'when Kim took your message she mentioned it to me in the bar. When Sonia got back, she told Kim to keep it as a surprise so, of course, we said nothing else. Trouble was that Jackie was serving at the bar that day and overheard Kim. Kim didn't realise until it was too late but told Jackie not to say anything to anyone else. I think Sonia wanted it to be a nice surprise for everyone, you know. She wasn't annoyed with Kim, or anything like that; the secrecy bit was no big deal! But you know what Jackie's like – she had to open her mouth at

27

the wrong time, didn't she? She made some remark to me in the restaurant about you this lunchtime, and there's bloody Pauline sitting almost next to her. You should have seen her face! The next thing I know, Kim's been called up to her office. Then later on, along she comes and asks me to pick you up. I didn't realise fully what was going on, otherwise I would have whisked her off out of harm's way. I only found out just before I left the house that Pauline had her.'

'The old cow!' exclaimed Karen. 'What's she up to?'

'She's probably miffed because she wasn't told about you and thinks everyone else was. I daresay we'll find out in due course.'

'Oh Val, I'm causing damned problems before I even set foot in the place.'

Valerie reached out and held her hand. 'Now look, you're not causing anything. Sonia wants you back; we all want you back. You're one of the family – it's her that's the odd one out! Don't you forget it, OK?'

'I'll try not to, but I can't understand,' said Karen. 'Why does Sonia keep her?'

'Oh, there are good reasons. The day-to-day running of the house definitely needs someone in charge of it. You know some of the girls have domestic work to do as part of their role in the scheme of things. Someone has to say who does what, and when, and to organise some of the private events. You know what I mean. And there's security. Can you imagine Jackie if she thought she could get a bloke into the place at night? Someone has to keep an eye on all that, and I have to admit Pauline does it very well. It's just that she uses her position to take it out on the more susceptible ones.'

'She wouldn't dare try it on you or Annette, surely.'

'Maybe not like that,' replied Valerie, 'but she could still make life awkward for us if we weren't careful. Annette sails a bit close to the wind sometimes but she's too important for Sonia's business operations for anything much to happen there.'

'But Kim, she doesn't strike me as being very submissive. She works with you in the beauty parlour and . . . and –'

'Yes, I know,' cut in Valerie. 'She's a very adaptable person in her own quiet way and more independent than most people think. But, as you say, she's not submissive like Jackie and one or two of the others – though even they use it to their own ends when it suits them.'

'And Mike?' asked Karen. 'Is he still odd-jobbing?'

'Yes, well,' said Valerie wryly, 'something must have been going on between him and Annette, even when you were there. She persuaded Sonia to let him star in one of her little productions with Cheryl. The one person who didn't realise what was going on was Mike. Annette got him into, let's say, a very graphic situation before he twigged. By that time it was too late. Since then, I don't think he's spoken to her. If she's in the bar, he'll eat in the conservatory and vice versa. Pauline takes the piss out of him too. She doesn't say much, just smiles at him knowingly.'

'Yes, I remember. Her smile was usually bad news for somebody.'

'Well,' continued Valerie, 'she's got poor Mike well under her thumb now. She's had him in two or three more little theatrical escapades since you left, all of them designed to humiliate. We all know he's not a born submissive but he enjoys his fantasies like most men, and now he can live out a few of them the way Sonia's customers do, but without it costing him a cent. He's got used to it being out in the open, I think, but the constant reminders and manipulation by Pauline don't please him too much at all, especially when she throws in remarks about Scotland Yard or the Inland Revenue. If she got struck by lightning he'd probably throw a party and I bet we'd all go to it, except maybe Jackie.'

'And Sonia,' added Karen.

'Yes, you could be right. I don't think Sonia knows about some of her little schemes and I doubt if she would have dared to take Kim away from meeting you today if Sonia had been around.'

'I'm going to have a fag,' said Karen, reaching into her shoulder bag. 'I don't suppose you . . ?'

'I will as we're outdoors,' said Valerie. 'I used to smoke a lot until I came to work at the house.'

Karen lit the cigarettes and said, 'Does Angie know I'm coming back?'

'No, I'm certain she doesn't,' replied Valerie. 'She'll be over the moon when you show up. She was quite upset when you left and I know she hoped you would come back. She always said so.'

Karen could see Angela in her mind's eye. Angela, with her blue-grey eyes, silver-blonde hair and understanding smile, had been the first person to befriend Karen when she began work at the house; the first person to show her sympathy and share her confidence when she felt so aside from everyone else because of her position, and when she first realised she was being drawn into a relationship with Sonia.

'Yes, well, I've missed Angie and all of you, and the warmth, and the sunshine.'

She looked up above the bright lights of the square to see the sweep of stars above them, blew out her cigarette smoke and watched it drift upwards into the evening air.

'We'll get going soon,' said Valerie, 'but there's time for another coffee if you fancy.'

The drive from Montpellier was a journey through darkness. For a while they talked but soon, consciousness and conversation became a burden and Karen found herself drifting in and out of wakefulness, sometimes aware of the ribbon of road in the lights before them, sometimes not. When they turned off the road and passed through the old stone gateway, Karen was fully awake.

The pool was in darkness though the lights about the main entrance of the house and inside the portico shone into the night.

'The Empire of Light,' mused Karen as they approached.

'What do you mean?' asked Valerie.

'The Empire of Light,' repeated Karen. 'It's a painting by René Magritte. I used to have it in an art book when I was a kid. It's always been one of my favourite pictures. The house reminds me of it; deserted and mysterious, with the lights just keeping the dark night at bay.'

'Well, I suppose most of them have gone to bed. It's gone eleven o'clock.'

'No,' observed Karen as they pulled up in front of the house. 'I can see through the french windows. There are a couple of people at the bar.'

'Mmm,' responded Valerie, switching off the headlights and squinting through the darkness, 'it looks like Kim and Jackie. As soon as we've taken your things up I'll have a word with them and find out what's been going on with Auntie Pauline.'

Apart from the two figures they had glimpsed through the windows, all was deserted as they ascended the stairs.

'Are you coming down for a nightcap?' asked Valerie as they placed the suitcases on the bed.

'No, Val . . . no, I won't. It's a bit late and I know you want to talk to Kim and Jackie. There'll be plenty of time in the morning.'

Valerie smiled and kissed her on the cheek.

Karen returned her smile and said. 'Thanks Val, for picking me up and everything.'

'That's all right, deary,' replied Valerie, squeezing her hands. 'And after lunch tomorrow, we'll give you a little welcome back treat. Come down to the beauty parlour at two o'clock, yes?'

Karen stared into her eyes for a few moments, remembering how she had been held prisoner down there on those two occasions and been pampered, shaved and driven almost wild with shameful lust, a lust which she then had been loath to admit but now desired to pursue. Was that not in part, after all, why she had returned?'

'Y-yes Val, er . . . two o'clock.'

Valerie opened the door to leave her, but turned as she was about to close it and whispered, 'Don't forget.'

The door clicked softly and Karen was alone.

Nothing had changed in the room. Sonia said she would keep it for her – for the time when she returned to the house. Karen began to unpack and was almost halfway through when she saw the white envelope trapped and sticking out from the right-hand drawer of the dressing table. She looked at it for a moment, wondering. When she moved closer, she saw that her name was written across the envelope in blue ink. She reached down to pull it free but it evidently would not move without the risk of tearing unless the drawer was opened. Karen pulled, released the envelope, and saw below it in the drawer a plain white box some 25 centimetres long. She regarded the box but did not touch it. Instead, she opened the envelope.

Inside, there was a folded note on pale blue paper. She opened the note out and read the neat script. 'Welcome home my dear. I'm sorry I could not be here for your return, but I will be back soon.' It was signed simply, 'S'.

'Welcome home,' breathed Karen, reading over the note again. 'I suppose it's the only home I've got.'

She replaced the note in its envelope and laid it inside the drawer, turning her attention next to the white box. She picked it up carefully, surprised that it was heavier than she expected it to be, and placed it on the top of the dressing table. The box was not sealed and she lifted the lid from it quite easily.

For some time she looked at the object inside the box without touching it. It was at least twenty centimetres long and five centimetres thick. The head, a realistic if moderately oversized representation of a circumcised penis, terminated a deep pink shaft which was not smooth but finished with small, soft, rubber teats. Towards the base, it flared out sharply and ended in a rubber ring. Below the ring, on a hard plastic cap, was a rotary switch. Karen lifted the dildo from its dark blue velvet lining, feeling her heartbeat quicken. She could see herself in the mirror, holding it, and behind her, the bed. She held it in her hands for a few seconds then reached with her fingers inside the ring and turned the switch. At once it began to purr and to move, vibrating ripples pulsating along the shaft from the head to the base. She took a deep breath and switched it off before putting it down next to its box. Beside the box, she placed the silver locket.

She turned on the radio and tried several stations until she found one playing cool jazz, then she began to undress, glancing at the object of lust as it lay where she had left it, silent and waiting. Some ten minutes later, she emerged from the shower, dried herself and entered the bedroom naked. She switched on the bedside lamp and a lamp next to the dressing table before switching off the main light. She walked back over and slowly, almost cautiously, took up the object which had so occupied her mind since its revelation. She could feel a burning inside her, a growing hunger which this thing in her hands could indulge and gratify. Why had Sonia, if indeed it was Sonia, left it there? Did she know her so well that she could expect her to make use of it? Perhaps it should not matter anymore.

Karen sat down on the edge of the bed, rose up and tilted the dressing table mirror down, then returned to the bed, now able to see her reflection. She turned the switch and the rubber organ once more came to life in her hands. In the mirror, she watched herself part her legs and bring the quivering pink head down into contact with the focus of her sensuality. It was cool against the heat of her sex but the head easily parted the reddened lips, finding them moist and yielding. She continued to watch her image, to see the bulbous head torment her with its demonic promise until its electric fire was spreading through her body. She fell backwards on to the bed, spread her legs further and pulled up her knees until her feet rested on the edge. The purring organ entered her easily. Indeed, she needed to encourage it hardly at all, for the moving ripples on the shaft, passing from head to base, caused it to enter her of its own accord as though it was an eager, living entity filling her with its lust. Letting down her legs, she twisted over, tightening on the pulsating shaft as she lifted herself on to her hands and knees with her behind facing the mirror. The currents were building up uncontrollably within and she knew she was approaching the time when they would surge up into every nerve of her body and take her over completely. Looking under her breasts and between her widespread legs, she could see it in the mirror, working inside her with an urgent life of its own. She snatched at a pillow and pulled it down under her head, clasping either end of it with her hands. But she wanted the shaft to enter deeper still, to extend throughout her, to become one with her. Then the golden light burned forth and she squirmed her body about, her hands crushing the pillow inwards under her face so that her cries were stifled within it while her body shook in repeated spasms.

When she withdrew the instrument of gratification, she was exhausted; not through the act itself but because her climax had fulfilled and terminated a long and tiring day. After this, there was nothing to do but sleep and dream, coiled within the womb of the bed.

In the darkness she relived fleeting moments, such as the taxi passing through London in the endless chaos of traffic. Then the airport, a dazzling, revolving sea of lights and people drifting before her closed eyes. Eventually, a velvet mask of peace and quiet descended about her senses.

Was the journey back to France all a dream? Was the conversation with Valerie at the little pavement café in Montpellier all in her mind? Karen turned over, part awake, slowly coming to and half expecting the apartment in London to materialise around her and the sound of police and ambulance sirens to intrude into her consciousness. She opened her eyes, looked about and saw the morning sunlight spilling through the Venetian blind. Just as on her first morning at the house all those months ago, the powder blue curtains were left open so as to dispel any doubts she might have had on waking.

She thought she had overslept, but the clock radio blinked to 7.15 as she looked at it. Outside in the warm air the birds were singing. There were no car horns, no sirens; there was only harmony. When she went to the bathroom, it still lay there in the sink where she had rinsed it, purposeful and unambiguous. She took it quickly out and dabbed away the few remaining drops of water with a towel. The open box still lay upon the dressing table and she carefully placed the dildo inside, fitted back the lid and put the box into the drawer, as close as she could remember to the spot where she had first seen it. She closed the drawer softly upon the shade of her guilt and wondered if whoever had put it there might not return in her absence to ascertain whether or not it had fulfilled its purpose. As for the 'who' in the equation, there were two likely possibilities. The first, that it had been left with the note, Karen now found darkly amusing. The alternative, that it might be a part of a devious scheme of Pauline's, she did not wish to contemplate.

In one side of the range of built-in wardrobes – the side which she had not looked into the previous evening and the side she expected to find empty – there were clothes and shoes. She stood for a little time regarding them, wondering why they were there, before reaching inside.

Among the clothes she saw dresses, tops and skirts, some colourful and casual, some glamorous, some more daring than she had ever owned herself. Some of the styles made her heart beat faster. Where was she going to wear these? On a low chest of drawers below the clothes stood the shoes, some of them smart but practical, some of them not at all conceived for everyday wear. She stooped and picked out a pair of open sandals in metallic PVC, with ankle straps and little silver buckles to hold them firmly in place. The heels were high and slim, so high that she could not imagine trying to walk any great distance in them. She picked out a dress from the end of the rail. The dress was black, short and made of frothy nylon lace. Its long sleeves ended in lace ruffles and the ruffled neck was cut very low and reinforced by curved wires sewn inside the material. It was intended to be worn with the breasts supported but exposed. Every one she examined was her size, though that meant little, for all of the girls were of similar build and height.

Pulling open the drawer below she discovered a feast of lingerie, underwear and stockings, all inside unopened transparent packets. She did not venture to undo any of them but could see quite easily that many of the styles were not from any high street shop. Her eyes beheld sheer nylon,

35

fine lace and some rather more exotic materials. She closed the drawer and the wardrobe doors, trembling slightly and seeing herself in the long mirror.

'I'm all right as I am for now,' she muttered, regarding her slim form in its pink cotton dress with deep, white belt and short sleeves, and her white, wedge heel sandals. With her light brown hair falling about her shoulders, Karen pulled open the door of her room and set out to renew old acquaintances.

'I knew you'd come back!' cried Angela, kissing Karen with enthusiastic warmth as she squeezed her arms.

Mike kissed her too, then dark haired Lorna. Jackie, sitting across the conservatory with an older girl who was unknown to Karen, waved her arm about in a circle and called, 'Hiya sweetie!'

Mike brought fresh orange drinks from behind the bar. They sat and talked, exchanging tales that could be exchanged, hinting at some that could not. At length, Karen asked, 'Where are the others? Where's Annette, Val and Kim?'

'Yes, well,' began Angela, 'Val and Kim are at the pool, Annette's in Paris on, er business with Rachel and two of the others, and Cheryl is supposed to be on the way back with Sonia.'

'And James? Is he still working in the annexe?'

'Oooh!' cried Angela with mock seriousness, 'I think he's got domestic problems –'

'She means his boyfriend's cleared off!' cut in Mike.

'Well, yes,' continued Angela, 'something like that. Sonia gave him a few days away to get himself sorted out.'

James, thought Karen, knew all their intimacies. Everything that was recorded in those secret rooms, he watched, mixed and edited then mastered on to tape, disk and film for reproduction and marketing. What a job, thought Karen. Yes, you would have to be a little different to cope with that.

'I'll go down as I am,' she said to herself. 'There's no point in putting on a bathrobe. Anyway, this time of the day it's going to look odd if I'm seen like that.'

Karen glanced at the clock. It said 1.50. Her heart was beating fast.

'It's different now,' she said to herself in the mirror. 'I know what is going to happen, and they know that I know. Christ! Why should I bother about it? They're at it all the time – Angela, Jackie, Lorna. What makes me so special, so bloody different?'

She ran her hands down over the gold, stretch lamé dress, over her breasts and down to her thighs, and stared hard at her reflection in the mirror. 'We know we didn't come back just for the weather, don't we?' The eyes flashed back at her, as though another being stood beyond the glass, a being who spoke the words and revealed to her what she would not as readily tell herself.

She twisted about before the mirror, seeing the short dress stretch and mould about her figure like a second skin.

'God,' she breathed, turning towards the door, 'why do I go on kidding myself?' She set off down to the beauty parlour.

'Come on in, deary,' said Valerie a few minutes later, pulling open the blue door and stepping aside. Karen looked at her and smiled back weakly. 'You look very glamorous in that dress,' she observed, as Karen entered the main room.

'It was in my wardrobe, with lots of others. I've never seen any of them before,'

'You'd make a stunning model,' commented Valerie, 'you really would.'

Sonia had once told her something like that, she remembered. The proposition had not seemed altogether unattractive even then.

Karen looked about the room where her suppressed carnality, like a jewel concealed beneath the darkness of a velvet cloth, had first been hinted at. Everything was as she remembered – the sinks and mirrors, the warm, low lights, the two hairdryers at the end of the room, the low bench with its hidden restraints and its covering of soft pink towel, and the oddly shaped chair, its voluptuous purpose obscured by the dark blue sheet.

'Where's Kim?' she asked.

'She's gone off to Béziers,' replied Valerie.

'Oh, to Béziers, so it's just –'

'Just ourselves,' cut in Valerie. 'Is that all right?'

'Y-yes . . . yes, I think so.'

Suddenly, one to one did not seem the same. With three, it was only a game and not as personal, but she knew Valerie so well that it should not have mattered.

'If you'd rather not bother . . .' said Valerie, smiling.

Karen looked her up and down. She wore a high collared catsuit of dark blue stretch vinyl. Below her curly black hair, two large gold earrings swung and her dark brown eyes were soft and understanding. Karen hesitated.

'No, it's OK, it's just that I expected –'

'Always expect the unexpected,' said Valerie, reaching round and easing down the zipper at the rear of Karen's dress. Karen allowed her to continue until the dress was loose about her body and pulled away from her shoulders to reveal her breasts. After a few moments, she was naked apart from her minimal black lace briefs and her sandals.

'I thought you might like a massage,' said Valerie. 'Something to make you feel at home and relaxed again.' Karen smiled. 'Take your shoes off, then sit down on the bench.'

Karen did as she was told, placing her sandals under the bench. Valerie moved around behind her but Karen remained staring ahead, trembling a little in anticipation. She heard a rustle and a clink of metal, but still did not turn. Then something was placed over her head, something which obscured the light from her eyes and caused her to raise her arms defensively.

'Val! What, what . . ?'

'Don't worry, lovey! You know I'm not going to harm you!'

She lowered her arms, feeling the straps tighten round and over her head and around her neck. The leather pads squeezed over her eyes until all was blackness. Passing through her mind was the thought that she could easily reach up and undo the harness if she so desired, so the whole thing must be only for effect. Hands continued to move about her head, then there was a metallic scraping, followed by a soft click, then a second and a third.

'Val, what's happening?'

'There we are', came the voice, 'nice and neat, and quite fantastic. It's a pity you can't see what it looks like.'

'Val, this isn't being . . . you wouldn't . . ?'

'If you mean being recorded, no, of course it isn't. You're the last person I would play a trick like that on. I'm not Pauline.'

'I know, Val, I'm sorry.'

Karen lifted her hands to feel the harness, running her fingers over the eye pads and around the leather straps until she reached the buckles. Her fingers stopped abruptly.

'Val – it's padlocked! What are you doing?'

'It's better if you can't remove it,' answered Valerie, watching her tug at the harness. 'It's all part of our little game.'

Karen still had her hands pressed to her face when Valerie reached around her and slipped a steel bracelet on to first one wrist and then the other before she could pull away. Karen instinctively tried to tug her hands apart but it was no use; the bracelets were quite secure. She lowered her arms and ran her fingers over the smooth steel bands, touching the short connecting links.

She sat saying nothing, her heart pounding over her chest, until Valerie took her arm and spoke into her ear. 'OK lovely, come with me.' She arose and a hand took her by the elbow. They began to walk, Karen taking hesitant and uncertain steps on the soft carpet.

She had sat with her back to the main door when Valerie put on the harness and so knew that they were moving towards the covered chair, the chair in which those few months ago she had rested, spread and helpless, while Valerie and Kim had carried out the permanent depilation of her sex. She anticipated that she was to be restrained in this sinister chair for a second time but she felt the cover brush against her as they moved by.

Next along the room, past the hairdryers and the kitchenette, was the shower room with its toilet and bidet. She slowed down, not wishing to appear willing to enter this last place for she was quite aware, from what she had seen in the past, of what the various items within might be adapted for. Valerie pulled on her wrists, not around to the left where she expected, but on to the end of the room where she remembered there were walk-in cupboards. She remembered also being told that one of these cupboards led to a room beyond via a secret doorway, a room to which Sonia had once taken her in the most intimate and personal of circumstances.

They stopped and she heard a door swing open. A guiding hand ushered her through the door and she could sense the space closing around her as she moved inside. The air was close and full of odours, the strong and distinct smell of leather mixing with the more subtle aroma of latex and other materials which renewed a number of memories. Karen moved slowly on, brushing against what she knew must be hanging garments, some cool or even cold to the touch, others soft and intimate like nylon or lace. Valerie stopped her and pushed by. She heard a key being inserted into a lock and a door opening. Warmer air greeted her, the odours of the cupboard disappeared and her feet trod upon a different carpet, not quite as soft or deep as in the parlour.

'Val, please,' she said again, 'what's happening? I thought we were doing a massage!'

'All in good time, deary,' came the reply from beyond the darkness as she continued forward. 'Lift your feet, you're stepping on to towelling.'

Karen did so and felt the material under her toes. Valerie moved her forward a little further before halting her progress and turning her a quarter way around. Since passing into this room, she had become quite disorientated and had no idea which way she faced or how close she might be to any other object.

She instinctively resisted as a hand closed about each of her manacled wrists and the voice said, 'Lift up – come on, right up!'

She allowed her arms to be pulled upward and felt her hands brushed against something cool and metallic. She realised it was a hanging chain. There was a soft click and the hands moved away from her, but she could not move her own arms down again. Between her hands she instinctively grasped the chain to which the handcuffs were securely attached, and waited in silence. Her right ankle was taken hold of and pulled outwards. She resisted, gripping the chain to keep her balance, but to no avail, for something hard and cool was quickly fitted about the ankle and held it fast. Her left leg was pulled aside next, increasing the tension in her arms and holding her body almost rigid as that ankle too was fixed immobile in its steel cuff. For a time she stood silent in her obscured world, hearing nothing but the creak of the chains which held her naked body helpless like an inverted letter 'Y'.

At length she whispered, 'Val, where are you?' There was no reply. 'Val, say something!'

In return to her plea, there was still silence. Somehow she knew that Valerie was gone and that she was alone. She stopped moving and listened. Her heart measured the passage of time but otherwise the silence was, like the darkness, total. Why had Valerie covered her eyes? Why was she not allowed to see? Was not being chained up like this enough? Perhaps Valerie had gone back to the parlour for something she had forgotten. Maybe she had gone to put on the rubber gloves she had worn before. She must come back soon. She must.

There was a sound. From somewhere behind her, something or somebody moved.

'Val, is that you?'

She could hear breathing, a faint rustling of clothes and the sound of something being placed gently upon a wooden table top.

'Val, please! Who-who's there? Say something, please. Ahhh!' she cried out as hands ran down either side of her body from chest to waist. The hands stayed on her waist and the feel of latex gloves, like a smooth, warm skin upon the fingers, was unmistakable. Karen trembled and

41

breathed in. It must be Valerie. It must be all part of the game they were playing. The hands left her waist and she sensed her moving away, only to feel the presence again moments later.

She tensed sharply as something liquid fell between her breasts and began to run slowly down over her stomach. The latex fingers at once began to spread it about her breasts and under her arms. It was warm and pleasant, and the aroma of spices entered her nostrils. She remembered this oil from the past. The hands did not play about the front of her for long, for the oil was next applied and spread on her back, the fingers smoothing it down to her waist and over the tops of her buttocks. Her thighs and legs received it next, the hands working the oil about from her upper legs to down below her knees. Her body was becoming pleasantly warm and the hands, now at her upper back and shoulders, were massaging more firmly and methodically, smoothing the oil deep into her skin. They progressed all about her, slipping over her breasts and nipples, pinching and squeezing, running down her stomach as far as the smooth and hairless area above her sex, over her thighs and behind – everywhere except that part of her where she at any moment expected the lubricated fingers must invade. The sensual attention of the hands was telling on her and she was starting to burn inside as well as out. She knew where the fingers were going to go but they were making her wait, withholding from her what her body was beginning to crave. She wanted to relax a little in the chains but could not for the strain it put upon her manacled wrists. The hands stopped.

A moment passed and she felt warm breath upon her face. She opened her mouth to speak but no words emerged, for lips closed upon hers and stifled her voice with voluptuous passion. It was not Valerie. A hand started to move down her stomach and the lips moved from her mouth to her neck.

'Sonia!' she gasped.

'Karen,' whispered the voice, close to her cheek.

Their lips joined again and the fingers found her sex, inflamed and wet with her own excitement. She moaned and tried to thrust forward to take the fingers deeper but there was no need for they stroked and slid further in and electrified her entire body, making her breath come in short gasps. She gripped hard on the chain between her hands, threw back her head and arched her back, twisting violently and crying out as the smouldering lust flared up to overwhelm her body and mind.

It was over and her limbs were free of the restraints. Karen remained, nevertheless, standing where she had stood since Valerie left her, one hand clutching the chain above while she flexed her arms and legs, aching a little because of the way she had been held. Still she was unable to see, for the head harness could not be removed until the small padlocks were undone, and the one who had intruded into her dark world had, so far, not allowed this.

She sensed a presence once more and a hand – Sonia's hand she knew – but minus its rubber glove, closed about her wrist.

'Open your hand,' came the voice. Karen did so and something small and hard was pressed into it. She closed her fingers about the small key. 'By the time you undo this, I shall be gone. Please remember that this never happened, it was all part of a dream.'

'Yes, but Val . . .'

'Valerie was never here – do you understand?'

'Yes,' breathed Karen, 'I understand.'

She reached up with the key and found the first small lock, at the back of her neck. It took a little time to undo it and a little more to release the others before she was able to remove the leather harness. Now she could see.

The room was lit only with the pink cornice lights but it soon became apparent that Karen was alone, alone except for the chrome and black leather furniture and fittings, all awaiting a willing or otherwise human form, each to restrain or contain in its own manner. She returned the way she had been brought, letting the secret door click shut behind her.

She passed between the racks of clothes and other items not so easily identifiable. In the dim light she could vaguely see now what before she could only touch. She stopped and held out her hands. Time seemed to be standing still.

She wanted to hesitate in the semi-darkness, with all of these intimate things crowding in upon her, cool and sensual against her nakedness, and to push between them and discover what lay behind. Perhaps, down there, was another door, a hidden door to be passed through in pensive silence, like entering a looking-glass world, a world of sinister and bizarre things, where time meant nothing, where the ritual was all. She breathed in the silence and the closeness, daring herself to remain longer. Listening.

There was nobody in the beauty parlour. Her gold lamé dress had been carefully laid out, with her shoes and lace briefs, upon the bench where she had sat. The oil had dried on her skin but the aroma lingered so she showered quickly before dressing. She did not want to go to the office wearing the gold dress. It did not feel appropriate. She told herself it was because of the time of day but knew it was because she wanted to become her old self again. The dress was too short, tight and revealing; all right for the evening or a trip out to an intimate restaurant, perhaps.

Once the parlour door had clicked shut behind her, she hurried along the corridor to the seldom used rear stairs. Turning the corner she came face to face with Pauline and stopped abruptly.

'Oh! I – I didn't see you,' she said.

Pauline's face broke into a smile, the smile of one convinced of ultimate supremacy over an opponent. She wore a long black satin gown with gold braided collar, its austere form contrasting with her large pale blue eyes, silver-blonde pageboy hair and soft features. She looked up and down Karen's body as a hangman might do when assessing the weight of the next candidate for the gallows. Karen lowered her arms as far as she could, being aware of the still visible marks upon her wrists where the steel cuffs had held her.

44

'How nice to have you back,' Pauline remarked, moving aside to allow Karen room to pass by.

'I'm sure it is,' answered Karen coolly before continuing upward, resisting the temptation to look back but wondering if the eyes at the bottom of the stairs were following her.

Sonia was working at her desk when Karen entered. She arose and walked towards her, smiling. This was a smile of greeting, a smile of fondness and more. She kissed Karen on the cheek and squeezed her affectionately, her dark eyes with their hint of the Orient looking into Karen's.

'I'm so happy you decided to come back, my dear.'

'I have to tell you, Sonia,' she sighed, 'there were times when I couldn't wait, really. And look here, I've brought back your locket.'

She held out her hand with the precious silver locket and its chain curled up on the open palm. Sonia regarded it in silence for a few seconds.

'No, keep it, please. Now you're here again, it's here too, so I can always see it when I want.'

'Yes, all right,' answered Karen. 'I'll wear it just on special occasions though. I won't let the others see it, I don't think.'

'No, perhaps you shouldn't,' replied Sonia. 'We'll keep it just to ourselves the way we keep other things to ourselves. I know you understand.'

'Yes, I understand.'

3

School Lessons

He was applying the last few drops of paint to the refurbished summerhouse when her voice reached his ears.

'Mike – there you are!'

'Hi!' he shouted.

Jackie strolled up to him, the sun filtering through the trees and shimmering gold upon her long hair. His eyes took in her slim form dressed in a white T-shirt moulding thinly over her breasts and a denim mini-skirt with a designer frayed hem.

'What are you doing out here in those shoes?' he asked, eyeing her blue stiletto heel sandals.

'Oh, it's OK,' she replied, grinning, 'they're pretty old but they'll clean up anyway. Look – er, she wants to see you at twelve o'clock. You've to go to her office and not look scruffy. Actually, I'm supposed to say "look reasonably presentable".'

'Did Sonia really say that?' he laughed. 'Don't look scruffy?'

'Sonia? It's not her I'm talking about, it's Pauline!'

'Eh? Pauline? Wants me – in her office – what for?'

'I've to say I don't know – sorry.'

He put down the brush and placed his hands on his hips. 'I'm not supposed to go up there, you know that.'

'Well you are now, lover boy,' she said, grinning impishly. 'I think she might fancy you!'

'Bloody hell,' he muttered, picking up the paint brush and wrapping it in a piece of polythene.

'Are you coming back now?' Jackie asked. 'I'll walk with you as far as the chalet if you are.'

He knelt down, tapping the lid back onto the paint can,

glancing at the lower part of her body. He looked at his watch. It was only five past ten. 'You fancy coming back for a drink?'

She smiled and folded her arms. 'I would, but I, er, I don't think we'd better just now.'

'All right, what's it about?' he asked as they set off towards the path. Jackie remained silent. 'Come on, I'm going to know soon enough anyway.'

Jackie stopped, turned to face him and took a deep breath. 'Mike, she'll kill me if she finds out. I daren't!'

He put down the carrier bag with its tin and brushes, took hold of her and kissed her. 'Look sweetheart, I wouldn't give you away, you know that.'

She looked up into his eyes, lips slightly parted, her fingers clutching his arms. 'You promise, Mike, you won't let on?'

'I promise. God's honour!'

'Come on, Mike, you don't believe in God!'

'OK, on my honour then. I'll swear on my honour if that's good enough.'

'Well ... they have a show arranged and, em ... the male model can't make it.'

'Can't make it – you mean he's had too much to drink?' said Mike, grinning.

'No, I mean he can't come.'

'It's the same thing, isn't it?'

'Oh, Mike!' she said, pushing him back. 'I'm trying to be serious!'

'Look,' he said, pulling her back up close to him, 'are you in it?'

'Er, yes, I am.'

He pressed his lips against hers, tasting her perfumed breath and feeling her warm softness against his body. His hand moved down and squeezed her behind.

'Then I'll look forward to it,' he whispered into her ear.

She sighed, relieved that he had not insisted on more information, wondering what he would say if he knew all of it. Perhaps it might not matter. She never quite knew with Mike.

* * *

47

'Give me a shout if you spot them, won't you, and I'll put the coffee on.'

'Yes, of course,' replied Karen. 'I'll keep an eye open.'

Sonia had said they were due at 11.30. It was now 11.35. But it was only minutes after Sonia had spoken to her that Karen saw first one and then a second white car appear, disappear, then reappear through the trees along the driveway.

'It looks like them,' called Karen from around the door.

'Do you want to bring them through?'

'Yes, I will, then I'll make myself scarce.'

'Not on my account,' responded Sonia, rising from her desk. 'You stay unless you wish otherwise.'

The two cars were pulling up to the front of the house when Karen stepped out into the porch. The car doors opened, accompanied by the sound of chatter and laughter. As the girls clambered from the cars, four from one and three from the other, something scurried past Karen's feet and disappeared up the main hallway.

'Oh, Pancake,' she said, laughing, as the ginger cat, disturbed from his daytime slumber in the shade, took to the front stairs in the pursuit of peace and quiet elsewhere.

The seven girls, each carrying a travel bag, approached the main doors. Karen saw they were all young, slim and attractive, two of them dusky skinned, none of them seeming to be over the age of twenty. None of them were dressed in any manner out of the ordinary, but wore tops and denims or summer dresses. She thought they had been speaking English, though with foreign accents, but now, as they greeted her with their smiles, they were all silent.

'Please come this way,' she said to them.

Some twenty minutes later, another figure approached the main entrance and strode into the hallway. He hesitated, having noted the two cars outside. He stopped again in the main hallway, listened to the babble of conversation and laughter flowing from the bar to his left and glanced inside. After a few moments he looked about, and seeing the main office to the right empty, proceeded a little further on and swung around to hurry up the main stairs.

Jackie had not, of course, needed to tell him where on the first floor Pauline's office was located. His earlier visits to the rooms there, originally clandestine but later 'official', had provided him with that information. He had never before, though, been summoned into her lair. He arrived at the door with mixed expectations.

'Come in!' sounded the voice, and he entered briskly, as if to make his visit appear no more than routine.

Seeing her at her desk to his right, he hesitated, glancing briefly about the room before proceeding onward to the waiting chair in front of her.

'Do you approve?' she asked, with a hint of sarcasm.

He looked around once more with contrived deliberation. 'No gibbet, not even a rack – I'm disappointed,' he said, smiling.

She regarded him coolly for a long time. 'They can easily be arranged,' she breathed, fitting her fingers together, prayer-like, under her chin.

He shuffled slightly in the chair, trying to maintain an amiable expression, suddenly doubting the wisdom of the remark.

'What has she told you?' Pauline asked, her large blue eyes fixed hard upon him.

'Told me? Who? Jackie?'

'Yes, Jackie!'

'Only that you wanted to talk to me, so here I am.'

'Good,' she said, smiling without a hint of humour.

He regarded her face and that part of her body visible above the desk. He had always thought of Pauline as a very attractive and desirable woman. Her legs in particular were an important element in his sexual fantasies, competing successfully with the rest of the girls in the house. No mean achievement under the circumstances! He imagined her naked before him, even as he sat in the presence of her intimidating gaze. He would have given much to penetrate the glacial facade and know what she thought of men in general, and of him in particular.

'We have a little problem,' she went on. 'There's a show arranged for this afternoon and our male star has turned his car over. He's going to be in hospital for a day or two in Marseilles, so he obviously won't be showing up here. Sonia's persuaded James to come back so it's important that we come up with something to make the show possible.' She relaxed back in her chair. 'You're the something!'

'What am I . . . er, what does it involve?' asked Mike.

Pauline looked at him without expression. 'Do the details matter? Isn't it all the same to you in the end?'

'No, it isn't,' he replied. 'Some things I don't mind doing, other things I do!'

'Well, let's say our little friend Jackie is starring in it, if that gives it more appeal.'

'There are some people downstairs. What are they here for?'

'Oh, them,' she replied with a wave of her arm. 'They're just here on business, visiting Sonia.'

'Look,' he said, 'I'm not sure I want to be pushed into anything I don't know about. You've set me up before and I don't care for it!'

'Then go and complain to Sonia. I'm sure she could find someone else to do your work – someone who isn't wanted by the UK tax authorities, that is!'

He leaned back in his chair and held her gaze. This might not be the best time to attempt to gain a rapport with her, but it was the first real opportunity he had encountered to date. If he was beset by doubt, it was because he had never been a man to take his life in his hands, except when it came to financial affairs, and he knew, as did Sonia and Pauline, how that had ended up. Still, he had never liked other people to get the better of him and what a *coup* it would be!

He hoped now, as he smiled back at her, that the acute nervousness he was aware of inside was not in evidence on the surface. He took a deep breath.

'I hope you don't mind me asking, changing the subject that is, but er, you don't have any male friends of your own here, Pauline. Don't you ever fancy going out to dinner in the evening?'

He felt an odd current passing through him as he spoke.

50

'Are you trying to proposition me?' she asked, her face betraying not the slightest hint of a smile. It was a challenge he had to meet.

'Yes, if you like. I've thought about it a few times. I know you're in a different situation to the other people here, but then so am I, and, er . . . personally, I consider you a very attractive woman. I just feel that, well . . . I don't get out all that much myself. So if you found yourself free one evening and you don't mind my company . . .'

Mentally, he swallowed hard. Was the unseen blow about to fall?

She began to laugh. He tried not to look perplexed. The rumour was that she did not possess the facility of laughter as nobody had ever seen it utilised.

'I'm glad you find it funny,' he said weakly, the blood rushing to his face.

She had triumphed over him.

'Well, well, a secret admirer! What would the rest of them think?'

'I don't know,' he replied. 'Would it matter?'

Her face regained its former composure. 'It would to me,' she replied with a hint of finality.

He considered further progress in this direction to be unlikely and so remained silent until she spoke.

'Two thirty,' she announced, 'at the first room on the right if you come up the main stairs. You'll take your shower in there first. Jackie and Lorna will be there.'

He left the office and hurried down to the entrance, feeling like a naughty schoolboy dismissed by the teacher after the uncovering of some misdemeanour. He could not have known how portentous that sentiment was. Meanwhile, the thought of what he might get up to with Jackie and Lorna fuelled him with enough enthusiasm to offset the rebuff. Fantasising about Pauline could take a back seat for the time being.

He did not knock on the door at 2.30, but tried the ornate brass handle and pushed it open. The small ante room was empty save for two green leather upright chairs. There was

51

no sound from beyond the inner door but he opened this with caution nevertheless. To his left and right were hung blue and green striped curtains, obscuring most of the room. Directly ahead, a door stood ajar. He continued on into the room, his feet silent upon the rich oatmeal carpet.

A curtain moved aside nearby and Jackie's face appeared.

'Oh, Mike, I thought I heard the door. Just go straight ahead for the shower. I'll see you in a few minutes. Put your towel around you when you come out, OK?'

'Er, yes, sure,' he replied, glancing at her.

She was dressed very much as she had been in the garden. There was no sign of Lorna. Jackie vanished back behind the curtain.

He thought, while under the hot water, that he should have taken the opportunity to ask about the curtains. There must be a reason for them; there must be something hidden behind. So many things in this house turned out to be hidden behind curtains.

When he stepped out barefoot on to the soft carpet, wearing only the blue towel about his waist, Jackie was back in view and with her was Lorna, her long raven hair swept back over her shoulders.

'Hello there!' Lorna said.

The two of them waited until he was with them, then both put their arms about him and alternately kissed his mouth and cheeks. He returned their kisses, slipping his arms about their slim waists and feeling his organ of lust stir beneath the towel. The three continued for some minutes with increasing passion until his arousal was obvious. At that point he began to pull Jackie's T-shirt out from under the waistband of her skirt, then up and over her head, freeing her young, firm breasts.

'Come over here with us,' said Jackie, pulling his arm.

Lorna took his other arm and they walked towards the curtain. Lorna pulled it aside with a smile and said, 'We've got a little treat for you!'

'Ah, no!' responded Mike, stepping backwards. 'Not this time we don't!'

The object of trepidation was a black timber X, some

two metres high, standing purposefully with black leather straps hanging from behind its four arms.

The two girls smiled at him and walked up to the sinister artefact. They stood at either side of it, each with a hand placed on top of its upper limb, and fixed their eyes on him. Lorna reached to the top of her blouse with her free hand and started to undo the buttons. He watched her intently as one by one they came undone and the blouse fell open. After the last button, she pulled the front of the blouse away to reveal her breasts. Like Jackie's, they were well developed and firm, with her nipples dark, hard and prominent.

He moved back towards them, urge overcoming caution, then stopped.

'Come on, you two, let's just get together. What's the point of that?'

Neither of the girls moved, but posed, swayed their hips and teased him to exasperation.

'Love us, love our cross!' pouted Lorna.

'OK, OK,' he said, raising his hands, 'I'll go along with it if you like, but I've got to check all of this out.'

He turned to the curtain from behind which the two girls had first appeared. This room was smaller than the other guest rooms he had seen and was brightly lit by natural daylight, looking out as it did from the front of the house. By one wall there stood a number of small tables and a stack of boardroom chairs. Opposite were two doors, neither of which would open when he tried the handles. The movable spot lamps above hung purposefully from their tracks. The small cameras were obvious as well, not having the elaborate furniture and fittings in which to be hidden from view.

There was nobody to be seen. He pushed back through the curtain. The two girls stood bare breasted in front of the wooden cross, hands on their hips, smiles on their faces, waiting. He approached them and was again engrossed within their arms and hot kisses. Once more he was aroused beyond prudence and gave himself over to them, kissing them in turn on the mouth and breasts, finding the zip fastener on Jackie's skirt and falling to his knees before her to pull the skirt down, while Lorna kissed him about the neck and shoulders. Jackie ran her fingers through his hair as he turned to Lorna and released her skirt too, pulling it frantically down and pressing his lips against her warm stomach. Intoxicated by their sexuality, he wanted to suck and tongue every part of their sensual bodies.

'Come on, young man!' urged Lorna, pulling him towards the wooden cross.

'Yes, come along!' added Jackie. 'Time for our little game.'

He allowed them to pull him towards the sinister object and turn him around so that his back was pushed against the cool, hard timber. Each of them took an arm and lifted it up against the wooden cross. He closed his eyes and let them encircle each wrist in a leather strap, which they passed through slots in the timber arm before buckling fast at the rear. They quickly passed straps around just below his elbows and fastened these too. It was obvious what their next moves would be and, having gone beyond the point of no return, he did not attempt any resistance as they pulled apart his legs and secured these at ankles and thighs to the lower members of the device.

Jackie and Lorna stood back and regarded him with obvious satisfaction. Mike, spread out and helpless, found his arousal all the more intense because of his inability to move and conceal it. The two girls turned around and Jackie, moving past him, pulled the rear curtain along its track all the way to the far wall. He had not bothered to look behind this other curtain because a gap at one end showed it to be close to the wall, but he now saw a school blackboard and easel, to the side of which was a desk and chair in a wide alcove. The other curtains were also drawn aside to the walls, lightening the room considerably, all the way through to where the wooden cross stood.

He fully understood the obligation he was under to take part in these rituals from time to time, but always maintained his preference for being in charge. Since becoming involved, however, he had also come to appreciate the element of uncertainty inherent in a situation like this. He had Annette to thank for all that. Had it not been for their clandestine meetings and secret revels together all those months ago, he would have seen none of these upstairs rooms and probably only have guessed what transpired within them. Now, he had become a convenient pawn in their games.

The girls stood before him, fully dressed again and waiting, when a sound to his right told him someone was entering through the main door. He twisted his head to see who the intruder was but was unable to turn it far enough. The figure passed behind him, watched by Jackie and Lorna, then Pauline's voice said, 'All right, you two, let's get these things arranged!'

He flexed hard against the straps, hoping against hope that they would give way and allow him to escape, but they would not. She was here! Why? She was the last person he wanted to see. She had never been present before when he took part in these sexual escapades. After the failed attempt to assert his masculinity over her, his humiliation would be complete.

She walked by him without acknowledgement, a smile on her face. The two girls followed her across the room. They pulled out the small tables and moved them across the floor to form a group of nine in front of the cross. To each table was added a chair.

'What's going on?' he demanded, having made his mind up that now was as good a time as any to speak out. Jackie and Lorna glanced at him momentarily. Pauline ignored him completely. 'Come on! Let me in on it, will you?'

This time, Pauline, making her way across the room back to the desk, looked at him coldly and continued on. She shuffled the easel and board closer to the wooden cross and dragged the desk forward. Turning his head to the left, Mike could see them more easily now. From a wall cupboard near where the desk had stood, she produced a school cane and a rolled up sheet of paper about a metre across. The cane she placed on the desk. The paper she unrolled and fixed with clips to the front of the blackboard.

On the sheet was printed, in full colour, an anatomical diagram, complete with captions, of the male sex organ. When he turned to look at Jackie and Lorna, they had gone. He heard Pauline open and close the desk drawer but she did not come into view. Instead, he sensed rather than heard her moving close behind him. Something flashed in front of his face and he instinctively opened his mouth in surprise. At once the red rubber ball was thrust into his mouth. The tightening strap across his cheeks and the sound of the buckle being done up at the back of his neck confirmed his predicament. He was effectively silenced. Pauline walked from the room, leaving him helpless and gagged to contemplate the forthcoming possibilities.

It was not long before a thought which had been for some time at the back of his mind became a conscious conclusion. There were nine desks. There were seven visitors plus Jackie and Lorna. But for the moment there was no one other than himself and the quiet surroundings.

The silence was broken by a voice and the door opened and closed and the two girls appeared before him. Both wore white blouses, blue ties and pleated blue mini-skirts. On their feet were white socks and wedge-heel brown sandals.

The words, 'For God's sake undo me before she gets back!' were perfectly clear in his mind but the, 'Ha, nnng!' which actually emerged meant nothing to Jackie and Lorna. It would have made no difference even if they had understood.

'Oh, poor old Mike!' cooed Jackie, moving close up to him, so close that her body was lightly touching his own. She placed her hands on either side of his torso, her nails pushing tightly into his flesh, and kissed his ear and neck. Lorna's hands squeezed through the towelling which still circled his thighs and her lips played their sensual game about his neck and ears from behind. He knew they were working to arouse him before Pauline returned, but despite attempts to think of other things, he could do nothing to prevent it even with the towel in place. It would be impossible to hide.

There were voices and laughter outside the door. Jackie

and Lorna hurried over to the group of small tables and took their places at the front. The door swung open and Pauline's voice rang out, 'This way, class! Come along now!'

The seven girls entered, looking younger still in the same style of school uniform as worn by Jackie and Lorna. Each carried a pale blue exercise book. They all glanced at him, particularly at the blue towel, and smiled as Pauline ushered them into their seats. He saw that Pauline had changed as well. She wore a mortar board and black lecturer's gown over a dark blue, two-piece suit.

She walked to the desk next to the chart and picked up her cane.

'Now then, ladies! I do hope you have all been attending to your homework! Please open your books!'

He was aware of their eyes, shifting from Pauline to him, looking at the bulge in the towel, and saw them prodding each other, smiling and making eyes at him. How much of it was contrived and how much was genuine mirth he had no way of knowing, but he suspected the former. These were far from being the naïve schoolgirls they were intended to portray.

'Pay attention, all of you!' Pauline tapped the board and pointed to various parts of the diagram, asking questions of different members of the class. Jackie and Lorna frequently met his gaze, both narrowing their eyes at him, and Jackie provocatively running her tongue about her lips.

The game of questions and answers continued for some minutes until one of the girls spoke and Pauline cut her short with a whack of her cane across the diagram.

'How many times have I told you?' she shouted. 'And still you can't get that right!' There was a moment of utter silence. Then Pauline, hand on hip, gestured at the recalcitrant pupil with her cane and ordered firmly, 'Step over here at once!'

One of the girls from the back chairs, a girl with grey eyes and long blonde hair, stood up and made her way to the desk. Pauline opened one of the small drawers and pulled out a pair of bright steel handcuffs from which, attached by a short chain, swung a leather collar.

'Turn around!' she ordered.

Pauline looped the collar quickly about the girl's neck, pushing her hair aside and fastening the steel buckle at the side, leaving the cuffs resting between her shoulder blades. She twisted each arm up behind her back and in a moment, the cuffs were snapped shut on the girl's wrists. The remainder of the class watched in silence as Pauline unfastened her skirt and pulled it briskly down to her ankles, revealing a pair of white cotton briefs. These followed the skirt down her legs to the floor.

'Lift your feet up and step out of them!' she ordered.

Mike, his head turned aside to keep his gaze fixed on the scene, saw her naked behind with her wrists pulled up together well above it. He attempted to adjust his position in the straps to make turning his head more comfortable. It had no such result. It did, however, cause the towel to loosen about his waist so that slowly, it began to move. He stopped squirming and for a time the towel stayed in place. His erection had died down over the last few minutes, but with the scene taking place nearby and the thought that he might soon be exposed to them all, it began to revive.

Pauline seized the manacled wrists and pulled them upwards, at the same time pushing the girl's head and upper body until she was bent face down over the desk with her naked behind on view to the others. Pauline, maintaining her grip on the girl's wrists and keeping the arms pulled away from her body, took up the cane with her free hand. She slapped the backs of the girl's legs with it and shouted, 'Open!' The legs opened until her most intimate parts were on view to everyone. 'Wider! Come on – wider!'

At last the girl's legs were spread as wide as she was able to spread them, her sex and her anus on full display. The cane rose, poised like a snake waiting to strike, then fell with a swish and a crack across the soft flesh. The girl shuddered and let out a sharp yelp. The cane fell once more and Pauline declared loudly, 'You will in future pay more attention to your lessons!'

The cane swished and cracked again and again, each stroke being followed by a howl of protest. The girl's buttocks began to glow pink with criss-cross weals and her cries became louder and longer. She began to struggle and twist her head from side to side with her mouth open and her eyes filling abundantly with tears. But her cries were not just cries of pain for she sobbed, 'Oh, oh, oh!' more in ecstasy than in agony, louder and longer as the cane swung remorselessly down. At length, she kicked out and her body shook repeatedly with a long, loud moan. The cane stopped and was laid aside. Pauline pulled her up to face the class. Her face was streaming with tears, her breath continued in short gasps and her eyes were shut tight. Pauline said nothing, but walked her over to the corner of the room, placing her, with arms still trussed up her back, face to the wall. Mike regarded her inflamed behind and could almost feel the burning on his own rear.

The towel began to slide. He pushed back hard with his pelvis against the wooden cross but it was coming undone from the side. Pauline had moved away from the girl and was returning the few short steps to the desk when the towel dropped down completely. There was a short burst of applause from the eight seated females as his semi-erect organ was exposed to their grinning view.

'Quiet, class!' commanded Pauline, looking him up and down with a suggestion of disapproval. 'Now, as you know, we have this wretch on loan for demonstration purposes ...' Jackie appeared to be having difficulty keeping a straight face. 'Does anyone care to tell me,' continued Pauline, 'what the next item in our lesson is?'

Four hands went up at once, followed promptly by the rest. Pauline eyed them without expression.

'Well, Claudia?'

An olive skinned Latin-looking girl with crinkled black hair, wide sensuous mouth and sparkling dark eyes arose.

'*Si signora – l'eccitazione ...*'

'No!' shouted Pauline, cutting her off in mid-sentence. 'So we all understand if you don't mind!'

'Oh, oh ... *scusi* ... yes,' she stammered, 'it is for the excitement of the man.'

'Stimulation!' countered Pauline.

'Ah, yes, stim-oo-lation.'

She picked up the cane and stepped over to the figure spread out helplessly on the cross. She looked at his penis, still maintaining its halfway house between rampant erection and flaccid indifference.

'This,' she announced, placing the end of the cane under the irresolute organ and lifting it up slightly, 'is all we need presently concern ourselves about. The rest of him is not important!'

He held his breath and closed his eyes, feeling the hard instrument pushing up under his most sensitive asset, trying not to think about what she might do with the cane. When he opened his eyes again it was to see eight amused faces. Amused, that is, in varying degrees. Some were merely grinning, while Jackie and Lorna appeared to be on the verge of convulsion.

'Control yourselves!' shouted Pauline, rapping the cane sharply down upon the table directly in front of Jackie. The mirth at once subsided. 'Now, I want each of you to show us your own approach to doing what you do best. Who is going to be first?' Eight hands went up simultaneously. 'Such devotion to duty,' responded Pauline, pointing to the middle girl in the second row. 'You!'

The girl stood up, tall and slim, her light brown hair swept back into a clasp at the side of her head and cascading over her right shoulder, almost down to her waist. Pauline moved aside as the girl stepped forward and halted in front of the helpless figure. She looked into his eyes, then lowered her head to his chest. Her tongue touched him lightly, making his body tingle as it played back and forth over his flesh, moving slowly downward. She put her hands on his waist and sank down on to her knees, her tongue darting about his navel, her teeth gently biting the soft flesh of his abdomen. His penis had quickly become erect and stood engorged and quivering against her neck. She brought her hands down across his stomach until her thumbs were pressed on either side at the base of the shaft. Her head moved down still further and she ran her tongue slowly, flicking from side to side, under the inflamed organ and up to the glistening head, one of her hands slipping down to caress underneath his testicles. He closed his eyes and tensed against the straps. The girl continued for some time, each pass of her tongue causing the object of her attentions to twitch visibly. Her actions were as much a torment as a stimulant, for what she was doing to him was at once too much and too little. He ached so much for relief that he began to wish she would stop. The pressure of the cane against her shoulder said that was enough.

Pauline turned to the other girls but before she had change to speak, Jackie's hand was raised high.

'All right,' said Pauline, 'but just be careful!'

Jackie smiled into his eyes mischievously as she stood up. He watched her move slowly closer, undoing her blouse button by button. When she stood before him, the blouse was pulled wide open and her breasts exposed. Still smiling, she ran her fingers over the rubber ball planted firmly in his mouth.

'I think I prefer you like this,' she whispered into his ear.

Her breasts were soft and warm against him as she ran her fingers up and down his waist and thighs. She also knelt before him and he watched her through half-closed eyes, taut with expectancy, his organ of lust aching for attention regardless of how many faces were turned on him. He did not have long to wait for she placed her hands on either side of her breasts and squeezed the shaft between them, keeping the swollen head visible between her cleavage, perceiving how it already glistened wet with expectation and feeling the pulse of his body concentrated in this one place.

At a gesture from Pauline, the remaining seven girls left their seats and gathered around in order to obtain a better view. Jackie held him firmly, running her tongue around the head of his penis and moving her breasts up and down against the shaft. He made no sound and gave no indication as to the state of his excitement as she quickened the pace of her movements. Nor did she hear the voice ordering her to stop, but continued with increased vigour.

As the cane rapped her shoulder, she felt his penis quiver and his body lurched hard against the straps.

'Stop that now!' came the order from above her, but it was too late. He groaned out loudly and, his loins shaking uncontrollably, spurted his passion repeatedly over her neck and breasts. There were cries of 'Oooh!' followed by a short burst of applause from the small group of on-lookers. Pauline affected a watery smile.

'What did I tell you?' she said through gritted teeth, close to Jackie's face.

'I . . . I'm sorry . . .'

'It wasn't her fault,' cut in Lorna. 'It happened too quickly.'

'Very well,' said Pauline, looking hard at Jackie, 'but we still have more to do. We'll break off for an hour then come back and continue as planned.' She turned to the figure standing obediently in the corner of the room, her hands still fastened up behind her shoulders. 'You can come and sit down here until we get back!' She smiled at Mike as the others, except for Jackie, left the room and said, 'I'm sure you'll both behave yourselves while I'm gone!'

Once through the main doors and in the ante room, Pauline gripped Jackie by the arm and pulled her around to face the inevitable wrath.

'You silly little bitch!' she rasped. 'You've delayed the whole thing unnecessarily! Go and get yourself cleaned up and be back here on time with the others. I'll talk to you later!'

'Later' proved to be at 7.30 in the evening, for after the events upstairs, Pauline had sat in discussion with Sonia and Cheryl in the main office for almost two hours. Pauline had summoned her up to her own rooms on the first floor and Jackie had entered in trembling anticipation, expecting the worst. She emerged unscathed, however, some ten minutes later and proceeded down to the ground floor. She entered the bar and waved cheekily at Angela, who was serving there for the evening, then continued on into the conservatory where she joined Lorna and Rachel at a table close to the french windows.

'God!' said Lorna, with no little surprise. 'I didn't expect to see you back so soon. Has she let you off?'

'Not exactly,' answered Jackie. 'She couldn't have a go at me tonight though because she's got letters to write and –'

'Letters?' cut in Rachel. 'Who to?'

'She has a friend in the Gestapo!' answered Lorna, with a look of grave conviction.

'Who needs the bloody Gestapo!' countered Rachel.

'Anyhow, she's busy tomorrow as well,' continued Jackie, 'so I've to stay in my room all day, including meal times.'

'Oh, the miserable old cow!' said Lorna.

'It could have been a lot worse,' added Rachel.

'Well, I happen to know they have visitors until five o'clock,' said Jackie, 'so she isn't going to be around to see what I do. I'll hang about until mid-morning in case she checks up on me then I'll be down at the pool with you lot, OK?'

'It's you that's taking the chance,' replied Lorna. 'By the way, what happened to Mike? I haven't seen him down here.'

'I saw him at the pool an hour ago,' answered Rachel.

'So she hasn't still got him in her clutches up there?' asked Lorna.

'Poor Mike!' laughed Jackie. 'The things he has to do!'

'Has to do?' questioned Rachel, with an expression of surprise. 'There must be millions of men who'd change places with him tomorrow. I know a couple of politicians who –'

'Well, maybe,' interrupted Lorna, 'but she goes out of her way to humiliate him, the same way she does with us.'

'So how did it end up today?' asked Rachel.

Jackie and Lorna looked at each other and laughed. Jackie pushed back her hair before speaking.

'Well, Francesca got in on the act and –'

'She can be quite outrageous!' cut in Rachel.

'Yes,' continued Jackie, 'and she was! I won't go into details but let's just say there was a bit of a misfire and he, er, it ended up all over the floor. Pauline locked away his clothes before she undid him and refused to let him have them until he got the soap and water and cleaned the carpet!'

'Well, someone had to,' said Rachel.

'Yes,' agreed Lorna, 'but she went out of her way to embarrass and belittle him in front of us – that's not fair, he's not that sort of person.'

'What can he do?' asked Rachel.

'I don't know,' answered Lorna, 'but I wouldn't be surprised if she was found floating face down in the pool one morning.'

Jackie said nothing, but turned her eyes away from them both. Her own needs, her own urges, were fulfilled by those very impositions which others might find so himiliating and the instrument of her perverse gratification was Pauline. As much as she might be swept by trepidation at the very sight of those cold blue eyes, the breeze which rippled the waters at the surface also churned the deeper currents of lust hidden beneath. She could forgive Pauline anything as long as there was something which needed to be forgiven.

4

Birthday Gifts

In the phantom world of half-consciousness, of neither light nor dark, there was a sound. Karen opened her eyes. It was daylight and the morning sun spilled insistently through little gaps and chinks in the bedroom blind. The light was both friend and foe. It announced the promise of a bright new day but dissolved the drifting half-world of the subconscious. But for her it was a special day and because it was special, she already felt lonely. Perhaps she would confide in Angela. Somebody should share it with her, it was only right.

There was a sound; she had not imagined it. Something rustling outside in the corridor. The clock radio said almost 7.40. It wasn't going to switch on for another five minutes and although today was Friday, a working day, she had already returned to the more casual routine of the house.

She sat naked before the mirror, running a comb slowly through her hair. The right-hand drawer of the vanity unit was part open and the white box could be seen. No one had alluded to it; no one had dropped the slightest hint. She had passed Pauline a number of times over the days since her return and there had been no sly remark, no knowing look. The instrument of carnal gratification which lay within the box had served her desires again the previous night.

From the selection of clothes provided for her, Karen chose a thin, sleeveless, saffron yellow cotton top, white flared mini-skirt and white sandals. Like the others, she usually only wore stockings in the evening. She pulled open the door, thinking vaguely of the day ahead, then stopped. Resting against the door frame was a large bouquet of pink and white roses, wrapped in cellophane and tied with a red satin ribbon. Around the bouquet were spread a number of envelopes, each bearing her name in a different hand. They knew.

She collected the cards and the flowers and turned back into her room, taking them through into the small bedroom and spreading them upon the multi-coloured bedspread. There were cards from almost everyone, including Cheryl, who she hardly knew at all, and, of course, Mike. The one exception came as no surprise. The flowers were from Sonia, the accompanying card bearing, in careful blue script, the words, 'Happy Birthday, XXX-S.'

Sonia must have told them. The gesture meant more to Karen than even Sonia might imagine.

She entered the main office at nine o'clock. Despite the easy-going lifestyle at the house, she had from the beginning remained punctual, and having returned, did not intend to let the habit lapse.

Sonia, wearing a biker jacket, black satin tights and ankle boots, was leaving her desk and walking towards the door almost before Karen was inside the room.

'Karen, my dear,' she said, smiling broadly, 'many happy returns!'

Sonia put her arms around her and kissed her on her lips. Karen returned her embrace with warmth. The kiss was a long kiss, even though they were visible through the windows from the corridor outside.

'Thank you for the roses, they're lovely,' whispered Karen.

'I'm very glad you liked them,' replied Sonia. 'You must share a bottle of champagne with me later, unless of course you had other plans.'

'Oh no, I didn't have anything planned. I didn't expect that . . .'

The dark eyes looked into hers. She felt a familiar stirring in her belly and loins. Sonia seemed to know her feelings and kissed her once more, this time only lightly.

'You're not going to work on your birthday. I'll sort everything out.'

'No, really, I don't mind, Sonia. Anyway, there are all the receipts to be –'

'I insist,' cut in Sonia. 'All that can wait until next week. You go and relax by the pool, but promise me you'll be in the bar by one o'clock, OK? I think the girls have something for you.'

'Yes, of course I will.'

'I can't be there myself, mind you – we have a couple of visitors – but most of the others will, I'm sure.'

Karen did not change but collected a book from her room, intending to sit by the poolside and read. When she arrived, two heads of long black hair bobbed up and down and glistened in the water, the sunlight catching their limbs as they circled about, oblivious to the world beyond.

'Hi, you two!' Karen called, pulling a chair out from beneath a sunshade.

Valerie and Lorna turned around, then stood up in the shimmering water.

'Happy birthday!' they both grinned.

'Coming in for a dip?' called Valerie.

'Not this morning.'

'OK, we'll come out!'

They climbed dripping from the water, their slim forms naked except for their minimal swim slips. Both were perfectly suited to the role of poolside glamour models and the scene lacked only a host of ogling photographers.

'You make me feel out of place and overdressed,' laughed Karen as they joined her at the table.

'You are,' said Lorna. 'You look like you're off to work.'

'I was, but Sonia gave me the day off.'

'I should think so too, on your birthday!' said Valerie.

'Oh yes – thanks for your cards. It was a lovely surprise. I didn't think anyone knew.'

'She told us all days ago,' said Lorna, grinning, 'but I bet you didn't get a card from Pauline, did you?'

'No, I didn't. I would have fallen over in amazement if I had!'

'Miserable old cow,' muttered Valerie.

'She's not old though, is she?' asked Karen. 'I was told she's around thirty. She doesn't look any more than that.'

'No,' replied Valerie, 'she just behaves like an old ... hey! Look who's here!'

They all turned their eyes towards the house. A figure approached them, her abundant auburn hair falling about her shoulders, the short, white cotton longsleeved dress fitting her slim body like a glove and her legs poised on white, high-heel sandals. In her hand she held a small gold and navy-blue paper bag.

'Hello, you lot!' she shouted, regarding them with green feline eyes.

'Annette,' said Karen, rising up from the chair and kissing her cheeks. Annette thrust the small bag into her hands and kissed her in turn.

'It's a little pressie for you from Paris, dear. It's lovely to see you back.'

'It's great to be back and I'm so glad to see you,' said Karen warmly. 'When did you get in? Have you seen Sonia?'

'Only about quarter of an hour ago. The taxi dropped me off at the gate. Sonia's in a meeting with Cheryl and Pauline, and a couple of rich-looking blokes. One of them's not bad looking either!'

'D'you know who they are?' asked Valerie, turning to Karen.

'No, not exactly. I think they're from Munich.'

'I feel overexposed with you two here,' said Valerie, looking down at her naked breasts. 'I'm going back into the water until you admit defeat and get changed.'

'Oh, look!' exclaimed Lorna. 'We've got reinforcements!'

Jackie approached, her light brown hair done up in a pony-tail, her body enveloped in a bathrobe.

'Hi everyone!' she said brightly, squeezing Annette's arm.

'Saw you walking along the path so I thought I'd make

the break. I got out the back way. You-know-who is in the main office.'

'She's been a naughty girl again, haven't you?' said Valerie. 'She's not supposed to be out of doors.'

'Oh dear!' said Annette. 'Breaking the dragon lady's laws again?'

'I'm not sitting in my room all day if I don't have to. She can get stuffed!'

'I wonder if she ever does?' said Annette, grinning.

'I'm going for a swim,' announced Jackie, pulling off the white bathrobe to reveal her body, naked except for her scanty blue and red slip, so minimal as to make it obvious that she had no pubic hair.

The three went into the pool, splashing and laughing in the warm sun and the crystal water. Karen and Annette sat talking and exchanging news under the sunshade. It was Karen who spotted the figure looking out from the portico.

'Oh dear – there's Pauline!'

Annette swung round.

'Bloody hell! I'll tell Jackie!'

She turned towards the poolside and issued the dreaded warning. The three clambered out, Valerie and Lorna taking up their bathrobes from the chair, Jackie hurrying along the poolside then off into the nearby trees.

'Where's she think she's going?' asked Valerie, as the fugitive disappeared from view.

'Not too far without any clothes on I shouldn't think,' remarked Karen, seeing the abandoned bathrobe.

By the time Pauline appeared, wearing a vivid red satin shirt, grey jodhpurs and black knee boots, Valerie and Lorna had pulled on their cotton robes and were seated at the table with Jackie and Annette.

'Where's she gone?' demanded the voice of authority.

Pauline stood between them and the sun, casting a dark shadow across the flagstones and the table before her. In her hand she clutched an ominous black plastic bag.

'She didn't tell us,' shrugged Valerie.

'She was here! I saw her from the upstairs window! She's in my charge, if you didn't realise it! I want to know where she is!'

'Haven't a clue, dear,' responded Annette.

'Haven't a clue, eh? Well, she'll have a clue when I find her and I'll –'

'Why don't you leave the poor kid alone for once?' cut in Valerie. 'She's not doing any harm!'

'That's right,' added Karen. 'She just came down for a quick dip. She was about to go back to the house.'

Pauline looked hard at her with an expression of near disbelief.

'I wasn't talking to you so there's no need to stick your nose in, is there? There's no need for you to be here at all!'

Karen felt an unaccustomed surge of anger welling up inside. She quickly stood up and moved around the sunshade to confront Pauline.

'Look! I don't care what your job is or how long you've been doing it! You're a bitter, spiteful bitch, Pauline, and that's no secret!'

Annette reached up to Karen's arm and pulled it gently. 'Pauline,' she said, 'why don't you just bugger off and leave us all in peace?'

'A brilliant idea!' added Valerie.

Lorna sat in silence, looking from one to the other.

But Pauline did not answer. Her gaze was fixed towards the tennis court. Mike and Angela were stood inside the wire netting, each with racket in hand, obviously talking to someone outside the enclosure who was obscured by the bushes. Pauline strode off around the pool and in the direction of the tennis court without further comment.

'Oh well – she'd have caught up with her sooner or later,' said Valerie.

'And Jackie knows perfectly well what happens when she disobeys the camp commandant,' added Annette. 'But you shouldn't let her see she's annoyed you,' she continued, turning to Karen. 'That's what she likes. It makes her think she's got the upper hand.'

'Yes, I suppose I should have kept quiet. It's nothing to do with me.'

'It's as much to do with you as any of us,' responded Valerie. 'I'm glad you spoke out to her. I wouldn't expect

Lorna to say anything because she's vulnerable, but you're not.'

They turned their eyes towards the tennis court. Mike and Angela were hitting the ball to and fro. Of Pauline and Jackie there was no sign.

Another minute or so had passed by before Lorna said, 'There's one of them now.'

Pauline was observed walking alone, cutting diagonally across the grass near the tennis court and approaching the front of the house. Conversation resumed, only to be interrupted again by the appearance of Jackie.

'Oh God! Now what?' groaned Valerie.

As Jackie came nearer, still virtually naked, it was obvious she no longer had use of her arms.

'So that's what she had in the bag,' remarked Annette.

Around Jackie's neck was a smooth steel collar. The others, gathering around, could see that there was a steel rod of little more than twenty centimetres in length attached to the back of it. At the end of the rod, a pair of swivel linked steel cuffs held Jackie's wrists together, pulled up firmly between her shoulder blades. She looked at them all in turn, her lips slightly parted and her breasts pushed out with their nipples pink and prominent.

'I-I've to ask for my bathrobe,' she stammered.

'This is out of order,' said Valerie. 'Restraints aren't supposed to be used outside the house. If Sonia sees this –'

'Sonia's out,' cut in Jackie. 'She's gone to Béziers railway station with Cheryl and those two men.'

'I see,' answered Valerie, looking at the restraint, 'and I suppose nobody else has a key for these.'

'No, and . . . look, I'm to go straight back, she's waiting for me. Please!'

'I'll take her back,' said Karen, picking up Jackie's bathrobe. 'It's not safe for her to walk around outside like this.'

Karen pulled the towelling robe around the girl's body and fastened the belt.

'It's her way of snubbing us,' said Annette. 'She knows we can't do anything about it.'

'I'm sorry about lunchtime,' said Jackie, as Karen led

71

her along the pathway. 'She wasn't going to let me out anyway.'

From an upstairs window, two narrowed eyes watched them approach the main entrance.

'Interfering bitch,' whispered Pauline.

There was a single, sharp tap on the door. Pauline waited a few seconds before moving. When she finally opened the door, Jackie stood there alone, the arms of the towelling robe hanging empty by her sides.

'So, Miss Prim and Proper's delivered you back, has she? Do come inside, or did you have somewhere else to go?'

Jackie walked into the room, looking straight ahead and remaining silent. As the door closed behind her, she caught her breath and opened her mouth. Ahead of her, draped over the green leather armchair, were a number of items in heavy black rubber. She could not tell how many or exactly what they consisted of. One thing only was certain; they were all intended for her.

Pauline tugged loose the belt and pulled the bathrobe away from her. Two thumbs slipped under the elasticated band of the G-string and pushed it down to her ankles. Pauline stepped over to her desk, threw the little garment down on to it and picked up the one thing Jackie dreaded. At the sight of the coiled black whip, she yanked at the cuffs and moaned, 'No ... please ... no!'

'You deserve a damn good dose of this!' shouted Pauline, pushing the whip under her nose then smacking her across the mouth with her other hand. Jackie felt her bowels churning.

'Now, get to the bathroom! We'll have no ceremonies and this isn't being recorded so be quick about it!'

Jackie did as she was ordered, Pauline following close behind. She trembled as she walked, expecting at any moment the angry sting of the whip. As she entered the blue tiled room with its harsh lights she saw what had been prepared, but did not hesitate. From its wall bracket, next to the oval blue bowl and some two metres above the floor, hung the rubber bottle. From it spiralled down the clear plastic pipe, which ended, resting on the sink, with its pink rubber probe.

'All right! You know what you have to do, so do it!'

Jackie, in silent obedience, faced the sink and bent forward, leaning against it and feeling the porcelain cold against her breasts. She spread her legs as Pauline laid aside the whip and took up the syringe. From a small jar she applied a clear jelly to the end of it with her finger. She moved behind Jackie and placed the nozzle against her anus.

Jackie did not resist as the cool probe entered her body, hard and insistent, pushing up into her rectum. She caught her breath and closed her eyes, feeling the invader move sensually inside her.

'Make the most of it,' remarked Pauline, as it entered as far as its flared base would allow.

Immediately behind the syringe was a small valve. With a quick twist of her fingers, Pauline released this and watched the bubbles skimming around the coiled tubing as the soap solution and water passed through. As Jackie's body stiffened, Pauline reached over and turned a chrome valve on the wall, directly above the lower bowl. Hot water gushed in a whirlpool from the inside rim. Jackie tensed again as Pauline slowly withdrew the instrument from her. She wanted to tighten her muscles on it, to keep it inside her, but in a moment it was gone and the dark turmoil within her bowels was beginning.

'On here, quickly!' came the next instruction.

She bent up from the sink and, guided by Pauline, lowered herself down over the gushing bowl so that she sat facing outward with her legs spread either side of it. She could see herself reflected fully in the big wall mirror opposite.

'Sit upright, don't slouch!' Pauline ordered.

Jackie caught her breath and closed her eyes as her body involuntarily evacuated its charge into the bowl, her bladder also releasing its hot amber contents in unison. Pauline watched her, revelling in the humiliation and degradation which she obviously knew such an act must ensure.

After being thoroughly rinsed, Jackie was allowed to rise. Pauline turned off the water before dabbing her dry with the towel.

'Please, my arms are hurting,' pleaded Jackie, but Pauline ignored her, picked up the coiled whip and said, 'Move.'

They re-entered the lounge-cum-office where the strictly manacled Jackie was brought to a halt.

'Now then,' said Pauline, standing before her, 'you deliberately and knowingly disobeyed me again, and in front of the others. In front of them! That was the worst thing of all!' Pauline moved around behind her and continued. 'If I was to tell Sonia you were becoming unmanageable, you know what would happen, don't you?'

Jackie remained silent.

'Well, don't you?'

The whip swished and cracked with a burning sting across her behind.

'Well, don't you?' yelled Pauline.

'Yes . . . yes,' Jackie whimpered.

'Yes! You would have to go from here and your father would be very, very angry with you!'

'Please don't . . . please,' begged Jackie.

'If I don't, then I have to ensure you cause me fewer problems. And that means further restrictions which you will have to accept as of now. Do I make myself clear?'

Jackie nodded. A nod was not sufficient. The whip hissed and cracked – once, twice, three times in rapid succession. Jackie shrieked and tottered forward.

'Do I make myself clear? Do I?'

The whip again seared her flesh.

'Yes!' screamed Jackie. 'Yes! Yes! Yes!'

'Good, then perhaps at long last we understand each other.'

She laid the whip down and walked over to her desk. Pulling open the drawer, she reached inside and took out a small silver key. Returning to Jackie, she held the key up in front of her face and said, 'I can leave you as you are until this evening, or I can undo you now and put you into

74

something more comfortable. Either way, I go out in ten minutes. Which is it to be?'

Jackie looked down with tearful eyes.

'My arms are killing me. I don't care what you do – just undo me!'

'You'll stand still and do as you're told?'

'Yes.'

'I don't know what to say to you all, apart from thanks,' said Karen, smiling. 'It's just, well, it's lovely!'

'Right!' said Mike, kissing her warmly. 'You'd better blow out the candles!'

Karen took a deep breath and blew. Everyone clapped and cried out, 'Happy birthday!'

'Now, you sit down, dear!' said Valerie. 'His lordship there is going to open the fizz and I'll cut the cake.'

'Who made it?' asked Karen.

'Kim,' replied Valerie. 'It's one of her many talents.'

Karen looked about the conservatory. Annette handed her a glass of champagne and said, 'It's a pity Sonia and Cheryl had to be away. I know they both wanted to be here.'

'And poor Jackie,' added Karen.

'I think your sympathy for her might be a little misplaced,' responded Annette, raising her glass. 'Cheers!'

'Yes, cheers! Maybe you're right, Annette, but I still think Pauline treats her dreadfully. I really do.'

'Well, don't let it bother you today. Enjoy yourself – I'm certainly going to!'

'Yes, I will. I think everyone is so nice to me here. Sometimes I don't understand.'

'It's our role in life to be nice,' said Valerie, appearing at her side and handing her a slice of cake on a paper plate.

'Absolutely,' agreed Annette. 'It pays dividends.' She pushed aside her long auburn hair and a mischievous smile flickered over her lips. 'We girls always try our best!'

Kim appeared, wearing a white sleeveless lace top, scooped daringly low over her full breasts. Beneath this, a short, tight, blue denim skirt and white stiletto heel sandals flattered her legs. Karen noticed Mike gazing hard at them over his glass from the other side of the room.

'Kim, it's the best birthday cake ever. Thanks!'

'You're welcome,' said Kim, holding her arms and kissing her. Valerie kissed her too. The kisses made her burn inside and for a moment, both pairs of eyes searched deep into hers. Karen wanted to kiss and hold them all at the same time.

Pauline glanced at herself in the mirror and adjusted the collar of her satin blouse before walking back across the room. She picked up the coiled black whip from the table and continued on to replace it inside the desk drawer. She turned to regard the figure seated in the green leather armchair.

The only visible part of Jackie was that part of her body from the waist to just below her knees. Her head and upper body were enclosed in an almost featureless skin of gleaming, heavy, black latex. The helmet was blank, except for two holes corresponding with the nostrils and, protruding below these, a short black tube ending in a rubber inflation bulb. Her arms were tightly confined within the garment and held folded in front of her. Enclosing her lower legs and feet was a single 'boot' of the same material. Unable to see, speak or use her limbs, Jackie remained statue-like in the chair.

'Can you breathe easily?' asked Pauline, bending towards the helpless figure.

'Mmm,' came the barely audible, muffled reply. At the same time, the head nodded up and down, causing the rubber bulb to jerk about and swing from side to side.

'Good,' responded Pauline, 'because you'd be an even greater nuisance to us if you suffocated than you already are, and Sonia would lose the income from your parents!' She turned towards the door. 'Oh, by the way. See if you can guess how much time has passed before I get back. It will seem a lot longer to you than it does to me!'

The door closed quietly and there was silence. In the silence, and in the enclosed darkness, Jackie began to dream.

In her dream she drifted down the river of voluptuous abandon and entered the secret grotto where the flames of lust
and sensuality burned. After a time, she began to squirm
slowly in the chair and tense her body within the restraints.

Karen had no doubts now about her assignation with
Sonia. Her only desire was that others should not know, as
Valerie surely did. And what of Valerie? Had she not
reached the heights of sexual gratification in the hands of
her and Kim? Could anything she did here, no matter how
outrageous, cause anyone to raise an eyebrow? Her friends
here loved her and she loved them. They were angels,
though even in this house of angels there was a Lucifer.
   Once, Lucifer had been the 'bringer of light', before the
mythical fall into darkness. How deceptive appearances
can be, for orginally she had thought of Sonia and not
Pauline as dark and devious. But then, she told herself,
everything looks dark if you can only see your own light.
She had known deep down, of course, that Sonia had tried
to manipulate her within a few weeks, or less, of her taking
the job. But it had worked for both of them, and now there
was something else, something special.
   After the little party, she had spent the latter part of the
afternoon talking to Angela. They had met at their favourite quiet spot, the old wooden seat under the tree, with its
view across the pleasant valley towards the distant sea.
Now, she was back in her own room, showered and standing naked before the mirror and brushing her hair down
before her breasts.
   She placed the hairbrush in the drawer, next to the white
box, and stepped over to the wardrobe. She touched the
more exotic garments within it; did Sonia want her to wear
any of those for their evening meetings? If not, why were
they there? Perhaps it was not all the work of Sonia. Some
of these things might have been chosen by Valerie or Annette. They would know that by now she would take no
offence.
   She pulled open the door and the drawer below the hanging clothes. Perhaps the champagne she had consumed

earlier on in the afternoon continued to suppress her inhibitions, for she had eaten only a light meal since. She decided to wear stockings rather than tights, so began to examine the rectangular packets to find something which appealed. She next turned her attention to the rack above and after some minutes, to the selection of shoes beneath. She placed the chosen items on the bed, hesitated with fleeting doubt, then closed the wardrobe door.

She first, and very carefully, pulled on the bikini briefs. They had looked black when she had held them, like a piece of nylon froth in her hand. Now they appeared as the merest shadow, their edges sharply defined by the black elastic. They fit like a gossamer skin, almost transparent, over her smooth vulva. The sheer black stockings needed more care in order to get the seams in line, but required no support, for the elasticated lace tops held them firmly in place on her thighs.

The shoes had needed even more thought and she still had some doubts about her choice. They were gold sandals with open toes and thin criss-cross straps intended to fit about the ankles. But the heels were some sixteen or more centimetres high and she knew that walking would not be easy. She sat down on the bed, thought for a moment, then pulled them on and fastened the straps. She stood up and looked at herself in the mirror, then walked up and down the room, cautiously at first but with increasing confidence.

'Oh well,' she whispered, 'I'm hardly going on a tour of the grounds this evening.'

She picked up the dress and pulled it on over her head. It was a low-cut dress of crushed velvet in Bordeaux red with shoestring straps over the shoulders. It fitted perfectly; tight about the bodice to define her breasts and slightly flared below the waist. The dress was short, but not unduly so, and would not reveal the tops of her stockings. She reached out once more for the hairbrush then the bedside phone rang. She hesitated for a moment. Who would call at this time? It was past 7.30.

'Yes?'

'Karen.'

It was not a question but rather a statement. It was the voice of Sonia.

'Oh! I didn't expect –'

'It's all right, my dear. I thought I'd catch you before you came down.'

'Yes, that's OK, I wasn't leaving for a few minutes.'

'All right – I wondered if you might feel more comfortable not coming in through the office door. There's another way if you prefer.'

'Em . . . yes, I had thought . . .'

'The door to the beauty parlour will be unlocked. It doesn't matter what anyone thinks about you going in there. You know the way through.'

'Yes, all right, that's no problem.'

'Good. The champagne is nice and cold. I'll see you soon.'

'Yes, I won't be long.'

Karen put down the phone and returned to the mirror to tidy her hair and apply a little lipstick.

She took the back stairs as she often did when she did not wish to be seen, treading very carefully in the exaggerated heels. The thought of another encounter with Pauline caused her some uneasiness, but the stairs were deserted and quiet. There were voices on the ground floor corridor so she hesitated before turning the last corner. The voices receded then vanished. She continued on.

Entering the beauty parlour, she found the lights switched on and the inner door ajar. There was nobody inside the main room but she walked through slowly, savouring the warm and inviting ambience, not wishing to disturb the quiet atmosphere because it was not her place to do so. It belonged to Valerie and Kim. It was their little kingdom and she was an intruder.

She emerged into the warm light of the room she had only visited twice before, and then as a half-reluctant prisoner of the person to whom she was about to encounter again. Not the Sonia of the day, the Sonia of her working world, but the Sonia of the night, the Sonia she had only glimpsed dimly during those early days at the house.

She walked by the chrome and black leather furniture, whose purpose she now fully understood, past the cage with its steel manacles and up to the ... she halted, mystified. There was no door, just a blank wall. Then a slit of light appeared in the wall and the door, disguised so as not to be identifiable as such, swung open.

'Come through, my dear,' said a voice from within.

Karen entered the warm privacy of Sonia's apartment, a womb of secrecy within a house full of secrets. Karen beheld her with open mouth but no words came forth. Sonia appeared as a sleek, black statue. Only her head, with its black pony-tail and her dark smouldering eyes, told that she was not a feline creation in black marble.

'Does it frighten you?' she asked softly, spreading out her fingers and running them up Karen's forearm.

'Frighten me? I-I don't know.'

'Well, come and sit down with me and relax for a while.'

Karen followed her across the room, seeing the rose-coloured lights gleam dully on her limbs. The catsuit fitted her like a skin, yielding with her every movement, enclosing her lithe body from fingertips to neck and down to her sleek black ankle boots with their slim high heels.

On the table sat a glistening ice bucket with its bottle of champagne already opened. At the table there waited two green leather chairs and before each stood an empty wine glass.

'Sit down, my dear,' invited Sonia.

Although the room was warm, Karen shivered. She sat down but continued to watch Sonia, who moved, pantherlike, around to the chair opposite. Why was she so bewitching? Even on the occasions of their previous intimacies together, when Sonia had explored and exploited Karen's body in ways she had never imagined anyone could, she had never appeared so menacing, so sinister.

Sonia pulled the champagne bottle up, wet and shining from its icy embrace, and filled the two glasses.

'To you, my dear!' she offered, raising the glass between them.

'Y-yes, cheers!' answered Karen, snapping out of her turmoil of silence.

They drank, and Karen sat in silence, her legs crossed and her dress riding high up her thighs. She dared not move to pull the hem down for she wished to make no signals. She sat as one being accused, not wishing to move or speak in case either action should draw the attention of the interrogator to something she ought not to divulge. She was again in the lair of one she knew so well and one who knew her body and mind better than anyone else. But Sonia was an enigma. She was like a casket which, once having become familiar, is opened to reveal another casket within, and then another, so that the secret is never revealed and may never be there at all. Karen thought that she had begun to know Sonia, until this evening.

'You are very uneasy,' whispered Sonia. 'As anxious as on that first day in England so long ago.'

Karen stared hard into her glass before answering. 'I-I'm sorry. I really don't know what it is.'

'And on your birthday, my dear. A day when everyone should be good to you and give you pleasure.'

'I feel as though you're a stranger tonight. The way you act. The way you look. I might be with someone I hardly know at all.'

'But, my dear, there are times when we should not be our habitual selves, when we are away from our work-a-day world, away from the sunlight and the open air. We should keep our secret world apart from all that; never speak of it, push it out of our mind until we have passed through the veil where no other can see us and we discover that which lives deep and abiding beneath our thoughts.'

'Through the looking-glass,' whispered Karen.

'Through the looking-glass,' repeated Sonia, her eyes dark and compelling. She took up the champagne bottle and refilled the glasses. 'But of course, when we have passed through the looking-glass, it is the world we have left behind us which ceases to be real. You have stepped over the threshold of that secret world a number of times since you came to this house. You have dallied for a time but never gone far beyond the portal – never further into the hidden places.'

'But I never knew the portal existed until I came here. What do you expect of me?'

'Expect? Why, only that you know your other self. The self that has never dared to speak.'

'Sometimes,' said Karen, draining her glass, 'sometimes it can be intimidating – the things I've seen here – that room.'

'And me,' said Sonia, smiling and running her splayed fingers, with their second skin of black, down the side of her face.

'Yes, and you. When I first saw you this evening, I thought you looked like a big cat awaiting its prey.'

'But does not a cat go out and catch its prey? You came here because you wished to, as you have before.'

Sonia rose from the chair and moved around to her. She seated herself on the edge of the table in front of Karen, looking down upon her, all but filling her view and holding her in her fathomless gaze.

'The door is only a few steps away,' she whispered closely. 'Perhaps you should leave while you can.'

'Leave? No! I –'

'Then shall we finish the champagne?'

Karen, with the demon of sensuality stirring in her belly, watched in silence while Sonia emptied the last of the frothing champagne into the glasses. She returned her eyes to Karen.

'Shall we drink this last glass to –'

'To what?'

'To our other selves in our other world – our secret world?'

Karen looked into her eyes for searching moments and breathed in softly. 'They must always remain apart.'

'Of course, my dear. Always apart, like day and night.'

'Then, yes, to our other selves. To our secret world.'

The smile passed as a shadow across Sonia's face. She reached down and stroked along the side of Karen's thigh, her fingers pushing softly into the sheer black nylon, running with electric sensuality up to the elasticated lace. Karen closed her eyes. This was not the real world. What did anything matter?

The empty glasses stood side by side upon the table. Sonia moved away silently. Why, Karen did not know. She sensed movements and saw shadows on the wall but did not move. Somewhere, in one of the dark corners, a clock ticked.

A hand was laid on her shoulder and a face appeared before her. Their lips met with perfumed fire and Sonia whispered, 'There's something I want to show you.'

Karen stood up, the effects of the drink becoming at once evident. She grasped the back of the chair for a moment, remembering that she still wore the sandals with their extra high heels. Sonia took her arm and they walked over to a long, low table placed against a wall. On the table stood a large maroon box, sprouting tissue paper, its lid propped up by the side.

'It arrived yesterday, as did this suit. Nobody has seen any of it before, just you and I.'

Karen touched her arm, running her fingers up the smooth gleaming black as far as her elbow. 'It's you, Sonia, exactly you. I've never seen anything like it. It isn't leather or . . . I don't know what it is.'

'It's a new material. It stretches, contracts and breathes – stays perfectly smooth too, as you can see.'

Sonia placed her hand on Karen's. The hand looked like a black snake which might dart at her at any moment. It was a hand which might go anywhere and everywhere. She found herself staring at it and felt a slight shiver within.

'And these other things,' whispered Sonia, pushing aside the white tissue paper which obscured the contents of the box, 'they are for you, my dear.'

'For me? Things for me to wear?'

Karen looked down among the confusion of tissue but could ascertain nothing.

'Yes, things to wear,' answered Sonia, lifting her hand up to Karen's shoulder.

The rich aroma of leather drifted up from the dark

interior of the box. Sonia's lips met hers with perfumed breath rising from a deep furnace. The shoulder strings of Karen's dress were pushed aside so that the dress loosened and released her breasts into the warm light. Sonia moved behind her, cupping the breasts in her hands and kissing her neck before relieving her of the dress altogether. For a time, they kissed, Sonia holding her arms tightly and pushing back her elbows. Karen did not resist.

'Turn around,' whispered the voice in Karen's ear.

She turned so that she was facing the wooden bed with its bright oriental cover. She heard the rustling of tissue behind her as Sonia reached down into the secret box.

Something closed about her neck, something large and rigid but lined with a softer material. As it tightened, it forced her head straight forward and slightly up, making it impossible to turn it to either side without moving her entire body. Sonia held the collar at the rear while quickly securing three metal buckles at the left side. Karen took a sharp breath as some object, cool and hard, touched between her shoulder blades. It remained resting there while Sonia took her wrists and pulled them behind her. Again she felt the same rigid material with its soft lining, this time holding her wrists firmly together. But there was something else, something she did not comprehend, resting against her lower back under the metal bar. She was soon to realise the nature of the restraint, for her arms were encircled from the wrists upwards and as each buckle was fastened, her elbows were drawn closer to each other. Inexorably, the sleeve tightened until her elbows were pulled fully back and held securely together.

'There!' said Sonia, moving away, 'You look wonderful, my dear.'

'I feel I'm set rigid from the waist up,' answered Karen. 'It's as well I'm double-jointed.'

'Oh yes,' came the reply, 'I remembered that.'

Sonia returned to the box and Karen stood in helpless apprehension, wondering what was next to be placed upon her. The next move was quick and unexpected. Something large pushed against her mouth and she involuntarily opened it to cry out, thus letting the object in. It remained there, firm and unmoving, as Sonia tightened the strap behind her head. Instead of a cry, a long 'Mmmm' of protest emerged from the plugged mouth. Sonia took her by the shoulders and moved her towards a large built-in wardrobe with large, mirrored doors. She came to a halt before this and Sonia turned her part way around. Karen stared wide-eyed at her reflection. The high collar about her neck and the slim strap which held the pink rubber ball in her mouth were of deep red patent leather with hand-tooled scroll work, as was the sleeve which she was just able to see, which pinned her arms so tightly and forced out her firm and ample breasts to greater prominence. She saw too what Sonia held in her hand, and gave forth another meaningless protest. Even Karen knew what a cat-o'-nine-tails looked like.

'I'll take care, my dear, don't worry, but this will be good for you in the end, you'll see.'

Karen attempted to move away but Sonia, with her free hand, grasped the steel bar which joined the arm cuff to the collar. Karen saw the whip being raised then closed her eyes tightly as the first stroke fell.

Searing hot as it was, she made no sound but jerked her body as it fell a second, third and fourth time across the thin shadow of nylon covering her behind. She watched Sonia in the mirror before her and saw the look of concentration on her face as she raised the whip with slow deliberation. She knew that she was not applying the instrument with anything like the force with which she was capable. But Sonia seemed to read her mind, for the strokes became harder. Karen began to struggle and pull in earnest, letting out a plaintive 'Aaaah!' which, after a further three strokes, became a muffled shriek. Her eyes, first welling with hot tears, now flooded wet anguish down her cheeks. Again the whip landed with a scalding crack and her protests became a continuous sobbing until her knees gave under her and she sank down, still held by Sonia, on to the carpet. Sonia released her hold and in a moment the strap about Karen's face loosened and the rubber ball was withdrawn, dripping, from her open mouth.

'Oh why!' she moaned. 'Why do you want to hurt me? Why?'

Karen remained on her knees as her other bonds were loosened and her arms, released from the severe restriction of the leather sleeve, fell aching to her sides. But that was nothing to the incandescent torment about her behind and her thighs and so she remained, bowed and weeping, while Sonia walked over to the low table. Moments later, Sonia was back by her side, and having placed something on the floor behind her, knelt down and circled an arm around her shoulders. She brushed the damp hair away from Karen's face, kissed her cool lips and whispered, 'My dear, you will soon understand.'

Karen looked into her dark eyes with reproach but did not refuse the second kiss, which made her shiver. The burning aftermath of the whip had started to spread through her loins and Sonia's kiss only intensified it.

'Let's make it all better now,' whispered Sonia, taking her arm and lifting it up from her side.

Karen saw what Sonia held before her and uttered, 'N-no, please,' but did not resist as her arm was pushed into the horizontal sleeve.

It was quickly done. With both arms folded inside the sleeve, the garment was pulled over her shoulders and about her body. Sonia deftly fixed and tightened the eight straps and buckles from top to bottom before standing up behind her.

'I'll help you,' she said, gripping Karen's shoulders. 'You'll be much more comfortable now.'

Karen saw herself in full view in the mirror once more. From neck to waist she was enclosed in a tight cocoon of deep red leather, decorated in the manner of the other restraints. It fitted her like a glove, smooth and sleek and held her arms firmly within. It was comfortable, as Sonia had said, but totally secure.

'Will you forgive me?' asked Sonia, holding her close and looking deep into her eyes.

'Yes ... I ... yes, but you won't ... I mean, you won't again, not tonight.'

'No, not tonight. Tonight was your initiation – your step a little further into the looking-glass world.' Sonia held her closer still until the dark, fathomless eyes consumed her and the warm breath dispelled her tears. 'Tomorrow you will think nothing of it, nothing at all.'

'No, nothing.'

Their lips met, soft and burning. Sonia's fingers slipped under the thin black elastic, between the gossamer nylon and the smooth as silk flesh until they discovered the jewel of their quest. Even through the black skin which enclosed her own body and limbs, Sonia could feel Karen's heat and sensuality and the gateway of her sex, yielding and eager.

Sonia hesitated and withdrew her hand. Guiding Karen gently, they moved towards the bed. Sonia sat on the edge and, with Karen standing in front of her, pulled down the little briefs until they were about her ankles before ridding her of them altogether. She reclined herself on the bed and pulled Karen across so that she lay in her arms face upwards. With their lips joined in passion, Sonia's fingers once more engaged themselves in the dialogue of lust upon the stage of her sex. Karen, her breath growing shorter, writhed against the straitjacket, flexing her legs and spreading them wider, willing Sonia to enter her deeper. But Sonia kept control of her, stroking the fire gently and not allowing the flames to erupt before their time. Karen squirmed against her, mouth agape, her rasping breath punctuated by intermittent soft cries which pleaded for release from voluptuous torment.

At last, Sonia allowed the flames of lust to break forth so that the prisoner in her arms stiffened and cried out as if in despair, her head shaking from side to side as the orgasm devoured her body.

They rested for a time then Karen sighed and opened her eyes. Sonia kissed her and they rose to sit on the edge of the bed.

'Sonia, I need the bathroom.'

'Yes, I daresay you must after all that champagne.'

Karen looked at her and then down at the smooth lines of the restraining garment about her body. Before she could speak, Sonia said, 'I won't be undoing that for a long time yet, my dear.'

'Oh, but I –'

'You must come with me,' cut in Sonia.

Karen gazed into her eyes for long seconds. They stood up and moved a short distance from the bed.

'Wait a moment,' said Sonia, turning away from her.

Karen watched her stand before the maroon box but could not see what she withdrew from it. When she turned and walked back, there was something glistening and deep red swinging from her hand.

'We'll slip this on for now,' said Sonia, moving around behind her.

'Please Sonia . . . I need –'

But before she finished speaking, the leather hood slipped down over her head, blanking out her vision and plunging her into enclosed blackness.

'Please Sonia!' Karen insisted as the laces were tightened and knotted securely at the rear.

Like the straitjacket, the matching hood moulded closely over her features, its smoothness broken only by a small cluster of breathing holes about the nose and mouth. Sonia tidied her hair where it bunched out from under the helmet at the back.

'All right, my dear, come along.'

Karen, still wearing the high-heeled sandals, walked hesitantly, guided by Sonia. She knew when they had entered the bathroom for the feel of the carpet was different. Sonia left her standing in dark silence and Karen could hear her moving about, water running and other sounds which were meaningless. After a time, invisible hands took hold of her once more and she was taken a few steps on before being turned around.

'Sit down carefully,' came the voice close to her ear.

She lowered her body slowly then stopped abruptly, feeling the chilling hardness of porcelain against her thighs. She pressed down against it as a hand pushed her back against the padded leather back support, forcing her to spread her legs either side of the bowl.

'Sonia! What are you doing? I just need to –'

'Relax,' came the voice, then there followed the rattle of buckles as a strap was passed first about her neck, then her waist, immobilising her over the bowl. 'A few seconds – that's all,' came Sonia's voice and, at once, Karen stiffened as a hand reached between her legs and something cool touched her behind. Whatever pressed against her anus was smooth and hard, but lubricated and insistent. She tightened her muscles to prevent its entry.

'Oh no – no don't!' she begged, but the intruder slid easily up, deep and cool into her rectum, and there remained as the hand departed.

Karen had never before experienced what happened next. She could not see the rubber bottle suspended from the bracket above her. She could not observe Sonia turn the small valve on the tube which snaked down from it. But she did cry 'Aaah!' as the soapy water began to discharge through the nozzle. The liquid was still passing into her when she heard the sound of water splashing and bubbling in the bowl beneath. She tensed again as the object was withdrawn from her.

'You'll feel much better soon, my dear,' came the voice, 'and you can keep on your birthday outfit for a good while longer!'

Karen already felt the urgent stirring within her bowels. It soon became an insistent turbulence. She began to twist against the restraints but realised that very soon, as though plunging from a dizzy height, she was going to lose control of her body.

5

The Fugitive

The day had begun still and overcast. Angela, having little desire for company after lunch and no inclination to remain indoors, set off across the gardens and over the rise to the seat beneath the tree. For Karen, this was a working day, though she and Angela had earlier passed a few minutes of conversation in the restaurant. The pool was deserted though on the tennis court, some distance beyond the house, two people weaved back and forth, rackets slashing the air. The auburn hair of Annette was unmistakable. The raven black hair, done up in a pony-tail, belonged to Lorna.

In the few seconds while she stood watching, a car flickered between the trees at the far end of the driveway. Though the blue light was not flashing, the livery of the vehicle was immediately recognisable. Angela looked on as the car came to a halt before the main entrance of the house. Only one figure emerged, though not a figure in uniform as she had expected. It was Inspector Gautier of the *gendarmerie*, apparently here on official business. What that business might be, Angela had no idea, though the inspector was on good terms with Sonia socially and on even better terms personally with at least one of her girls, as well as Angela herself.

Sonia did not have any problems with the *gendarmerie*.

By the time Angela had walked over the rise and out of sight of the house, the sky was beginning to clear. The far side of the valley was bathed in sunlight and the distant sea shone like liquid metal. Angela breathed in the warm air and its hint of the sea and, positioning herself comfortably on the bench, pulled from the bag her lighter, a packet of cigarettes and the paperback novel brought back from London and given to her by Karen.

Apart from the electric buzz of the cicadas a small distance away and the occasional call of the birds, this place was silent and idyllic. Soon, Angela was lost in the intrigue of the book, puffing occasionally on her cigarette, the soft breeze gently coaxing the silver-blonde fringe of hair above her blue-grey eyes. She was unaware of the figure approaching.

'Angie!'

Her head turned in surprise. 'Oh! Mike, I didn't hear you.'

An agitated Mike, hands thrust deep into pockets, stood before her.

'I'm sorry Angie, I didn't mean to –'

'What's up?' she asked, uncrossing her legs and moving aside her things to make space for him by her side.

He sat down and let his head fall back. 'That car outside the house,' he said, out of breath.

Angela laughed lightly and squeezed his hand. 'The *gendarmerie*, dear. Is that what you're bothered about? It's only Inspector Gautier to see Sonia. If they were after you they would have arrived in force with flashing lights and a fleet of helicopters!'

'OK, but I only saw the car when I was going to get a bite to eat. It could have been full of them for all I knew!'

'Mike, you're not getting paranoid are you?' She continued to hold his hand.

'Yes I am,' he grinned. 'I think I need something more to worry about in life than Pauline.'

'Has she been having a go at you? I thought Jackie was getting it all.'

'No, but ... look, as I appear to be safe again for a while, give me a fag and I'll confess something to you that'll have you in stitches.'

His eyes took her in as she turned around to retrieve the cigarette packet. He looked at her shining blonde hair, wound around and fixed at the side of her head in its light

91

brown clasp, her loose-fitting white sleeveless top, low cut with her firm breasts pushing away the small buttons, her short mid-blue skirt, almost a tennis skirt, in nylon satin and her long legs with their gold sandals. She turned to him and held out the packet.

'Since when have you smoked?' she asked grinning.

'I don't usually. Only in times of stress.'

'Stress! God, Mike, I can't imagine any bloke having fewer reasons for stress than you, unless you miss the traffic jams and the rat race. Anyway, what's the big confession? I'm all ears?'

'You'll keep it to yourself?' he asked, affecting a grave expression but at the same time moving closer to her and taking her hand in his.

'Everyone seems to confide in me, Mike,' she replied. 'I'm very discreet – but then, aren't we all – or should I say nearly all?'

He gazed meaningfully into her eyes for a few seconds.

'OK, here goes.' He cleared his throat in preparation for the announcement. 'I tried to get off with Pauline!'

Angela opened her mouth to speak and her eyes searched into his before any sound came. 'Michael, you fibber! I don't believe you!'

'It's true – I did!' he insisted, releasing her hand and putting his right arm around her shoulder. 'And I got a metaphorical sock in the mouth.'

'Well, I've seen you weighing her legs up now and then but I mean ... she'd eat you alive! Not just you – anybody!'

He looked into her eyes, without expression, for a number of seconds.

'All right!' he said, grinning and kissing her on the lips. 'I was just joking. I knew you wouldn't believe me.'

'Some things are simply too far-fetched,' she said, returning his kiss.

'Would you believe something else?' he asked, placing his other arm around her.

'I did come here to do a bit of reading, but go on.'

'Oh well, I'll push off if you prefer!'

'Not until you've told me another pack of lies,' she whispered, moving her face closer to his.

'OK,' he whispered back, gently squeezing her breast and kissing her ear. 'You're the loveliest lady in the world.'

'I thought that was Jackie,' she responded with forced sarcasm.

His eyes widened for a moment, then his face broke into a grin. 'She has a vivid imagination.'

'And a big mouth,' said Angela, 'but never mind.'

His hand moved to the front of her top, and while their lips met once more, he picked open the buttons one by one until the material was pushed aside and her breasts exposed to the warm sunshine, the pink, hard nipples testifying to her arousal.

She ran her fingers through his hair and whispered, 'Mike, this isn't the place.'

'There's only us around,' he whispered.

'No,' she insisted, as his lips and tongue played about her breasts. 'If Karen gets out early, she'll probably come here.'

'It'll do her good,' he responded.

'Mike!' she urged, as his hand stroked up the top of her thigh and found the edge of her small blue briefs.

'All right,' he whispered, 'near the tree. No one can see unless they walk around and look.'

Once partly enveloped by the foliage, Angela sat naked, apart from her sandals. He knelt before her, holding her head in his hands and catching his breath sharply as her cool fingers, working their way up the leg of his white boxer shorts, closed with cool deliberateness around the heat of his erection, causing the head to thrust out against the thin cotton like a tent post against canvas. After long seconds of voluptuous manipulation, she pulled down the shorts, easing them over the reddened and swaggering organ while he struggled up to remove them completely. At once, he placed his hands beneath her knees and lifting up her legs, pushed them back and far apart to display her sex fully before falling upon her. He held her tightly while his tongue darted and coursed between the inflamed lips of her most intimate place, proclaiming itself upon the stage of her sensuality.

The level of her arousal soon became obvious, not only from the glistening heat of her sex but from her repeated moans, coming ever louder and longer. He raised himself up and moved quickly forward, poising for a moment over her as if to savour the forthcoming assault, then drove into her up to the root. She wrapped her legs tightly around his body as though to pull him in further still and with each stroke forced her fingers harder into the flesh of his back. They bucked and pitched together as one, oblivious to the surroundings and caring nothing if another should pass by and chance upon them. When the boiling tide of lust overwhelmed them, her cries rose into the sky and drifted upwards to join those of the birds, wheeling and swooping against the blue expanse in cryptic games of their own.

'It was just a routine visit,' said Sonia. 'They're on the lookout for someone and they've left a description with the local people as well as us.'

She put down the glass and looked out through the conservatory windows across the gardens. The sun was lower, slanting across the gardens and through the windows. Around the table with her sat Valerie, Lorna and Pauline; Pauline affecting a demure, almost benign aspect, with Valerie also giving no hint as to the harsh words which had recently passed between them.

'Apparently,' continued Sonia, 'there were three of our fellow countrymen involved in a robbery at Lyon. They took jewellery from two shops and cleared off in a stolen car. They were spotted heading for Marseilles but the police lost them near Avignon when they abandoned one car and pinched another. They were seen again between Nîmes and Montpellier but people have been reporting them from all over the place, even as far as Toulon, so the police didn't put themselves out too much in this area. Anyhow, they got drunk and abusive at a bar in Montpellier and someone called the coppers in for that. Before they turned up, the three of them had cleared off. They were chased along the N109 through Clermont and crashed their car on some back road a few kilometres from here. Two of them were rounded up immediately and the other one is still on the loose.'

'I suppose he's armed and dangerous,' remarked Valerie.

'It's a she,' replied Sonia. 'Their female accomplice, would you believe?'

'Oh well,' added Lorna, 'I suppose she'll get nabbed before long. Where can she go?'

'I think someone ought to let Mike know,' said Valerie, grinning. 'I saw him through the window after the police car arrived. He took one look at it and headed for the hills.'

Pauline smiled but remained silent.

'Poor old Mike,' mused Lorna, 'he's probably spent an afternoon of utter misery wondering if they're on to him.'

'Oh, I wouldn't say that,' commented Valerie, peering out through the french windows. 'I can see him over by the pool. He looks happy enough to me!'

Sonia glanced at the window. 'Well, each of you can tell the others. The inspector asked me to type out a description in English and circulate it to everybody. Karen will have run a few copies off by now to leave at the bar.'

'Who do I tell about it?' asked Kim, her soft face shadowed by disquiet.

'I suppose it ought to be Pauline – it's the kind of thing Sonia pays her to deal with.'

'Yes, I suppose so.'

'If you like,' said Valerie, 'I'll talk to her later.'

'Oh, Val, no, it's up to me. I'm supposed to keep an eye on things. I'll check if the old bag's in and go straight up.'

'All right, but I want you back down here in half an hour – we have three appointments this afternoon. If she starts on at you or tries any funny business, I'll be up there, OK?'

'So what are you saying?' asked Pauline, eyeing Kim coolly across the desk.

'I'm saying it's been pinched. I know I shut the windows last night and I know where everything was. Angie and Rachel reckon stuff has gone missing too but we've never needed to keep records.'

'And who,' asked Pauline quietly, 'do you consider has been taking it?'

'I-I don't know. Why should anybody here want to steal cheese, bread, fruit and other stuff when they can just ask for it any time at the bar?'

'Why indeed?' asked Pauline, with a humourless smile. 'Well, if it isn't any of you lot then obviously it's someone from outside, so you should have taken more trouble to secure the kitchen.'

'But we've never had to, not here, nobody would ever steal anything . . . and . . . and there's the stuff by the pool – bits of food and drinks cans. Mike always clears up and hoses everything down in the evening. None of us would –'

'Quite so,' interrupted Pauline. 'Then we know who it might be, don't we?'

'Yes, that's what we all thought too.'

'We all! And how long have "we all" known about this before telling me?'

'It's not like that,' answered Kim. 'It looks like it's been going on for a few days. But it's not until people mention it to each other that anyone realises that something could be wrong. That's why I've come to you now.'

Pauline sat back and regarded her for a few seconds.

'All right,' she said at last. 'Then I'll talk to Sonia. I'll arrange for some of us to keep an eye open between the house and the pool. If the little bitch comes back again, we'll nab her and see what Sonia wants to do with her.'

'Let's hope it's not an old tramp or a gypsy,' said Kim.

'I doubt it,' responded Pauline. 'I very much doubt it!'

'What time is it?' asked Valerie in a low voice.

'This watch is barely luminous,' answered Mike, squinting down at his wrist in the darkness. 'It's nearly quarter to one.'

'Are you staying all night?'

'I don't think it's worth it,' he whispered. 'Maybe I'll hang around until three or half past. What about you?'

'I'll stay as long as Pauline. She's keeping an eye on the back of the house until half two.'

'Has she got her whip and spurs?'

'No, she's got a gun.'

'A gun!' he hissed.

'Shush,' responded Valerie. 'Sound carries at night. It's a shotgun. She has to have something – it might be a man we're after despite what everyone else says.'

'It might be a bookkeeping error too. Nobody seems all that sure about what's gone missing.'

'Oh, I don't know. I wouldn't be standing under this tree for hours if we weren't.'

'Well,' answered Mike, 'at least it's a warm night. Look at those stars – aren't they fantastic?'

'Yes, it's almost a stage set. Everything is so absolutely still, like an enchanted evening.'

They stood breathing the silent air until Valerie said, 'I wonder where he's off to.'

'What! Where?' hissed Mike, clutching her arm.

'Steady deary, it's only Pancake.'

They watched the shadowy feline stroll by, ignoring their soft calls completely, before vanishing into the obscurity of the nearby bushes.

'Perhaps he's the culprit,' suggested Mike. 'We might think he's curled up most of the time doing bugger all when he's really figuring out plans to improve the quality of his menu.'

'You could be right – if he'd developed a liking for fruit and if he was able to get into the fridge and open plastic containers. Any more good ideas?'

Mike smiled into Valerie's face, then peered about into the darkness.

'Look at the moon on the pool. It's like a mirror.'

'Since you mention it,' whispered Valerie. 'I wouldn't mind a swim right now.'

His arm slipped about her waist. 'Why don't we, one evening? When everyone else has gone to bed.'

'Quite an opportunist, aren't you, dear?' she joked, squeezing his arm in the darkness.

'Well I suppose –'

He released his hold on her and peered towards the swimming pool.

'What is it?'

'I thought I heard – yes! Look at the water!'

'There's someone in the pool,' said Valerie.

'Let's sneak around behind the trees and – no, I'll go while you fetch Pauline. If it is a bloke, we might need the gun.'

'All right,' said Valerie, 'but be careful just in case. Give me a couple of minutes.'

Valerie disappeared across the grass in the direction of the darkened house. He waited and listened. The sound of splashing drifted intermittently through the night air. At length, two figures emerged quietly out of the gloom.

'We're back,' whispered Valerie. 'Anything happened?'

'No, they're still in the water.'

The other figure, bag over one shoulder and shotgun tucked under one arm, said nothing. Pauline was dressed in a black catsuit and short boots. Only her face and silver-blonde hair caught the moonlight, giving her head the appearance of disembodiment against the blackness of the trees.

'OK,' said Mike, 'you two go along this side and I'll sneak around the other where the sunshades are. As soon as they see you, they'll head towards me, yes?'

'All right,' answered Pauline, 'you'd better go first, then we'll follow.'

Mike stooped low and moved away silently across the main pathway before they lost sight of him. Pauline gestured to Valerie and both walked quickly, keeping by the bushes, towards the pool. As they approached the poolside and moved out into the open, the figure in the water stood up, black against the moon-rippled surface, then swam quickly the short distance to the steps on the far side and started to climb up and over. Valerie and Pauline waited as the fleeing shadow moved among the poolside tables and chairs, disappearing behind the sunshades.

Pauline hurried quickly towards the end of the pool, followed by Valerie. They had just turned the corner when a
shriek cut through the darkness, followed by the clatter of
an overturned chair.

Mike's cries of, 'OK! OK! We're not going to hurt –'
were cut short by a desperate yell of, 'Get your bleeding
hands off me! Let me go!'

Pauline laid the shotgun down on a nearby table and
produced a torch from her shoulder bag. In the beam of
light the girl cringed, held from behind by both arms. She
was naked. Her skin glistened wet in the torchlight and her
hair was plastered about her face and shoulders.

'Well, what have we here?' asked Pauline, looking into
her frightened eyes.

'Tell him to let go of my arms!' she pleaded. 'I haven't
done anything!'

'Where are your clothes?' asked Valerie.

The girl did not reply but her eyes darted from Valerie
to Pauline. Mike nodded towards a chair. 'There they are.'

Pauline shone the beam of light on to the clothes and
stepped over to examine them.

'I see. These filthy old things.' She turned to Valerie and
said, 'It might be a good idea if you go and alert Sonia
while we sort this one out. She'll be waiting up in the
office.'

Valerie hesitated, looking from Pauline to the girl then
back again, before turning without a word and walking
away into the darkness towards the house.

'We'd better get her dried and dressed,' said Mike.

'There's nothing to dry her with,' replied Pauline, reaching again into the bag, 'and those clothes are only fit for
the incinerator.' She stepped towards the girl, something
metallic glistening in her hand. 'Turn her around!'

'What?'

'Just turn her around and hold her arms while I put
these on. Quickly!'

'Hell, no!' shouted the girl, writhing and struggling.
'You're not putting no bloody handcuffs on me, you old
cow!'

99

Pauline at once seized one of her wrists, fitted the steel bracelet on to it and snapped it shut. Mike, showing not quite the same degree of enthusiasm, helped to pull her around and despite her expletive protests, held the other arm in position while her wrists were secured together behind her back in the steel embraces of the handcuffs.

'Take them off me!' screamed the girl, twisting about in a futile attempt to release herself.

'I think we can call it an evening now, don't you?' said Pauline. 'You can leave her to me, if you don't mind.'

'Well yes, if you say so.'

'I do say so!' replied Pauline coolly.

Mike turned and walked slowly away, glancing over his shoulder at the two figures illuminated in the soft moonlight. Pauline replaced the torch in her bag and turned to the naked captive, now visibly shivering.

'You can follow me back to the house or you can spend the rest of the night out here. It gets cooler as the night goes on. Well?'

'I haven't any choice, have I?' the girl answered dryly. 'You're going to turn me in, aren't you?'

'That's not up to me,' responded Pauline, picking up the shotgun. 'I only work here, as they say. But if you're going to move, you'd better move now. Right now!'

'All right! I'll come with you but let me put my pants on first!'

'Now!' shouted Pauline, then turned away from her and walked towards the black silhouette of the house.

'Wait! Come back!' came the voice from behind, but Pauline carried on walking.

Halfway between the pool and the house, Pauline stopped and turned around. The slim figure also came to a halt, a few metres behind her.

'I knew you'd see reason,' she muttered and continued on.

A few minutes later they were in Sonia's office.

'So,' said Sonia from behind the green shaded desk lamp, 'you're the one on the loose? Until now, that is.'

'I didn't have anything to do with it, honest! I was hitching a ride and these blokes picked me up. Look, just get these bleeding handcufs off me and I'll shoot off – I haven't done any harm to anyone, see!'

Sonia rose slowly from the chair and looked hard at her.

'There is one thing I will not tolerate in my office or anywhere in this house and that is swearing!' The girl looked from Sonia to Pauline then around the room as if for some consolation. 'Well,' continued Sonia, 'you are wanted by the police and I understand there is a reward for anyone who hands you in. Now, you wretched girl! What are we supposed to do with you other than that?'

The girl looked back at her with moistening eyes and quivering lip. 'I don't know. I dare say you'll do whatever you think.'

Sonia regarded her in silence for some time. Her hair was fairer than Jackie's but she was about the same age and build, though her features were sharper and her demeanour that of one having much more experience of life than her years would indicate. Even in her bedraggled state, or perhaps because of it, she was very obviously what Sonia's 'lesser gender', the male of the species, would regard as most desirable.

'I think we'll sleep on this one,' said Sonia eventually, 'and decide what to do with her later. Put her somewhere secure and comfortable until the morning. Better give her something to eat and drink first, I suppose, as she hasn't yet had the opportunity to steal it.' Sonia walked around the desk and stood before the girl. 'I'll talk to you in the morning, but for the time being, you'd better do exactly as you're told. Inspector Gautier really wouldn't mind what time of the day or night I phoned him – understand?'

'Yes, right then, I'll behave, honest, but I can't eat or sleep in these, can I?' She twisted her arms around to show the handcuffs.

'Leave it to me,' said Pauline. 'I'll put her into something more comfortable. She won't be going anywhere, I can promise you.'

'Good, I'm sure I needn't doubt you on that account, then we can all get some sleep.'

* * *

101

At 7.45, a key turned in the lock. Pauline entered the half-light of the room carrying a small tray upon which rested a glass of orange juice and a chicken sandwich. The girl was already awake, and sat up in the bed with the sheet pulled up over her breasts. Her eyes followed Pauline as the tray was placed on the bedside table and the curtains were pulled open, flooding the room with light.

'What's happening?' asked the girl, regarding the black leather suited figure framed in the window with apprehension.

'You're to have that,' answered Pauline, gesturing towards the tray, 'then take a shower and make yourself presentable. Afterwards, we'll get you dressed and ready to meet Sonia in my office at nine o'clock prompt. I take it you have no objections?'

'How am I supposed to use a shower with these on?'

The girl pulled up the bedsheet to reveal her ankles, each enclosed in a smooth steel band and held close together by a chain of little more than ten centimetres in length.

'I'll undo them before you go into the bathroom.' Pauline opened the door of a large fitted cupboard. 'There are clothes, shoes and underwear in here. I don't care what you put on. I daresay most of it will fit you.'

'Yeah, I had a good look inside last night,' said the girl, munching on the sandwich. 'There's kinky stuff in there as well – the sort of gear perverts wear.'

'How nice of you to say so,' said Pauline, smiling. 'I can see you are going to enjoy your stay here enormously; unless we give you to the police of course.'

'Here no, just give me a chance, right? And ... you couldn't let us have a fag, could you?'

'You'll get all the chance you deserve,' answered Pauline, ignoring altogether the second request.

At 8.45, the key again turned in the lock and Pauline re-entered, this time carrying a black plastic bag.

'How's this?' asked the girl, turning to face her.

Pauline rested the bag on a nearby chair and regarded her for a few moments. The girl wore a sleeveless top in dark blue crepe nylon cut well down at the front to display the tops of her firm breasts. Her mini-skirt was of silver-blue stretch vinyl and fitted her lithe figure snugly. Around her waist was a wide belt in white vinyl and below the skirt, sheer black seamed tights and silver vinyl high-heeled sandals with small blue bows.

'They're my favourite colours,' she said, 'blue and silver.'

Her straw-blonde hair hung down her back, straight and shining, its fringe conspiring to soften the streetwise look of her blue eyes and alert features.

'Fine if we were going to a disco,' observed Pauline, opening her bag, 'but we're not and most people don't wear tights during the day. It's the climate, you know.'

'Yeah, I know,' she replied, pivoting herself around in front of the long mirror. 'Still, the blokes like them, especially these open body ones – if you get my meaning.'

'I don't think you quite understand yet, do you?' said Pauline, emptying the contents of the bag on to the chair. 'Pull your hair over your shoulder to the front and turn towards the window.'

'What? What for?' She regarded the black leather object bunched up on the chair with straps and buckles hanging from it over the edge of the seat. Her eyes turned to Pauline and to what Pauline held coiled about her hand. 'Here! What the bloody hell's this? Get away from me!'

Pauline stepped quickly over to her and the whip struck out like a rattlesnake around the girl's behind.

'Ow! My arse!' she screamed, lurching towards the window and looking back in startled fear.

'We can do this the easy way or the hard way,' said Pauline with expressionless clarity. 'Personally, I'm just as happy to do it the hard way; I enjoy the practice!'

'Look!' exclaimed the girl. 'I don't want any bother!'

'Then do as you are told! Now!'

The girl moved slowly and timidly back towards her, her eyes constantly darting from Pauline's face to the whip.

'Good, right. Now, pull your hair forward over to the front and . . . yes, that's it . . . and place your arms behind

103

your back with the palms of your hands flat together. Good. Now, if you move I'll most certainly give you three strokes, not one!'

The girl stood, visibly trembling but obedient as the cool leather pouch slid up and enclosed her hands in its snug embrace. A small buckle rasped as the strap passed through it and tightened about her wrists. The whirr of the heavy zip fastener moving upwards told her why the leather sheath was pulling insistently about her arms and drawing them closer so that her breasts were made to stand out more prominently. The zipper ceased its ascent, level with her shoulder blades, so that most of her arms were encased in the sleek, black leather.

'What is this?' asked the girl, twisting her head around. 'What the hell's it for?'

Pauline pushed the free ends of the straps, which hung from either side of the leather sheath, under the girl's arms, drew them out at the front, pulled them up and crossed them over her chest.

'I would have thought by now,' she answered, passing the straps over the girl's shoulders and pulling them down behind, 'that the purpose was fairly obvious.' Once passed through buckles at the top of the sheath, the two straps were tightened and fastened, holding the restraint securely in position. 'It couldn't be better if it was tailor-made,' remarked Pauline, picking up the whip and looking at her watch. 'And we're in good time for your interview.' She walked over to the door and pulled it open. 'This way, madam!'

'Here, look! I can't go about the place wearing this – it isn't right – and my skirt's riding up!'

Pauline looked hard at her and slowly uncoiled the whip.

'You'll wear the bondage glove all day if I say so. And you chose what you're wearing, not me, remember? Now move!' The whip hissed and cracked across her behind. 'Now!' repeated Pauline loudly as the girl shrieked and all but jumped towards the waiting doorway.

As they entered Pauline's apartment, Sonia, wearing biker jacket and black satin leggings, arose from the green leather two-seater by the window.

'Ah, how nice to see our young guest again.'

'Yes,' agreed Pauline, 'and so tastefully attired.'

'What is this place?' asked the girl, looking from one to the other. 'Some kind of bleeding hospital? More like a loony bin if you ask me!'

Sonia slapped her across the mouth, causing her to gasp and turn her head.

'Before we continue, I will repeat what I said last night. You will not swear in this house – ever!'

Pauline prodded the girl to elicit an answer.

'N-no, right, no swearing.'

'Good,' continued Sonia. 'Now, the police seem to be in possession of your handbag and any documentation you had in it. You must have taken leave of your companions in some haste.'

'Yeah, I scarpered quick.'

'And I gather that your name is Rose. Is that your real name?'

'Yeah, Rose. It's my real name.'

Sonia pulled over a green leather stool and placed it before the two-seater and a single easy chair. Pauline sat in the chair and Sonia returned to the two-seater.

'Sit down, Rose,' ordered Sonia, indicating the stool.

The girl backed up slowly against the stool and in attempting to shuffle herself on to it, succeeded in pushing it back until it fell over with a thump.

'If I can't use my arms I can't hold the blee ... I mean the stool steady!'

Pauline stepped over, lifted the stool back on to its legs, and held it in position.

'Now sit down!'

Rose obeyed, turning about awkwardly and adjusting her position until she felt balanced, with her legs at a right angle to her captors.

'Please turn and face us,' ordered Sonia.

The girl looked from one to the other, her mouth opening slightly as she shuffled awkwardly around, keeping her legs as close together as possible.

'My skirt's pulling up,' she muttered and began to blush.

'The little bitch hasn't put any knickers on!' declared Pauline, looking from Rose to Sonia with an expression of mock astonishment.

'Oh, and why is that, Rose?' asked Sonia. 'Why have you nothing on under your skirt?'

Her mouth opened but no sound emerged for a few moments, though the flush of embarrassment still persisted. 'Er, well, me and my friends used to do it as a bit of a dare, like ... just a bit of fun ... but I didn't know you were going to fasten my arms up, did I? It's not my blee ... er, not my fault, is it?'

Sonia and Pauline regarded her in silence for a very long half-minute.

'It seems to me there are a limited number of choices to be made and we will have to decide here and now,' said Sonia. 'We can simply give you some clothes, ordinary clothes that is, and let you go. We can hand you over to the police, or we can keep you on here. Those are our options.' The girl remained silent. 'Your options are not so easy. If you decide to go, you stand a good chance of being spotted and arrested. I'm sure the second option doesn't appeal very much, so that leaves you with the third choice, doesn't it? And that is rather a difficult one since you don't know anything about us.'

'I don't want the police,' said Rose. 'But then you haven't said what you're all about, so I don't know what to think, do I?'

'It might be better if you find out gradually,' mused Sonia. 'But let me put it this way. You're not only a common thief, but a coarse and ill-spoken slut. We can offer you a chance to stay out of trouble and to better yourself with proper use of those assets which you have taken so little trouble to conceal this morning. There is –'

'What!' interrupted Rose. 'Sell myself like a sodding tart! You're out of your bleeding mind if –'

Sonia and Pauline had risen simultaneously as she spoke and this time it was Pauline who brought the palm of her hand hard across the girl's mouth. Sonia held her by the shoulders and looked hard into her startled eyes.

'You are already a tart! And as far as selling yourself is concerned, you just give it away, I have no doubt! And when I consider the company you seem to like, it doesn't look to me as though you even have the wits to give it to anyone who's worth anything!' She turned to Pauline. 'You've probably got something to keep her quiet, haven't you?'

Pauline nodded and walked towards the curtained-off chamber at the rear of the room.

'Now then,' continued Sonia, 'you're going to learn that when I say I do not tolerate swearing, I mean exactly that! And whatever happens to you after this morning, you are going to learn a little humility – something to remember us by even when you end up again with the kind of riff-raff and no-hopers you're so obviously attuned to!'

Sonia looked up as Pauline approached from behind Rose and nodded.

'Here! What are you up to?' protested the girl, but it was to be her last meaningful objection for a time, as Pauline reached quickly around and thrust the rubber ball into her mouth. Sonia at once gripped her head and held it still, while Pauline tightened and buckled the strap behind.

'Do you want this?' asked Pauline, gesturing towards the whip, which lay nearby.

'No, something a bit less drastic and a pair of scissors, large ones if you have them.'

Rose uttered a series of muffled protests through the gag and slipped down off the stool before Sonia. Pauline returned and stood behind, as though to prevent her from backing away. She handed over the scissors and, as Rose cringed in abject fear of what she might be about to do, Sonia tugged the blue nylon top from under the girl's belt and quickly cut through it up to the neckline. In a moment, the shoulder material was cut too, and the ruined garment was wrenched away from her body and tossed aside, leaving her naked from the waist up.

Sonia placed the scissors next to the whip and began to unfasten the white belt at the girl's waist. As the belt loosened, Pauline tugged down the skirt so that Rose stood before them wearing only the sheer, black suspender tights and silver, high-heel sandals.

'Over the back of the chair with her!' ordered Sonia, and both of them pulled Rose across to the seat, earlier occupied by Pauline, and stood her behind it.

'All right, I'll take that – you lift up her arms,' said Sonia.

Pauline handed her the three-tailed strap then, seizing Rose's leather-sheathed arms, pulled them up and away from her body, forcing her to bend forward over the padded back of the seat.

'Now, next time you want to be abusive,' pronounced Sonia, 'just remember this!'

The strap descended with a sharp crack against the girl's flesh, making her whole body jerk and prompting a loud 'Aaah!'

It descended again and again in rhythmic strokes, each crack followed by an even louder shriek of protest to accompany the weeping and kicking back of her feet.

'And that makes six!' announced Sonia with the final stroke.

The diffused red weals on Rose's behind glowed an angry pink.

'I think you've been very lenient,' commented Pauline coldly.

'All right, let go of her,' ordered Sonia.

The girl stood up slowly, an intermittent moan coming through the ball gag, her face streaked with tears.

'Do we have any tissues?' asked Sonia.

Pauline strode to her desk and returned, holding out the box. Sonia pulled one out and, placing it under Rose's mouth, released the strap at the back of her head and eased the wet rubber ball from her. She looked at neither of her captors but stood with her head bowed, shivering and crying quietly.

'Right, so there will be no more swearing or you'll know what to expect,' said Sonia. 'Agreed?' The girl silently nodded her agreement. 'Now, as I was going to say before you so rudely interrupted, there is an opportunity here for you to leave behind the totally pointless existence you have been leading, to keep out of trouble and get to know the sort of people who have a little more to offer than the average lager lout! Are you even remotely interested?'

Rose looked up at Sonia, her eyes still wet with tears.

'I don't have much choice, do I?'

'You have the same choice as you had before we found you, plus the extra one. So you're actually a lot better off than you were last night.'

'If I opted for staying, what would I have to do?'

'Well,' replied Sonia, 'you will certainly have to become more ladylike in both speech and presentation. It will take a period of time for you to adapt – you will have to get used to certain disciplines.'

'Literally,' added Pauline, with studied nonchalance.

'We'll return you to your room now,' continued Sonia, 'then Pauline and I will discuss a few things and talk to you later on in the morning.'

They moved to either side of Rose and guided her towards the door.

'Hey, wait!' she protested. 'What about taking this thing off my arms?'

'You mean the bondage glove? No, you'll keep it on until we're ready to remove it. I'm sure it's quite comfortable. And bear in mind that if you stay with us you will certainly become more familiar with that, as well as other items.'

'Her language is dreadful,' said Sonia, now back in the two-seater by the window. 'I suppose it can only get better!'

'With the right kind of encouragement,' remarked Pauline.

'If she's going to stay, we'll need to formulate a regime and a timetable for her to keep to. Have you any suggestions?'

'Well,' answered Pauline, 'she will need constant supervision at first. I think we should consider splitting that between myself, Cheryl when she's here, and, I suppose, Valerie.'

'You don't quite hit it off with Valerie, do you?'

'We've had our disagreements, but she's got her job to do and I've got mine.'

'She could help Valerie in the parlour a bit, especially when Kim's not around,' suggested Sonia. 'And helping in the bar might suit her temperamentally.'

'Yes, that would keep her occupied some of the day, and I could teach her some manners, and get her used to a few other things!'

'Yes, I can imagine.' Sonia smiled. 'But don't be too harsh with her, she may not be another Jackie.'

'No, perhaps not, though it seems to me they're not too dissimilar.'

'And I think she would do well to spend a bit of time with Karen. She needs elocution lessons and encouragement to read.'

'If you say so,' responded Pauline. 'It will give them both something to do.'

'Now, now! I know you've never liked her but she's taken a burden off my back and I was more than glad when she decided to return. We all have our parts to play. You should know that as well as anyone.' Pauline stared across the room and did not reply. 'She can't keep that room,' continued Sonia. 'I suggest she moves in with Jackie or Kim. They're all about the same age and she'll have a friend to turn to.'

'Better if it's Jackie,' said Pauline. 'That way I can keep an eye on both of them and Jackie can let me know if she gets up to anything. Jackie's got a double bed too, so they can share that except when she's entertaining a guest. Unless the guest wants the two of them, that is.'

'She may, of course, not wish to stay after an hour or so in the bondage glove. Though I have a feeling that the alternative still won't hold much appeal.'

After they left her, Rose had stood for a minute or so in the middle of the room, waiting in silence for something to happen. Nothing had. She had walked over to the long mirror on the door of the wardrobe and seen herself, almost a stranger, looking back. She had turned partly around and twisted her head to look at the restraint which enclosed her arms and held them straight down her back. For a time she had watched herself struggle and twist her arms about in the leather sheath until it became even more obvious than before that no amount of effort was going to release her from it.

Apart from the persistent itch just to the right of her nose, an itch that grew in magnitude because she was unable to attend to it, Rose did not find the restraint as disagreeable as she might have thought before her unwilling acquaintance with it. She began to wonder if security in one sense could not mean security in another, though she had come to realise that the house, at least the parts of it she had seen, was not a prison for there was no indication that people could not come and go as they wished.

'What the hell do they get up to here?' she muttered to herself as she gazed out through the Venetian blind. The room she occupied was at the rear of the house and so her window did not overlook the pool or the tennis court, but gave a view of the rolling countryside and the vineyards beyond the distant road.

She was still aware of the attention her behind had received from the strap. The soreness had given way to a pleasant burning, a burning which reached within her body and deep into her most intimate places. Did they know, she wondered, that it would have that effect on her?

A key turned in the lock. She moved aside from the window and looked over her shoulder as the door opened and the two figures entered.

'Oh, you're still with us,' said Pauline.

'Yes, I'm still here. What did you expect?'

'Please come over here,' ordered Sonia in a low voice. Rose obeyed and stood before them. 'You now have to decide what you are going to do. Do you wish to go on the run again?'

'No, can't say I do.'

'Well, I will say again that if you remain here you will have a number of benefits but you will have to do as you are told. By that I mean that you are going to learn to speak properly, present yourself as a lady and behave with good manners. I am making myself clear, I take it?'

'Like I already said, I haven't no choice, have I?'

Sonia nodded to Pauline, who stood just behind Rose. Pauline swung the strap down with a rapid stroke across her already tender buttocks. Rose, her mouth springing wide open in startled surprise, let out a high-pitched yell and lurched forward, almost colliding with Sonia.

'We're starting from this very moment,' said Sonia. 'Would you care to try again?'

Rose, her lips quivering, gazed at Sonia and took a deep breath.

'I-I have not . . . not got any choice . . . have I?'

'Well, that's an improvement anyway,' remarked Sonia, 'but "I don't have any choice, do I?" would have a more natural flow even though some might regard it as less than perfect English.'

'Please,' entreated Rose, glancing at Pauline and back to Sonia. 'I'll try my best, honest I will.'

'But you understand the path we have to take at least, and there will be plenty of incentives to aid your progress.'

'There certainly will!' added Pauline.

'All right,' continued Sonia, 'you will be under Pauline's jurisdiction but you'll spend time with some of the other girls and you'll help with domestic duties. Believe it or not, we will actually pay you to be here. It won't be much, but then you won't need to spend much either. When you do not come up to scratch, you will be punished and you can expect to have your freedom curtailed – literally – as it is now. You will soon come to understand what this is all about and what it can mean to you. You will have plenty of opportunity to run away. If you do, you will forfeit the money we put into your account, and when you get caught, we'll just say we didn't realise who you were. It might sound implausible, but I think the police will accept our version.'

'I'm sure they will,' said Pauline knowingly.

'Do you wish to ask me anything before I go?' queried Sonia.

'Y-yes,' answered Rose, clearing her throat. 'I need to ... I mean, with –'

'With what!' demanded Pauline.

'With my arms fastened behind me, I can't go to ... I mean I want to go –'

'We're trying to say we want to use the toilet,' said Pauline sarcastically.

'I'll leave you to it, if you don't mind,' said Sonia. 'Everything is more or less ready, isn't it?'

'Just the rubber bottle to be filled,' answered Pauline, taking Rose by the shoulder. Rose glanced anxiously at the bathroom as she was pushed towards the door to the outside corridor. 'Not that one madam,' said Pauline, 'there's a special one prepared just for you!'

'And the things they've done to me,' said Rose, 'you wouldn't believe!'

'I would,' answered Jackie, lying next to her in the dark.

'You mean it's happened to you as well?'

'I wouldn't worry about it,' answered Jackie, 'and I wouldn't mention it to anyone else either or you'll really be for it, I can tell you.'

'Yeah, right. But apart from all that, it's really posh here, isn't it? I mean, the old girl, that Sonia, must be loaded.'

'We don't do too badly.'

'Yeah, you've got everything – nice house, swimming pool, food and wine. Just one thing missing.'

'Don't tell me,' said Jackie.

'Well, I have to say it, don't I? It's all women here – except for that bloke who grabbed me by the pool. Who's he?'

'That's Mike. He's a nice guy.'

'He looked all right – a bit old for us though.'

Jackie did not reply for a few moments. Then she said, 'Rose?'

'Yeah, what?'

'Maybe you'd like to ... maybe there's something you need to help you sleep.'

113

Jackie's hand slid across Rose's stomach under the bed-clothes.

'What do you mean?' she asked, but did not push the hand away.

Jackie moved closer and whispered in her ear, 'Just a little something.'

Rose turned towards her and touched the side of her face, at the same time feeling the fingers move down with electric deliberation to the base of her stomach and stroke through her pubic hair.

'Here, what are you doing?' giggled Rose, squeezing Jackie's arm.

Jackie did not reply, but continued on until her fingers touched the heat of Rose's sex, found her unresisting, and gently entered it. Rose sighed, pressing her lips suddenly against Jackie's and reaching down with her own arm to find that which she knew must be found.

'It's awkward like this,' whispered Jackie. 'Let's get up.'

They pushed back the light covering from the bed and struggled up on to their knees so that they faced each other in dark intimacy. With arms entwined they began again to kiss. Soon, they were engaged in the dialogue of lust, each finding the sex of the other moist and welcoming its invasion. Jackie and Rose swayed gently back and forth, biting and kissing, both breathing loudly as each stroked the rising flames within the willing body of the other. Any doubts Rose may have held about entering into this world of sensuality had vanished like a snowflake over a furnace. And a furnace was what each of them was becoming, ready to erupt molten fire as each entered deeper and harder into the other. At last the fires broke free. They grasped each other and both cried out loudly as the flames of lust engulfed them completely.

They remained locked together in the darkness for some time afterwards, each listening to the beating of the other's heart.

After a while, Jackie stirred and said, 'You could have a good time here Rosie, you know that?'

6

Enforced Servitude

'What's going to happen? What are they going to make me do?'

'Look Rosie, don't worry about it. Go back to sleep.' Jackie peered through the darkness at the radio alarm. 'It's not even four o'clock, you know.'

'Well, just tell me something, Jackie. I don't want to be treated like a bleeding servant just to keep me from the hands of the fuzz!'

'Rosie, you have to wait and see. Just remember, you've been all this time out in a sea of troubles. Why not give yourself a break? I don't want to say anything, but you'll be all right, believe me. There's one thing though, and you really will have to take notice or you'll end up on the run again.'

'My language?'

'And more Rosie – the way you express yourself.'

'They said I had to talk posh.'

'No, it's not simply a matter of talking posh, it's . . . oh, you'll find out. I just hope it's the easy way and not the hard, though sometimes I –'

'Sometimes what?'

'Oh, nothing,' sighed Jackie, 'it's just me.'

They said no more, but moved closer together, and in each other's arms drifted like two soft white feathers into the abyss of sleep.

'She's just drying herself,' said Jackie, as Cheryl and Valerie entered the room.

'She was supposed to be ready by now,' remarked Cheryl, lowering the plastic bag to the floor.

'I know but she's not used to –'

'Never mind,' cut in Valerie, 'we're not in any rush.'

Jackie eyed the plastic bag, knowing from past experience of her own what its contents were intended for. She stood slightly back from the two and regarded them for a few moments. The dark haired Valerie, with her gypsy eyes, and the Nordic Cheryl, with her short, waved blonde hair. Both were beautiful in their own way: Valerie warm and vivacious, Cheryl a siren from arctic climes. Jackie saw that they had on identical outfits, outfits suggesting the nursing profession but shorter and styled in blue vinyl, with black seamed stockings and high stiletto heel shoes to complete their attire.

'It's being recorded then,' remarked Jackie.

'Yes,' answered Valerie, 'Auntie Pauline's orders.'

'It's a good job she's not here now,' remarked Cheryl. 'She's very keen on punctuality!'

As if in response to Cheryl's comment, Rose appeared at the bathroom door, swathed in a white bathrobe. At the sight of Cheryl and Valerie she stopped dead and regarded them with an anxious stare.

'Well, come along!' ordered Cheryl, picking up the bag and walking over to the small dining table.

Rose approached cautiously, clutching defensively at the bathrobe and looking at all three in turn.

Jackie smiled at her and said, 'Rose, they're not going to eat you.'

'Oh . . . er, yeah, right, I've had my shower.'

Valerie pulled Rose's hands away from her front. 'Now, let's have this off.'

Rose looked at her with apprehension as Valerie pulled away the belt and Cheryl upended the plastic bag.

'Look, I haven't got anything –'

'No,' replied Cheryl, pulling the contents of the bag out on to the table, 'but you will have in a minute!'

Rose was hardly aware of the bathrobe slipping away from her body as the sinister black garment with its array of straps and brass buckles settled down with a sigh on to the table, exuding the rich and unmistakable aroma of leather.

'Sit on here,' ordered Valerie, indicating a nearby stool. Rose obeyed.

Cheryl picked up the garment and moved around behind her. She offered one side of it to Valerie, who pulled it around the front of Rose, at the same time taking hold of Rose's right arm and pushing it into the horizontal sleeve which ran across the inside. Cheryl gripped the upper part of the arm while Valerie took Rose's left and guided it into the other end of the waiting sleeve.

'That's it,' said Valerie, 'right inside and cross them over.'

Rose hesitated, glancing from Valerie to Jackie, but at once the garment was pulled tightly around her shoulders and upper body, forcing her arms completely into the internal sleeve and holding them folded across her middle. Two pairs of hands worked quickly at the back, to the rasping and clicking of buckles, and the straitjacket pulled and tightened about her body. A few moments later saw Rose encapsulated from neck to waist in shining black leather, her arms held immobile inside with her fingers pressed around her elbows.

'Well, that wasn't too difficult,' remarked Cheryl. 'Come on, get up!'

Rose, her face a mask of bewilderment, struggled to her feet, while Cheryl reached over to the table and collected the other items which had occupied the plastic bag.

'Hey! What are you doing?'

Rose backed away from Cheryl, but Valerie held her from behind.

'Just think of this each time you open your mouth,' said Cheryl, dangling the three-tailed strap in front of Rose's face. 'Now, what were you going to say?'

'I-I wasn't g-going to say anything,' stammered Rose. Valerie pulled the bathrobe about her and fastened the belt about her waist, leaving the arms hanging empty at her sides.

'All right,' said Cheryl, 'let's go downstairs.'

'Come along, deary,' added Valerie, propelling Rose towards the door.

* * *

117

'Is it all ready?' asked Valerie as Kim appeared from within the bathroom.

'It sure is,' replied Kim, regarding the anxious-looking Rose.

Cheryl closed the inner door while Valerie unscrewed the cap from a small bottle of methylated spirits and applied some of the contents to a paper tissue. She turned to Rose, who would have backed away had not Cheryl held her firmly by the shoulders.

'Hold still,' said Valerie, and began to wipe the area of skin about Rose's mouth.

Rose glimpsed Kim in the big wall mirror above the sinks and work surface. Kim too was attired in the approximation of a nurse's uniform. She stood behind Valerie and was occupied in opening a small packet from which she withdrew a strip of shiny white tape. She pulled the backing paper off the tape and, as Valerie turned to her, handed it over carefully and took away the used tissue.

'All right, dear,' said Valerie, 'close your mouth nice and tight.'

'Wait!' objected Rose, looking at the small oblong of tape.

'Cheryl, the strap!' said Valerie.

Rose immediately closed her eyes as well as her mouth. Valerie, not waiting to give her chance to express second thoughts, applied the tape promptly over Rose's lips, squeezing it down hard and rubbing it outwards with her thumbs, while Cheryl held the girl's head steady from the rear.

'Neat job,' observed Kim as Valerie stepped back. Rose opened her eyes and let out an anxious 'mmmmm'.

Rose was then ushered along the length of the beauty parlour, past the sinks, past the odd-shaped chair with its dark blue cover and past the two hairdryers standing like sentinels a short distance from the bathroom door. When they entered the warmly lit, blue tiled bathroom with its pink rugs, Rose looked about her. She saw the shower and the sink with their luxurious fittings, saw herself in the large, bronzed wall mirror, then saw the low-level bowl with its attached restraints and the pink rubber bottle hanging to one side above it with the clear plastic tubing coiling down from the neck. She let out a long, protesting 'mmmmm!' and attempted to pull back, but all to no avail.

When, on the previous day, Pauline had taken her to a similar room, she had seen the same equipment. Then, she had not realised what it was intended for until it was too late. Now, she knew only too well what they were about to do with her and there were three people to witness her humiliation. As the straps tightened about her legs and body, holding her straddled over the bowl, she determined that at the first opportunity she would flee the house and take her chance on the run. The coiled pipe spiralled down in Valerie's latex gloved hand as Rose watched it with helpless apprehension. However, the action of the smooth and lubricated nozzle entering her anus and pushing coolly into her rectum gave her a sensation in her loins she had not expected nor experienced the previous day. It was a sensation she found disturbingly pleasant.

Once the warm liquid had passed into her, Valerie withdrew the instrument. A moment later the water was turned on in the bowl to cascade and bubble around beneath. Rose could feel the insistent pressure churning and building up inside. Cheryl, Valerie and Kim left the room. Whether it was out of consideration for her feelings or whether it was normal practice under such circumstances, Rose did not know. Nor did she care, for she closed her eyes and moaned softly through the tape as she lost control and her body rapidly discharged its contents into the whirlpool below.

No more than five minutes had passed before Valerie returned, this time alone. Rose was rinsed, soaped intimately by the latex fingers and rinsed again before Valerie released her from the bowl. Cheryl and Kim stood waiting by the bench when Valerie and Rose entered the main room. The bench, some two metres long, and a little under half a metre wide, had been obscured by its pink towelling when they had first arrived, but the towelling was gone now and Rose could see the padded black leather gleaming dully.

Valerie and Cheryl, with the strap tucked neatly into her belt, took her by the shoulders, pushed her down on to the bench and turned her around until she lay flat upon her back. Kim busied herself at the range of cupboards opposite.

'Are we nice and comfortable?' asked Valerie, looking down at Rose.

The girl made no sound but looked from Valerie to Cheryl, who moved around and stooped either side of her. From under the bench they pulled two long straps, one of which was passed over Rose's enclosed upper arms and chest, the other about her slim waist. Rose felt the straps tighten and pulled up her knees as the buckles were fastened. A moment later, both her ankles were grasped and pulled wide apart. Her lower legs were forced over the sides and underneath the bench. Hidden straps were quickly passed around her ankles, securing them firmly to the underside of the bench and keeping her thighs held well apart by its width.

'I sometimes wish this thing was higher,' said Valerie, as she and Cheryl pulled themselves up.

'Yes,' replied Cheryl, 'it's a bit undignified in these uniforms.'

Apart from the limited movement of her head, Rose was totally immobile and exposed before the three of them. What they were about to do to her she did not know and could not ask. She only knew that whatever it was, there was nothing she would be able to do to prevent it. She watched Valerie easing on a new pair of skin-tight, translucent rubber gloves.

Valerie pulled over a small chrome and black leather stool and sat down next to Rose. Kim passed something to her as Cheryl looked on. Rose could not make out what the object was until it began to emit an electric whine.

'She doesn't have much anyway,' remarked Valerie, running her rubber gloved finger through the fine down of straw-coloured hair over Rose's vulva. Rose stiffened and lifted her head. She at last realised they were going to shave her, and tensed against the restraints once more as the cool

120

head and metal cutters made contact with the firm but tender flesh directly about her most intimate place. The cutter moved back and forth, its fine toned vibration penetrating and warming her loins. If dignity had ever been high on Rose's list of priorities, her present situation would have precluded any feelings of pleasure to be gained from what was taking place. But dignity and decorum had never intruded unduly upon anything in which she had been involved and were not about to do so now. She relaxed and closed her eyes.

Once the hair was gone, the foil head of the shaver began its work to remove the fine stubble and leave the skin silk-smooth. Rose sighed inaudibly through the tape.

'Are we removing it permanently?' asked Valerie.

'I don't know,' replied Cheryl. 'Did Auntie Pauline not say?'

'Not to us she didn't, no.'

'Well then, I think I'll make an executive decision on the matter,' continued Cheryl. 'Let's do it anyway.'

'All right,' answered Valerie, turning to Kim. 'Plug it in will you, deary.'

Rose opened her eyes for a moment and looked about her. She saw the ultrasonic depilator as Kim handed it to Valerie, and though she suspected what its function was, did not feel that the effort of attempting a protest would have altered their intentions.

The high-pitched whine of the depilator passed into Rose even more than the vibration of the shaver had as Valerie continued her work. She wondered if they knew what it was doing to her; if it was deliberate or if it was through her own susceptibility.

After a few minutes, as the instrument was pressed in electric ecstasy immediately above Rose's clitoris, Valerie half-smiled and said, 'You know, I think she's going to come!'

'God,' answered Cheryl, 'don't tell me she's as bad as the other one. Are you going to let her?'

'Yes, why not,' said Valerie, smiling. 'We don't want her to think life is all trial and tribulation.'

121

The depilator continued to feed and fuel Rose's lust. She began to moan, softly at first, as she felt the glow within her body begin to intensify. Soon, she no longer cared who was watching and began to twist her head about and tense against the restraints. Cheryl, Valerie and Kim watched her as her muffled moans passed through the tape, louder by the second, until her body stiffened like a rock and shuddered repeatedly as the fires of orgasm overwhelmed her.

A few minutes later, Rose stood before them again, this time unsteady after her restraint on the bench, still wearing the straitjacket, still unable to speak.

'Now then, madam,' said Cheryl, 'Val and Kim are going to make you look presentable. After that, we have a nice little outfit for you to put on and then you can begin to earn your keep in a modest way.'

Valerie and Kim guided her across the room to the range of sinks and the panoramic mirror. There, they eased her into one of the small swivel chairs with her reflected image before her. She relaxed and watched as Valerie began to brush her hair in long, slow strokes. To Rose it felt good and she did not wish Valerie to stop.

'She has nice hair,' remarked Kim.

'It's not been properly looked after,' responded Valerie. 'It would be lovely if she bothered to keep it in good condition. I suppose being on the run didn't help.'

When the brushing had finished, they took the long swathe of hair and wound it tightly about and over her head, keeping it in place with pins and finishing it with a large black clasp at the side.

'It's made her look like Angela,' remarked Cheryl.

'Yes,' replied Valerie, 'she's much more like Angie than Jackie, though you wouldn't have thought so before, would you?'

Valerie reached for the bottle of methylated spirits and unscrewed the cap. She poured some of the liquid on to a tissue and pressed it against the edge of the tape which still sealed Rose's mouth.

'You'll be able to speak in a minute, dear,' said Valerie.

'And make sure you think before you do!' added Cheryl.

The tape at last came away from Rose's lips and Valerie dabbed about her mouth to ensure that no adhesive remained on the skin. Kim had meanwhile arranged a small number of jars and tubes in front of the chair. Some of these, at least, Rose recognised and saw nothing to prompt further misgiving.

First they applied moisturising cream and massaged it soothingly about her face and neck, then foundation cream. Rose said nothing but continued, with an expression of almost amused interest, to watch them in the mirror. After the sparing application of face powder and eye make-up came the lipstick, which Kim put on to her so expertly.

'Rose pink,' said Valerie.

'Very appropriate with a name like hers,' added Kim, who then turned and walked towards the large cupboards.

'She's very quick today,' muttered Valerie.

'From street urchin to glamour model in one easy step,' put in Cheryl.

'What's it all in aid of?' asked Rose at last.

'It's the first stages of you becoming more of a lady and less of a slut,' answered Cheryl coolly.

'All right, get up,' ordered Valerie, putting her arm around Rose's shoulder. Rose obeyed, with Valerie's help. 'Is that outfit ready?' asked Valerie, turning to Kim.

'All powdered and ready,' answered Kim, gesturing towards the bench.

The bench was again covered with its pink towelling and over this was draped an as yet unidentifiable garment in black. Valerie began to undo the straps down Rose's back, loosening the straitjacket until Cheryl, standing in front of her, was able to pull it away and drape it over the chair.

'Thank God, my arms are –'

'Take these to the bathroom,' said Valerie, handing Rose a flat, clear plastic packet. 'Use the toilet if you wish and don't forget the bidet, then put them on and come back here.'

'And if you do anything to that make-up,' added Cheryl, patting the strap, 'you won't sit down again today, I promise!'

123

When Rose reappeared, she had on a pair of sheer, seamed, black open crotch tights. That was all. She approached them cautiously, looking from one to the other. Valerie lifted the garment from the bench and held it out to Rose.

'You're having this on, but be very careful with it.' Rose took it in her hands and examined it. The odour of latex, like the soft, cool feel of the material, was unfamiliar to her but the garment was obviously a dress of most unusual style. 'I'll help you into it,' said Valerie, taking hold of the top of the dress. 'Step into the skirt. We'll ease it up, then I'll do up the zip at the back.'

It took some time to get the dress on for Rose found it difficult. And then there were the black sandals in patent leather, with their criss-cross ankle straps and stiletto heels of unaccustomed height. Kim had to fit these on to Rose's feet as she stood supported by Valerie, for standing was what she was obliged to do.

The dress fitted Rose's slim figure like a tight black skin with a subtle sheen. It was short – at least as short as anything she had ever worn.

'You won't be sitting down in this,' Valerie had said. Now Rose knew why.

The short, flounced sleeves and the low scooped neck were trimmed with white lace, as was the small, white cotton semi-circular apron fitted high on her waist.

'That will be yours from now on,' said Cheryl. 'You'll wear it whenever you're on duty.'

'But . . . but . . .'

'But what?' asked Cheryl.

'But,' continued Rose, 'I haven't anything on under it.'

'No,' replied Cheryl, 'you haven't and you won't. You are not allowed to sit when on duty and if you reveal part of yourself that you shouldn't, you will be punished. I'll punish you if I see anything and if Auntie Pauline is there, you'll really know about it!'

Rose, as if in anticipation of possible infringement, pulled down on the tight hem of the dress. Rose had noticed the two pairs of steel cuffs by the nearest sink and had wondered briefly if their presence concerned her. It did. Cheryl picked up the smaller pair.

'Hands out!' she ordered. Rose hesitated. 'Now!' said Cheryl sternly. Valerie pushed one of Rose's arms forward. Rose complied with the other. 'Good girl,' said Cheryl, fitting the steel cuffs on to Rose's wrists and snapping them shut.

Rose looked hard at the cuffs and pulled her hands as far apart as the ten centimetres of steel chain would allow. Cheryl picked up the second pair of cuffs and placed them into the pocket of her tunic.

'Those can wait until we're upstairs,' she said.

Valerie and Kim pulled a long white cotton gown around Rose and fastened it with tapes down the back.

'What's this for?' asked Rose.

'It's just until you are up on the first floor,' answered Valerie. 'Outfits like yours aren't supposed to be worn down here. It's against the rules.'

'Come on,' said Cheryl, taking Rose's arm, 'we'll use the back stairs.'

They had barely turned the corner from the stairway on to the first floor corridor when Cheryl brought Rose to a halt. She tugged away the tapes at the rear of the gown and, moments later, it was gone from Rose's body, leaving her standing in the bizarre outfit.

'All right,' said Cheryl, 'now let's see how you get on with these on, shall we?'

She reached into her tunic pocket, brought out the bright steel cuffs, knelt down in front of Rose and ordered, 'Bring your feet closer together.'

Rose obeyed, felt the cool grip of metal around each ankle in turn, and heard the soft click as each was secured in place by its internal lock.

'How can I walk in these?' asked Rose nervously, looking down at the twenty centimetres of chain which joined the cuffs.

'Other people seem to manage well enough,' answered Cheryl. 'You just have to be careful and take short steps. Once you are used to wearing them you'll do it automatically.'

Rose looked into Cheryl's eyes with an expression of mild trepidation, then down to her manacled wrists.

'Get used to them?' she asked weakly.

'I'm going to bring Angela down now,' said Cheryl. 'Don't move from here and remember to stand up straight. If Pauline catches you slouching, she'll have just the excuse she's looking for.'

Cheryl turned and disappeared up the stairs leading to the second floor, leaving Rose to stand alone at the end of the deserted corridor. Rose wondered what she would do if someone came out of one of the rooms and approached her; someone she had not met before. Would she look at them? Would she speak or simply turn away? Without the distraction of another person, her thoughts and feelings turned inwards. She became more aware of the tight rubber dress about her body and of how it enclosed her with warm intimacy. Where it stretched about her thighs it gave her an odd sensation, particularly when she moved her weight from one leg to the other and the latex slid across her shaven sex.

There were voices on the stairs. Moments later two figures appeared. One was Cheryl, the other looked at first to be a slightly older version of Rose herself, for their complexion and eyes were not dissimilar though the other's hair was lighter and the eyes greyer than Rose's. The way the hair was styled and fixed by its clasp at the side was identical to her own.

'Rose, this is Angela,' announced Cheryl. 'Angie – Rose, our new maid.'

Angela smiled warmly and held out her hand. 'Hello Rose.'

Rose swallowed hard and her face flushed brightly with embarrassment. 'Oh ... er, I can't properly ... I'm, I'm ...'

She lifted her manacled hands to touch Angela's. Angela lifted her other hand to take both of Rose's.

'Don't be shy, dear,' said Angela, her smile broadening. 'We all wear what you're wearing from time to time on domestic duties, if we've been bad girls, that is.'

Rose looked at Angela's outfit and was not reassured, for she wore a plain, white, satin, long-sleeved blouse and close-fitting turquoise blue trousers of the same material, with a wide, black vinyl belt. The contrast between this and her own outfit was not calculated to make Rose feel any easier.

Angela saw her looking and smiled. 'Never mind, you look very glamorous.'

'I'll let you get on with it,' said Cheryl. 'And watch her language, won't you?'

'We're not still recording I take it?' asked Angela.

'No, the show's over for now,' answered Cheryl, then she turned about and left them.

'Right,' said Angela, 'you're with me until lunchtime. You can have the easy jobs and just hold a few things for me. By then, Cheryl or Pauline will be back to collect you.'

'Oh . . . what happens at lunchtime? I mean, I don't have to wear –'

'No, you'll get changed and go down to the restaurant. After that you'll be in the office or the library with Karen for elocution lessons and –'

'Eller what?' cut in Rose as they reached the first door.

'Elocution lessons – how to speak correctly.'

'And then,' said Rose, 'and then, I'm down with this Karen to sit and read, and answer questions. She was really nice to me, like Angie was. Then I had a really nice slap-up dinner in the bar and got to help out serving them all drinks, like in a pub.'

'So you might not run away this week?' asked Jackie in the darkness of the bedroom.

'Well, I dunno. I thought when I was wearing that dress and them handcuffs – I thought of all the things they've done to me. Oh yes, and the other thing, the beauty parlour; I didn't like to say at first, you know, but they've gone and shaved me cunt so it's –'

'Rosie!' shouted Jackie, sitting upright in the bed. 'Rosie, please! You have to try, really you have! For my sake as well as yours, even in private. Please – promise!'

127

There was silence for long seconds.

'Jackie, love, I'm sorry. I will try, honestly, but I've only been here a day or so. It's all so strange.'

'I suppose it must be, but I don't want you to end up in the hands of the police.'

'No, me neither, but I did think earlier that I might clear off out of it first thing tomorrow. I never even dreamed of a place like this – wouldn't have believed it possible, you know. And why do they want to make you all helpless so you can't use your arms?'

'Rosie, it's all play-acting and theatre. You'll understand after a while.'

'Do you like it all then? I mean, doesn't any of it bother you, those weird outfits and all?'

'No, Rosie, not most of the time. Not really. Sometimes ... sometimes it's well ... I don't quite know how to explain. You're either into it or you're not, if you see what I mean.'

Rose was silent for a few seconds.

'Well, I can see it's a way of getting off sometimes – you know.'

'Getting off?'

'Yeah – yes, with the right sort of people, it could be dead sexy and –'

'Oh yes,' cut in Jackie, 'I see what you mean. Yes, Rosie, it can be very sexy.'

'And those rooms on the other side of the corridor. Angie said they were secret and not for me to see. What's inside them? Do you know? She wouldn't tell.'

Jackie laughed softly in the darkness. 'Yes Rosie, I know.'

'Well?'

'Well, what?'

'Oh, come on, Jackie! I hate bleed ... I mean, I hate secrets!'

'It's a bit awkward. We're not supposed to discuss anything like that with anyone who doesn't work here.'

'Blimey! I thought I'd seen enough already in that Pauline's room, not to mention the beauty parlour. It can't matter all that much now. Let's go have a look, all right?'

'No, we can't. I don't have a key anyway. Only Sonia has a master key and other people have to go and ask for it. Pauline can get into a couple of them – so that's it I'm afraid.'

'Bet I could get in easy.'

'What d'you mean?'

'Those locks,' continued Rose in a low voice, 'they wouldn't give me any bother, if you know what I mean.'

'Are you saying you pick locks?'

'Could be I've done a few in my time.'

'Rosie, I'd be in dead trouble if we did anything like that. They'd throw me out!'

'Throw you out! Is that all?'

'No, that isn't all. You just don't understand. It's the worst thing that could happen to me, it really is!'

'Aw, come on! Why would they do that just for going into somewhere you already know about? Tell you what, I'll get in, right, and if anyone sees us we'll say you followed me and tried to get me out. How's about it?'

'Well . . . I suppose, if we're careful, and it's an evening when Pauline is away –'

'Atta girl!'

'And Rosie, it's not just me I'm bothered about. I don't want you to get into hot water either. If we're going to be friends, I don't want anything to cause upset.'

Rose reached up and squeezed Jackie's arm. 'You're a good pal, Jackie. I'll try not to let you down. And . . . and the other night, what we did, that was real good fun that was.'

'I'm glad, Rosie,' she answered, turning and looking down in the darkness at the vague form of her companion.

Rose eased herself up against the pillows and kissed her on the lips. Jackie placed her hand on the side of Rose's head.

'Rosie,' she whispered, 'I've got something we could play with if you fancy.'

'Yeah, what?'

'Well, switch on the bedside lamp, it's on your side.'

'Right, if I can find the . . . ah . . . there!'

The room filled with soft, subdued light from the small, pink-shaded lamp. Jackie, in her nakedness, eased herself from the bed and took a few steps to the nearby chest of drawers. She pulled open the top drawer, rustled tissue paper and lifted something out, keeping it concealed from Rose but grinning mischievously over her shoulder as she pushed the drawer shut with a soft thump.

'Well, go on. Show us!'

Jackie spun around suddenly with a beaming grin, holding the object up in front of her with a triumphant 'Da-daaah!'

'Oooh-er!' responded Rose, with a high-pitched laugh. 'How did you get hold of that?'

'Oh, easily,' said Jackie, returning and placing the object of their attention on the bedspread. 'You can easily find goodies like this around here if you know where to look.'

Rose reached out and touched it, lifting it up slowly. 'I've seen them in sex catalogues,' she mused, 'but I've never, well . . .'

'I'll put it back in the drawer, if you're not keen.'

Rose looked up at her with mouth slightly open. 'No,' she said softly. 'I'm game if you are. How are we going to . . .?'

Jackie picked up the double-ended dildo by one of its amply proportioned shafts and ran her fingers over the bulbous pink head. 'Shall I show you the best way to use it, Rosie?'

Rose reached out to touch it. 'It even feels real, except it's bigger than any I've seen.'

'Well?'

'Yeah, go on then. Let's give it a go.'

'OK, you just sit on the edge of the bed and I'll sit next to you, yes?'

Rosie slid to the edge of the bed and waited. Jackie sat beside her and with the instrument of lust held in one hand, placed her arm around Rose's waist. Rose turned and kissed her on the lips and Jackie's arm tightened about her.

'You're good fun, you are, Jackie,' breathed Rose into her ear.

Jackie released her hold and climbed further up on to the bed until she was propped up against the padded head-board behind Rose. She parted her legs and pulled Rose back between them until she was leaning with her back against her. Jackie reached around Rose and played with her breasts for a time, kissing and biting her gently on her cheek and neck. Rose relaxed, let her head fall back and closed her eyes. After a minute, Jackie reached down under Rose's thighs and began to pull. Rose obliged her efforts by lifting and spreading her legs until her feet were on either side of Jackie's. Jackie's left hand fell upon the dildo, which she took up by one of the pink shafts. The other shaft she brought down between Rose's legs until the cool rubber head found its mark and Jackie felt her body stiffen. Rose's hand joined hers around the shaft and they moved the head of the dildo back and forth until Rose began to sigh and push it harder against the moist lips of her sex. Jackie knew that Rose was aroused and eager enough for it to enter her but would not allow her to take charge of the situation until she began to tug harder. Then they were of one intent. Rose sighed again as both hands helped the shaft into her so that it entered fully, up to the flared-out join between the two opposing organs.

Jackie released her and pulled herself out from behind, allowing Rose to fall back on to the pillows. Now that she lay almost flat, Jackie climbed astride her. Not so that they were face to face, as Rose had expected, but the opposite way about, so that Jackie's thighs were spread above her face. Jackie squatted frog-like over her and, pulling away Rosie's hand, began to work the rubber cock back and forth inside her. For Rose, the situation was novel and sur-prising though it in no way diminished the growing carnal urgency within her. On the contrary, it not only fuelled her lust but drove her to do that which she had never before imagined she would ever do. She took hold of Jackie's thighs and pulled down until her sex was close enough. Rose's tongue began its work, teasing voluptuously about the clitoris, finding Jackie already inflamed and eager and tasting her excitement. The fires began to rise up higher

131

within both of them as they worked upon each other. Then, to Rose's surprise, Jackie stopped and lifted herself clear. But it was only a momentary cessation, for without speaking, she lifted and pushed Rose's legs back, almost against her chest, so that the exposed half of the dildo protruded upwards and inviting. Jackie shuffled forwards and lowered herself down on to it without further ado, allowing it to enter her as completely as it had entered Rose so that it united them both in urgent intimacy. She leaned forward, allowing Rose to wrap her legs about her and letting their lips meet.

Together they wrestled in voluptuous passion – panting, kissing and biting – each unspeaking but each urging on the other with the action of her body until the flames of lust burst forth to engulf them at once. Rose began to cry out first but then Jackie threw back her head and, forcing her sex hard against Rose's, let out a loud wail as if in anguish, each of them writhing in burning abandon against the other.

When they withdrew the glistening organ from within themselves, Jackie took it to the bathroom and placed it in the sink. She returned to find Rose unmoving and with eyes shut, still lying upon the bed. She sat on the edge and laid her hand upon Rose's arm.

'All right, Rose?'

Rose stirred and opened her eyes. 'God help us – I never had one like that before.'

'It's fun, isn't it?' asked Jackie, stroking her hair.

'And you say you get paid for it and all,' laughed Rose.

'You're funny, Rosie, you really are.'

'I'll try extra hard now,' said Rose, 'just for you.'

A few minutes later, they lay once again in the darkness and neither spoke for some time. Each was aware that the other was wide awake.

At length Rose said, 'If we get the chance tomorrow –'

'Chance for what?' asked Jackie.

'Well, what we did before, I mean . . . with that thing.'

'Go on,' whispered Jackie, finding her hand under the sheet.

'Well, if we did it again, if you want, that is, we could swap around the other way.'

'Yes, I don't mind.'

Rose turned and moved towards her and their lips met, warm and eager. 'You're good fun, you are, Jackie.'

'And you,' replied Jackie, putting her arm around Rose. 'But if you want to try –'

'Yes – what?'

'Well, if you feel like it now, I wouldn't mind.'

'No, nor me,' replied Rose, as their lips met again.

7

The Night Has Eyes

'Remember last time we sat here?' asked Annette. 'You felt a bit unsettled about your future. Did your trip back to England sort anything out?'

'I suppose it did,' said Karen, 'but you all helped me decide: you, Val, Angela and the others.'

'So the crimson world of sin has its good side after all?'

'I can't say yes or no to that anymore but I tell you, sitting here under the tree at this little table on a day like today doesn't leave an awful lot to be desired.'

'Yes,' replied Annette. 'I remember how much you enjoyed it last time. That's why I thought we'd come back again.' She examined the red and white checked tablecloth. 'I wonder if they've changed this since we were last here!'

'Oh, Annette, of course they have!'

'Karen, sometimes you take things too seriously. Have another glass of wine.'

'Oh, thanks I will. Anyway, you'd take things more seriously if you had my upbringing.'

Annette smiled and glanced about at the people passing by, going about their unhurried business, talking and gesturing about the everyday affairs of life.

'That's what I like about this part of the world, you know. They don't seem to worry too much over time or take a lot of notice of . . . oh! Look who's drifting along towards us.'

'Oh yes,' observed Karen, 'it's Mike. Shall I call him over or are you both still . . ?'

'I don't mind,' said Annette, 'we got over our little disagreement some time ago and he's found a new role in life since. I can assure you, Karen, he endures his ordeals like a man and thinks of nothing else but queen and country.'

'Annette,' said Karen, smiling, 'you're so cruel!'

'Cruel! Me! Nobody's done him more favours than I have since Sonia rescued him from the tax man in England. He just took a long while to appreciate how –'

'Hi, you two!' cut in the voice.

Annette turned. They both smiled up at him, shading their eyes against the sun.

'What are you doing prowling around Béziers today?' asked Annette.

'Not a lot,' he said, pulling up a chair. 'I thought I'd look at some clothes.'

Annette affected an expression of open-mouthed astonishment. 'New clothes! God – did those old jeans of yours get up and run off on their own?'

'Hey, come on! What's the point in me being fashion-conscious with the job I do?'

'Oh Mike,' said Karen, 'she's just teasing you. You ought to know by now.'

'Yes,' he said, grinning and eyeing her mischievous green eyes and seeing the sun glint on her rich auburn hair. 'I'll get my own back one day, you'll see.'

Annette poked out her tongue.

'What are you going to buy?' asked Karen.

He looked into her soft brown eyes and saw the warm breeze move the hair about her cheek. 'Well, something casual. Maybe some shorts – a couple or more T-shirts and, er, I haven't seen my sunglasses around for the best part of a week so it'll be a new pair of those too.'

'They're probably behind a pile of dirty dishes,' murmured Annette. Karen grinned at them both. Mike protruded his tongue at her. 'I know just the place you should go,' she continued. 'La Grenade. It's hardly more than five minutes walk from here.' She turned to Karen. 'You got your swimwear from there. Tell him what a super shop it is.'

Karen remembered the boutique only too well, and yes, she had made a purchase there and got a little more than she had bargained for. She felt herself blush slightly and cleared her throat. 'Er, yes. A very good shop – lots of nice things to choose from.'

'And if you work for Sonia,' said Annette, 'you can put your stuff on the house account and get a better price as well. I'm surprised you didn't know that.'

'Nobody told me,' he answered. 'There are probably all sorts of other things I don't know.'

'Poor old Mike,' said Karen, smiling. 'Go and get yourself a drink and sit here for a while.'

To be seen sitting with two such desirable women was an invitation he was not about to refuse. Minutes later, he was back at the table with a glass of beer.

'Don't forget today is early closing, will you?' said Annette.

Mike looked at his watch. 'I'm OK for a while. No rush.'

'Well, I have a bit to do yet,' said Annette, draining the last of her white wine and pushing back the chair. 'If you don't mind, I'll get round to the *boulangerie* now in case they sell out. I'll drop into La Grenade and tell Louise and Marielle to expect someone in dire need of smartening up!'

'But Annette!' exclaimed Karen. 'We already have enough –'

'Don't worry, dear!' cut in Annette pointedly. 'I'll only be fifteen or twenty minutes.'

Annette turned without another word and left them at the little table. Karen watched her disappear then turned with a smile to Mike.

'Well, at least you're talking to each other again.'

'Hmmm, yes,' he answered, rubbing his chin. 'I suppose this shop is genuine? I mean, with a name like Grenade!'

'It just means pomegranate. You must have walked past it often enough, the number of times you've been here.'

'Yes, I probably have. But I drive to Montpellier if I want to get myself anything personal, and then it's usually books and records. This shop – Sonia owns it, does she?'

'I'm not sure if she owns it,' answered Karen. 'At least, not the business: that belongs to Marielle and Louise. I think Sonia owns the property. She has business interests all over the place, including two or three shops in Paris.'

'God, I thought I was the financial expert. When I dealt with her in London, it was only her affairs in the UK and Holland. I only found out about her operation here much later. That woman is full of secrets.'

'It's just as well you did find out,' said Karen.

'So, I'm safe going to this shop? It's not one of Annette's set-ups, with cameras hidden all over the place?'

'No, I'm sure it isn't, not here. But, er, the girls will pamper you something rotten if you let them.'

He smiled to himself, leaned towards her, and asked, 'Look, why don't you come and have a drink with me down by the pool this evening? We could have a midnight swim and a bottle of wine under the stars.'

Karen knew as well as everyone what an opportunist Mike had become. She knew equally that he was never forceful or insistent and that it was not in his interest to cause offence. She looked thoughtful and clasped her hands out of sight under the table. 'Erm, not tonight, I can't.'

'Oh OK, I just thought I'd ask.'

Karen had never, mainly because of her relationship with Sonia, spent any time alone with him, although he had in the past suggested that she might do so. Now that her relationship with Sonia was re-established, Karen wondered if such a firm commitment was a good thing, and if she ought not, if only for appearance's sake, show a little more interest in the opposite sex, as she had in England. She looked into his eyes. 'How about tomorrow evening? I can make it then if you like.'

He was taken aback momentarily, having regarded her last remark as a rebuff. His face broke into a broad grin. 'Oh, fine! Tomorrow it'll be then. Around eleven o'clock if that's not too late.'

'No, I'll be there.'

He relaxed back into his chair and picked up his glass, wishing not to appear too self-satisfied at having established a liaison with one who had previously given no cause for encouragement. They exchanged small talk for a time and watched the passers-by in the sun until Annette reappeared in her yellow cotton dress, her brown leather shoulder bag swinging at her side.

'Where's all the shopping you had to do?' asked Mike as she rejoined them at the table.

'The sh– oh, the shopping! I popped it into the back of the car. There wasn't much.'

He smiled at Karen and raised his eyes briefly, not wishing to render his disbelief too obviously but wanting her to see that he suspected Annette of some petty machination. He knew where her car was parked. He knew there would not have been enough time for her to do the things she had claimed.

Annette smiled at him and said, 'Don't worry about closing time. Marielle and Louise will be there all afternoon. So you can go after lunch instead of before.' She eyed his empty beer glass. 'As it looks like you'll be going to the bar in a minute, I'll have a prawn salad and an orange juice, please. And whatever Karen wants.'

The two girls stared at him, Annette in wide-eyed seriousness, Karen awaiting his reaction with barely suppressed humour.

'Oh, all right, Mike, I'll have the same please. If you can't say it all in French, I'll write it down.'

He looked from one to the other and broke into a wide grin. 'Ah well, caught out again, I see!'

'Oh, come on,' said Karen, reaching down for her shoulder bag, 'we'll both chip in. It's not fair –'

'No!' cut in Annette, placing a hand on Karen's arm. 'You'll encourage him to be even more tight-fisted than he already is. Anyway,' she continued, smiling up at the mildly bewildered Mike, 'he came out to spend a bit of money so he ought to be glad to be buying lunch for a couple of dolly birds like us!'

The early afternoon was hot and the pavements almost deserted when Mike strolled up to the front of the boutique. To all intents and purposes it appeared closed. He moved nearer to the window and peered inside at the displays. At last he pressed the doorbell.

Soon, a face appeared and regarded him from behind the glass pane of the shop door. Her features were somewhat angular, her eyes a wide, pale blue and her lips full. The long straw-coloured hair fell about her shoulders as she stooped to draw back the bolts and unlock the door.

'*Bonjour*,' she said, smiling into his face as the door opened.

'Mike,' he said, pointing at his chest in case it helped her to understand.

Unlike Annette, he had not taken up the French language with any dedication and had no idea if the two who ran the shop spoke English.

'Aah! *Monsieur* Mike,' she said and held out her hand. 'Please come in, we are expecting you.'

He squeezed the outstretched hand, passed into the shop and heard the rattle of the bolts behind him. The shop was cool and intimate with its racks and displays of colourful garments closing in about him. Shafts of sunlight speared across the displays, picking out flashes of brighter colour here and there.

'I am Marielle,' she said, smiling up at him. At that moment another figure appeared and Marielle turned to her. 'Ah, Louise, *voici* Mike.'

Louise offered her hand too and he clasped it with a meek 'hello', feeling moderately embarrassed at his inability to converse properly in the language of the country where he lived as an exile. The two girls, in their loose-fitting blue skirts and white cotton sleeveless tops, were obviously sisters, perhaps three or four years older than Karen and Annette. They were, of course, beautiful. Everyone associated with Sonia appeared to be beautiful. They reminded him a little of Rose, though in her case the age difference was even greater.

'You look at some things and we make you a coffee, yes?' asked Louise.

'Oh, yes please,' Mike answered.

Louise left them and returned to the back of the shop. Marielle grinned mischievously and indicated a rail hung with men's shorts.

'Annette says English people have no style for dressing and that you are an even worse example. She says we must help you because you are a big "oof". What is an "oof" please?'

'Ah! Well . . . I think the word is "oaf" . . but never you mind, I'll talk to her about it later!'

'Very good,' said Marielle. 'So, you choose the shorts here. Annette says you need sunglasses. They are over there.' She looked over him carefully and a frown crossed her features. '*Mon Dieu*! Those trousers, they are very old. You have brought them from England, no?'

'Well . . . well, I . . .'

'We have upstairs very good trousers. *Mademoiselle* Annette says you need everything!'

The look of bemused disbelief which, for a moment, characterised Mike's expression, gave way to a guarded smile as Louise appeared from the rear of the shop with a cup of coffee.

It was nearly three quarters of an hour later when, after a number of purchases and a lot of advice from Louise and Marielle, Mike watched them check off each item at the counter. He had turned to gaze at the pictures of exotic locations above the displays and was wondering what else Annette had said to them, when Louise and Marielle approached. He opened his mouth in surprise as an arm closed about his waist.

'Now we will go back up, yes?' asked Louise.

Marielle linked an arm into his.

'W-what?' He looked from one to the other. 'What . . . er, what are we –'

'Oh, *Monsieur* Mike, now you can freshen up, we give you your rub-down on the table and then you put on some of your new things.'

'Yes,' added Marielle, 'you are a friend of *Mademoiselle* Sonia. You must leave our little boutique feeling happy.'

'*Absolument!*' confirmed Louise, as they pushed him towards the stairs. 'Always we take care of people from her house.'

'Yes, but . . .'

The shop and its two proprietors had taken on a new

dimension. As they climbed the narrow wooden stairs he wondered if treading the path of caution might not be wiser. After all, if Annette was involved . . .

When they reached the first floor room with its Venetian blinds, big wall mirror and more racks of clothes, he looked about, recalling that he had seen nothing previously and saw nothing now that would be out of place in any shop.

'This way,' cooed Louise, taking him by the arm. They walked towards the curtained-off area at the far end of the room which he had earlier supposed to be private. 'In there,' said Louise, indicating the left side of the curtain, 'is a *toilette*, and in the room next to this is the shower. You will use please and then we will be ready for the treatment. Just bring your towel, nothing else.'

'Hey, wait!' he said as they turned to go. 'What am I . . . I mean, what are we . . ?'

Marielle and Louise swung around. Each placed her arms about him and each kissed him in turn on the lips. 'Now be a good boy, *Monsieur* Mike, and do as you are told,' pressed Louise.

When he entered the right-hand doorway behind the curtain, it took him almost a minute to assimilate the surroundings. With the long wall mirror, the sinks and the hairdryers, it appeared to be a hairdressing salon. The furniture, in chrome and black leather, was disturbingly familiar. The even greater resemblance of this room to the equally luxurious, if slightly larger, beauty parlour at the house escaped him, as the parlour had always been out of bounds. He noted the low bench, the chairs and the oddly draped piece of furniture beyond them. Opposite to the mirrored wall and beyond the bench stood a narrow table, finished in leather with a small black leather cushion at one end.

Inside the warm, comforting luxury of the shower he began to imagine himself back at the house, an experience which gave rise to ambiguous feelings. Nevertheless, he was fairly convinced that he was in for more than just a 'rub-down'. Life seemed to be like that of late.

141

Refreshed and dried, and with the heavy pink towel tucked firmly about his waist, he pushed cautiously through the door to see if anyone was outside.

'Ah! *Monsieur* Mike!' came a voice as he entered the room. 'Here we are waiting for you!'

The two swivel chairs in front of the mirrors swung around to reveal Louise and Marielle.

'Oh my God,' he heard himself mutter as they rose to face him.

Both wore loose-fitting black nylon chiffon blouses with long sleeves and high necks. About each of their waists was a wide, deep red, vinyl belt and beneath this a flared mini-skirt in shimmering black satin. Their legs were sheathed in gossamer black, seamed nylon and their feet in red vinyl sandals with high stiletto heels. They were at once inviting and intimidating.

'I think you like this,' said Marielle, smoothing her hands down her thighs then reaching out to kiss him.

Louise joined her sister and kissed him too and he saw their hands, sheathed in translucent latex surgical gloves. They held him and passed their hands over his shoulders, about his arms and around his body. The weight of the towel could not suppress his enlarging erection. He put his arms about both their slim waists and they about his. They kissed him about the face and neck and he returned their kisses with eagerness, feeling the sensual warmth of their bodies and smelling their enticing perfume. Without speaking, they guided him gently towards the padded table with its stout wooden legs, which he observed had been moved away from the wall.

'Please, now lie upon here,' said Louise.

He saw the soft, warm light of the room shining in their eyes and found himself obeying without question. The table was no more than 75 centimetres high, so easing himself on to its black leather top was not a problem. Once on his back, his arousal was obvious though the two girls appeared not to notice and walked around to face each other on either side of him.

The table was too narrow for him to rest his arms at his

sides, so he lay them loosely across his middle with his fingers clasped. But Louise and Marielle each took one of his wrists, pulling it away and downwards. He was wondering why he should allow himself to be manipulated by two very glamorous but total strangers in this way, when his misgivings became academic. A cool leather strap quickly encircled each wrist and tightened before he could pull free and the rasp of the buckles confirmed what they had done. He at once, and part instinctively, tried to sit up but was able to raise only his head from the small leather pillow. This proved to be a mistake for their plans were well laid. Two hands pushed under his head and held it, while two others thrust the rubber ball into his mouth and passed the straps around and behind. The ball gag was quickly tightened and secured before his head was lowered back on to the pillow. With each arm strapped to a table leg and unable to speak he watched intently as they took his feet and pulled these over the sides of the table as well. In a matter of seconds, all four limbs were secured and the two girls turned to him.

'Ah, you are nice and comfortable now?' asked Marielle.

He neither nodded nor made a sound, but tensed as Louise began to tug away the towel. She did not remove it from under him but once having exposed and freed his erection, let the ends hang over the sides of the table.

'*Ah, c'est beau,*' cooed Louise, running her fingers up the swollen shaft. Like a surge of electricity, it made him catch his breath and tighten the muscles about his pelvis. Marielle ran her fingers about the base of the shaft and under his testicles. It became the magnetic centre of his body, the beginning and the end, for all of a sudden nothing else could possibly matter. Then Marielle moved away, leaving Louise to carry on with her voluptuous manipulations.

When she returned, she smiled at Louise and at their captive. In her hand she held up a large white tube which she began to uncap, watched by Louise as well as Mike.

'Now for the treatment *Mademoiselle* Annette says you wish to have. We will do it!'

She squeezed the tube and he let out a stifled 'Mmmm!'

143

as the white cream spiralled coolly and abundantly about the base of his penis.

'I think that is enough now,' said Louise and began to massage the thick cream into his pubic hair.

Eventually, it lay like a mousse on the skin above his groin and though Marielle maintained his erection firmly by squeezing and stroking below the head of the penis, he was beginning to experience a prickling and mildly burning sensation where the cream lay. Louise walked over to the sink and moments later returned holding a box of tissues and a small, white plastic spatula. He had, of course, realised even as the cream was being applied, what its purpose was. He realised equally, from his experiences at the house, that attempting to express any objections or to free himself from the restraints would achieve nothing.

With his head propped up on the small pillow, he was able to see as well as feel as Louise removed the cream with the spatula and Marielle held the head of his penis with an expression of amused concentration. When she had finished with the spatula, Louise wiped around the smooth and hairless skin with a warm, damp cloth.

'Très bon,' said Louise, smiling. 'Now the little soldier looks very smart, just the way Annette says you would wish to have him. Perhaps next time you will not be too shy to ask Mademoiselle Valerie and she can take away the hair permanently.'

If they could see the expression on his face, they chose not to acknowledge it. His feelings of mild outrage did not, however, diminish his physical excitement nor his anticipation, for now that all traces of the depilatory cream were gone, the two girls bent forward and each ran a tongue up and down the gorged and inflamed organ from root to head and back again, seeing it quiver with each electrifying passage. The tension was, for him, becoming almost unbearable. He craved relief above all else. What they were doing would keep him hovering upon the edge but never achieve it. He began to twist against the straps in the hope of imparting to them his growing frustration but they continued this fiendish, sensual dialogue with him for some

144

minutes longer. When they stopped it was only to change tactics, for instead of tonguing, they began kissing, pressing their warm lips against his penis and moving slowly, inexorably upwards until they reached the moistened, quivering head. He closed his eyes tightly in expectation. Then they stopped.

Marielle slipped her cool, latex fingers about the foreskin. Louise smiled and said, 'Oh, the little soldier has stood to attention so well. Now, perhaps it is time to give him the discharge from duty.'

'I think so,' answered Marielle, working him gently up and down as Louise slipped a caressing hand beneath his testicles.

They understood instinctively how close he was to crisis point and Marielle stopped her work with only a few urgent heartbeats to spare. He moaned quietly in despair at the cessation and, with half-opened eyes, watched as Marielle peeled the thin latex glove slowly and deliberately from her right hand. For a few moments, she smiled and swung it before him, while Louise began to stroke once more, with her finger, the prime focus of his sensations.

Marielle opened the aperture of the glove and eased it down over the aching penis. The cool, sheer latex enclosed him with a voluptuous caress and, for a few seconds, the two girls stood smiling and regarded it, protruding upright before them.

Once more, his body responded with a tremor as Marielle's hand closed around the glove and his swollen organ and began to work it purposefully. This time he knew she would continue until . . . until . . . Then the inevitable happened. Every nerve in his body was seized in electric fire. He tensed rock hard against the restraints, groaning loudly, and ejaculating rapidly and copiously into the rubber glove.

It was over, and Marielle removed the glove. Louise began to undo the straps, saying, 'Ah! You English. You desire the pleasures so much but you are so afraid to admit to them!'

He stepped out of the shop into the warm afternoon air and the bright, sunlit street, wearing smart, new fawn

145

slacks and denim shirt. In one hand swung a red carrier bag, across which, in bold, green script was splashed 'La Grenade'. With his free hand, he adjusted the sunglasses with their reflective lenses and looked up and down the street, hearing the bolts of the shop door rattle shut behind.

The streets were not busy in the afternoon heat but the bars and cafés were doing a brisk trade. He was thirsty after his 'ordeal' in the shop and, though the girls had offered him coffee, he had declined the offer and left them. Perhaps they were right about the English, or at any rate, about him, for he retained a sense of unease, wondering if he ought to feel gratified or humiliated about his treatment at the hands, literally, of Louise and Marielle. What if the tables had been turned and he had been in control? He shrugged his shoulders and carried on.

Minutes later, he hesitated outside a small bar and looked inside at the crush of people.

'Hey! Smarty pants!' came a voice from behind.

He turned to see a smiling Karen and a grinning Annette strolling towards him.

'Hi there!' he responded.

'Oh, that's better!' said Karen. 'Those things suit you perfectly.'

'Surely you haven't been in the shop all this time,' put in Annette with a searching look.

Mike was glad to be wearing the sunglasses so as not to betray his expression.

'We've been all around the art gallery,' added Karen as they walked on.

'I bet he's been trying to take advantage of those two innocent little sisters,' remarked Annette.

'No, not me. I wouldn't do anything like that,' he offered, half seriously.

'No, of course you wouldn't,' said Karen, smiling.

'No, of course he wouldn't,' mocked Annette, with an expression which said everything to him but meant little to Karen. 'He's such a smoothie, aren't you, Mike? Real smooth!'

Karen hesitated to look into a shop window. Mike and

Annette walked a short way on. He turned to her and hissed, 'Annette you're a bitch!'

'I know,' she said, 'but I'm ever so good at it, aren't I? And just think what you'd be missing if it wasn't for me!'

'Missing! I tell you what I'd be missing, and that's the risk of being recognised by someone who's seen one of those damned videos!'

'Oh, don't be silly, Michael. Nobody has ever recognised any of us and we must be in dozens of them. I bet you wouldn't remember anyone you'd seen in one either. You don't realise how lucky you –'

'Back again!' cut in Karen's voice just behind them. 'You're not having a row, I hope?'

'Of course not, are we, dear?' Annette grinned and tucked her arm into his as they walked on. 'I was just telling him how lucky he was to get out of that shop in one piece. Louise and Marielle only look innocent.'

'I though a minute or two ago you were telling me they were,' remarked Karen.

'I was only kidding,' answered Annette. 'I reckon there are people who've gone in there and never come out again.' She smiled up at Mike. 'I bet you had quite a close shave, didn't you, dear?'

'Am I missing something?' asked Karen, taking his other arm.

He looked at them each in turn as they walked, his mouth fixed in a broad smile. Annette was right of course. He was lucky. He imagined what some of his old acquaintances back in London might think if they could see him now, walking along this sunlit street, arm in arm with these two beautiful and sensual young women. At the moment, he could forgive Annette anything. He glanced at her long auburn hair, burnished in the afternoon light, and then at Karen, her hair the colour of corn falling over her shoulders. He recalled her promise to meet him at the pool the following evening and his smile became broader still.

'So what's brought on this sudden attack of style consciousness?' came the voice from beside him.

Mike looked up from his magazine. 'Oh Val, I didn't see you, sorry. Are you sitting down for a bit?'

'If you don't mind my company for half an hour I will, thanks.'

Valerie placed a glass of orange juice down on the table and pulled up a chair. He regarded her shapely form in her thin, deep blue nylon halter-neck top, figure-hugging pencil skirt in gold lamé and her sheer black stockings. He sighed inwardly.

'Well, what's come over you?'

'Nothing . . . I, erm, just thought I needed a few things. No special reason.'

'I see,' said Valerie. 'Nothing to do with Annette and Karen in Béziers yesterday by any chance?'

'Well, I er . . . I was out shopping around anyway. They mentioned this little place between the market and the theatre – The Pineapple or something like that.'

'Oh yes. La Grenade. I'm sure you got your money's worth if I know Louise and Marielle.'

'Yes, I certainly did,' he muttered, glancing again at the magazine.

Valerie smiled to herself over his forced nonchalance on the subject of the boutique. There was a suppressed giggling from behind and she turned to regard the two figures huddled together by the yucca plant between the conservatory and the bar room.

'So that's where she is. I did wonder.'

'Yes,' answered Mike, glancing at Jackie and Rose, 'they're thick as thieves, aren't they? I'm sure they're hatching something.'

'It'll be fun and games if they do. Pauline's not been too happy of late. I think she's waiting for someone to step out of line so she can bare her fangs and pounce.'

'Oh, why's that?'

'I thought everyone knew,' answered Valerie, leaning forward and lowering her voice. 'She didn't want Karen back here, apart from anything else.'

'Why, it's no skin off her nose, is it?'

'No, not to a normal person it wouldn't be, but I think

148

the fact that Sonia has a close confidante makes her feel a bit marginalised when she thinks she ought to be seen as undisputed second in command.'

'Yes,' Mike breathed, 'I can understand that.'

'So she'll take it out on anyone she can, I suppose.'

'Speak of the devil,' grinned Mike, glancing into the bar room. Valerie looked briefly aside only to observe the approach of the silver-blonde hair and red lips everyone knew so well.

Pauline's body was almost entirely concealed beneath her long black gown with gold braided high collar and wide cuffs on full-length sleeves. Two middle-aged men followed her through the bar and into the conservatory, each of them wearing a plain, lightweight, sand-coloured suit and dark glasses. As they sat down at the end of the room, Mike looked at Valerie with thinly disguised amusement and said, 'Looks like the mandarin and the mafia, doesn't it?'

'Shush,' whispered Valerie, 'we're supposed to be entertaining them in a bit.'

'Who are they?'

'Er, I'm not sure to tell the truth; I believe they're from Brussels. The less you know about some of Sonia's visitors, the more important they are likely to be. I think these two are banking and finance but it doesn't matter too much as long as they're reasonably presentable.'

'Like me,' he smiled.

Valerie looked at him with amusement in her dark, gypsy eyes. 'Well, I supose you've gone up a few notches since yesterday.'

'I always used to be well dressed, you know,' he answered. 'Always a suit and tie. It was such a drastic change for me coming here. I suppose I wanted a complete break from the way I used to look.'

'But now you've succumbed to the hail of innuendo and shifted back a bit the other way.'

'There were a few comments, yes,' he said, leaning forward. 'You might not believe this, but it's not all that easy being the only bloke in ...'

His voice trailed off as Lorna entered the room, her long raven hair sweeping down over her bare shoulder. About her slim, curvaceous body was a short black chiffon dress, the top held up by shoestring straps, pushed out by her firm breasts and gaping at the sides, the ruffled, flared skirt accentuating her long legs in their gossamer lace nylon. On her feet were delicate gold stiletto heel sandals. His mouth remained slightly open.

'You were saying?' asked Valerie, with a bland expression.

He returned to her. 'Yes, well, you might not understand but it isn't that easy, that's all I'm saying.'

'Michael,' sighed Valerie with an expression of mild anguish, 'I know what you must be going through, I really do.' She placed one of her hands on his. 'Look, if I can help you, I will. I'll have a few words with Sonia. If you can pick up enough French, I think she has a little fancy goods and souvenir shop down on the coast that needs a manager. It'll get you away from all of this and you'll be able to chat to the tourists.'

'Just you dare say anything!' he hissed as her face broke into a wide smile.

'You're so gullible sometimes, aren't you, deary?'

'You're almost as bad as the other one,' he answered.

After a time, Valerie looked at her watch and said, 'I think I'll get a move on now.' She pushed back the chair. 'And what about you? Are you off anywhere this evening or are you staying here?'

'Me? Oh, no,' he answered, picking up the magazine. 'I'll hang around for a bit then go for a stroll.'

'Well,' she said, leaning over him with an expression of concern, 'you be careful and don't talk to any strange women.'

There was no moon but the starlight reflected in the still, clear water of the swimming pool. The chirping of night-time insects broke the silence. Karen pulled back a chair, eased herself into it and placed the folded towel on top of the table before her. She had encountered no one as she left the house, though it would not have mattered greatly. Going out for a midnight swim was not an uncommon practice, though it was less usual to go out alone. The air was warm with barely the hint of a breeze. She leaned back, folded her arms across her purple beach dress and took in the sweep of the stars, the myriad lights of heaven.

There were footsteps. Someone was approaching along the pathway, whistling. A figure appeared in the gloom at the other side of the pool and began to walk around it.

'Hello!' she called softly.

'Hi!' came the reply as he approached the cluster of tables and chairs. 'Been here long?'

'A few minutes, that's all. Isn't it lovely?'

'It sure is,' he said, 'especially now you're here.'

Mike, in his jeans and white T-shirt, placed a paper carrier bag on the table next to her towel, then sat down.

'What have you brought in that?' she asked, leaning forward a little to peer over the edge. 'Not just your towel.'

'Towel, a bottle of cold white wine and two plastic cups. How's that?'

'Mmmm, sounds good, but I think we should go in the water before we polish it off, don't you? Boozing and swimming don't go well together.'

'Nope, quite sensible,' he said. 'Just a cup each now and the rest afterwards.' He pulled the bottle from the bag and handed her a paper cup. 'Cork's already out.'

'Oh, you were sure I'd be here then?' she asked playfully as he poured the wine.

He looked into her eyes, seeing the light of the stars. 'You said you would be. Why should I doubt you? Cheers!'

'Cheers,' she replied, raising the cup.

They made small talk for a time, discussing the house, the girls, Rose and, of course, Pauline. At length, he asked her, 'Why don't you and I get out together more often? You're with the others but not one of them, and you know my situation. Sonia couldn't object if we went around together more could she? I mean, you've no obligations the way –'

'Look Mike, we've been over this before. I really do like

you a lot, but I don't want to get involved, for either of our sakes, that is.' She looked deep into his eyes. 'If I didn't think much of you, I wouldn't be here now, would I?'

'No, I don't suppose you would,' he said, squeezing her hand.

They got up and, pulling off his own clothes until he stood in his swimming shorts, Mike watched Karen slip out of her beach dress in the night air. She wore what he hoped she would; the minimal little swim slip she had bought in Béziers when she too had visited La Grenade. Her breasts stood full and firm in the dim light. She placed the dress over the back of the chair, then turned to Mike and smiled. 'OK?'

'OK,' he answered, and they walked hand in hand to the edge of the pool. They jumped in together, the splash resounding into the night. They swam back and forth, sometimes separate, sometimes together, plunging and circling until, eventually, they met near the shallow end and stood with the water at chest level, facing each other. Karen was not sure about which of them put their arms around the other first, but after a long and fervent kiss, she felt his arousal against her sex. Again they kissed and she drew in her breath sharply as his lips closed upon her breast and his fingers slipped down between her G-string and smooth flesh to find the wellhead of her sensuality. With his free hand he tugged at the cord around her waist.

'Let's get out of the water,' she breathed.

He released her and they pulled themselves up the steps and out on to the poolside, glistening in the night and dripping wet. He took her hand and they walked past the tables and on to the grass, where they stopped and faced each other closely. He kissed her and passed his arms down her body, beginning at her shoulders and letting his thumbs and fingers squeeze her hardened nipples before running down her slim waist. He eased down the scanty slip, lowering his body as he went, running his mouth down her stomach until he was on his knees and he could kiss the heat of her sex. She ran her fingers through his hair and sighed. He wanted to savour her, for until this evening she had seemed remote, aloof and unreachable. When he rose to his feet, she helped him remove his shorts and now it was his turn to catch his breath as her cool fingers closed firmly about his erection. His hand returned to her sex and each began the fiendish game with the other, pausing only to ease themselves down on to the grass so that Karen could spread herself and he could reach deeper into her moist and eager warmth. Soon, hearing her breath shortening and feeling the way her body moved, he clambered between her legs, lifting her knees up and apart. She needed no further encouragement, but lifted her legs higher and, as he thrust deeply into the goal of his lust, brought them around his back so that they were locked tightly in the tournament of love. They heaved together under the night sky, her breath becoming louder with each stroke. He hoped she was close to fulfilment for the dark flames were coursing throughout his own body and he knew he could not hold himself back for long. She began to moan, at first softly, but her moans rapidly became louder and the grip of her arms and legs about him suddenly tightened. He felt the breath almost driven from his body as she cried out loudly and held him as if drowning in the surge of her own pleasure. His release came within moments of hers and he too cried out into the darkness.

'Come on!' she exclaimed, as they pulled themselves up from the grass. 'Let's have another swim and wash away our sins!'

'Sins?' he responded, chasing after her. 'I don't feel sinful! I feel good!'

She turned as they reached the edge of the pool and kissed him. 'I'm only joking, stupid! I feel good too!'

They clasped each other's arms and swung about, until Karen, with finely judged timing, laughed and pushed him hard so that he fell backwards with a loud slap into the water. Moments later, she was by his side in the pool. There, they swam, circled and splashed about until Mike said, 'Hey, we're making too much noise. Someone will be wondering what's going on.'

She bobbed up in the water beside him, her hair floating about her shoulders. 'We've got some wine left, haven't we?'

'Yes, around two thirds of the bottle, I think. Shall we go and see it off?'

This time they dried themselves with their towels then sat, naked, back at the table, savouring the cool wine.

'This'll do you good you know,' Mike said, grinning at her.

'What do you mean?'

'Letting yourself go for once, that's what I mean. You should do it more often.'

'Mike, you assume a lot, don't you? I do have a life of my own; I just don't go around telling everyone about it.'

He reached out and took her hand. 'Look sweetheart, I'm sorry, I just meant that . . . well, that you don't do much, like going out in the evenings. I'd take you out to dinner every week if you'd let me. I'm not tight-fisted as a certain person made out earlier either.'

'Mike, there are things I really can't talk about. You have to understand, I'm far from unhappy here. If I wasn't happy, I wouldn't stay. I appreciate your concern, but, believe me, it's not that simple.'

They continued to talk and eventually finished the wine. He watched her soft eyes as they talked, saw her bedraggled hair in wisps across her face and felt again the blood warming in his veins and the organ of his sexuality begin to stir and invoke his attention. He leaned across the table and took her hands in his. She leaned to meet him and they kissed. If he had been in any doubt about the renewal of her enthusiasm, those doubts were cast aside now as she repaid his attentions with a passion equal to his own.

Neither spoke as they arose and walked back over to the area of grass where they had before abandoned themselves. He lay on his back, looking up at the stars and she propped herself up at his side, tracing her fingers down his chest and over his stomach. He heard her laugh softly.

'What is it?' he asked, pulling her down until they were face to face. 'What's so funny?'

'You're . . . . I mean, like me, you haven't any –'
'Hair,' he cut in.
'Yes. Have you been . . . has Valerie –'
'No, she hasn't. And never you mind; it's a long story.'
They continued to kiss until she raised herself up and stroked his penis with her fingers before gently enclosing it with her hand and working it slowly back and forth so that he tensed involuntarily. He raised his hand and began to stroke between her legs, feeling her moist and very warm. She moved further around and lowered herself down. He let out a sharp moan as her warm lips slid over the head of his penis and down the shaft, drawing him into her so that he felt there was nowhere else he should ever want to be. Almost instinctively, he reached out and took her leg, pulling her across him. With equal spontaneity, she eased herself into position so that, with her thighs either side of his head, his mouth was close to her most intimate place. His tongue immediately found its goal and played about her clitoris, tormenting and teasing her as she enveloped his gorged erection as far as she could, sometimes lifting up and twirling her tongue about the head, making it quiver like a mouse in a trap.

The currents of lust were quickly rushing over them and once more fuelling their ardour. She began to work him with her hand as well as her mouth and he, in turn, thrust his tongue deeply into her sex, alternately withdrawing it to dart about and probe her anus, feeling her body react as though touched by a hot iron.

All self-control flew from them both, as a bird of prey liberated from a cage, their passions boiling forth simultaneously as his tongue revelled in her climax and she enveloped him completely in her mouth. He ejaculated as though the very life was flowing from his body and their stifled moans once more passed into the dark air.

For a third time they got back into the pool, not swimming now, but weaving slowly about and floating on their backs, looking up at the speckled sky.

'I think we should call it a day now, don't you?' Karen asked.

'Yes, OK,' he answered, finding her hand. 'I really haven't enjoyed any evening the way I've enjoyed this one.'

'You've been good fun,' she replied.

'Perhaps again soon?' he said.

'We'll see.' She laughed, heaving a spray of water at him from across the pool.

He returned the gesture and sent a cascade towards her, high in the air. It arched across the pool and over the pathway towards the trees, where a few drops spattered and slowly trickled down the toe of a booted foot, hidden in the blackness of the bushes.

The night was not as secret as they would have wished.

8

Acts of Vengeance

'You're on your own today then,' remarked Rose, sitting down at the coffee table opposite to Karen.

'Yes, Sonia left yesterday afternoon.'

'Was that her car I saw, that posh green job?'

'That's the one,' said Karen.

Rose looked down at her fingers then back to Karen. 'You're a good sort you are, Karen – you and some of the others. Everyone has been all right to me – well, nearly everyone. Her upstairs, she's a real old cow, she is.'

'It's her job, I'm afraid,' replied Karen, 'though I think that . . . oh, never mind. Look, you have all morning with me, don't you?'

'Yeah, then after lunch I'm on duty upstairs.'

Rose stabbed her finger up at the ceiling. Directly above, as they both knew, was Pauline's suite.

'When you're up there,' asked Karen, 'wearing those clothes, and other things, do you . . . I mean, does it bother you?'

'What, all that pervy gear? Er, I dunno . . .'

Her speech trailed off and Karen saw her face redden. Rose gazed down at her hands and remained silent.

'I'm sorry Rosie, I didn't mean to embarrass you. There's no need to tell me.'

Rose looked up. 'When they put some of those things on me, well, it's a bit weird like. It makes me feel funny. I can't explain it.'

'You mean, er, not altogether unpleasant?'

'If you like,' answered Rose, her embarrassment clearly intensifying.

'Rose,' said Karen, 'it doesn't matter. I understand, I really do.' Rose's face brightened and she pushed back the hair from her forehead. 'I was going to suggest,' Karen continued, 'that we do our lessons outside. There's a seat over the rise, about five minutes walk away. You can see the sea from there and we can have a fag. I'll grab a couple of sandwiches and Colas from the bar on the way out.'

'Sounds great!' replied Rose.

'All right, get your book and I'll switch on the answering machine. Angie's behind the bar. If anyone wants me, she'll know where to find us.'

Rose waited, clutching a copy of *Jane Eyre*, as Karen locked the office door. They began walking towards the main entrance when Pauline appeared from the bar. Karen would have simply ignored her and continued on, but she approached them directly and addressed Rose.

'I trust you won't be late this afternoon. I do value punctuality.'

Rose glanced at her nervously and replied, 'No, I'll be back on time, honest.'

At that point, they expected her to continue on but she did not. Instead, she turned her attention to Karen and looked her coldly in the eye. 'There's something I wish to talk to you about. It would be in your interest to come up to my office later.' Her face broke into a broad smile, a smile which Karen had long ago come to understand meant trouble. 'Around three o'clock, if you're not too busy, that is,' she ended sarcastically.

Karen held her gaze and replied, 'I'll see.'

Pauline's smile broadened until her eyes wrinkled, then she turned and walked briskly away down the corridor.

'What's up with her?' asked Rose.

Karen thought for a moment. 'I don't know. She usually doesn't speak to me at all.'

'You can tell her to sod off, can't you?' said Rose. 'She can't boss you around, can she?'

They returned to the house at 1.45. The air was warm and still. The afternoon sun blazed across the swimming pool, where Jackie and Kim could be seen bobbing up and down in the water. At the entrance, Rose stopped and gave her attention to something just to one side of the main door.

'Oh look, isn't he cute.'

'That's Pancake, Valerie's cat,' said Karen. 'You must have seen him around before.'

Rose began to tickle the sleeping ginger form behind the ear, causing him to stir and stretch a little. 'I used to talk to him when I was sleeping out in the garden. He kept me company but I didn't know his name. I used to feed him too – did you know?'

'No, I didn't, but I know you'll be in trouble if you're late upstairs. Don't give her any excuses, Rose.'

'No, I won't,' said Rose, pushing open the door, 'and thanks for all the trouble you're going to.'

'It's no trouble, Rose,' said Karen, smiling.

Karen spent some time in the office finding minor or unnecessary tasks to do, pretending for a time that she was not at all concerned about Pauline's invitation – or was it a summons? At three o'clock she stopped and looked at the phone on her desk. It would be easy enough to speak to Pauline on the internal line. Easier than going upstairs into her territory. But that was backing down and Karen had long ago decided that she would never do that.

At five past three, she was locking the main office door and moments later making her way up the front stairs to the first floor corridor. She walked with deliberate slowness, determined to demonstrate, if only to herself, that she was going up on her terms and not on Pauline's. As she turned into the corridor, she was confronted by two figures. Although Karen had glimpsed some of the girls doing maid's duties before, this encounter came as a shock. She could not walk by, pretending she had not seen them, as had happened in the past. Nor could they ignore her as they were supposed to do. They stopped, face to face.

Both Rose and Lorna wore the gleaming black, skin-tight latex dresses with their abbreviated little skirts. Their legs shimmered in gossamer black nylon and each had on the black patent leather sandals with their exaggerated stiletto heels. There the similarities ended, for Lorna's limbs were free and, had she not been forbidden to do so, she no doubt would have spoken a few words to Karen. Rose was not so fortunate. Her lips were held open by a red rubber ball, planted firmly in her mouth and held in place by a thin leather strap which was seen to be padlocked at the rear. About her waist was locked a wide leather belt, bearing a bright steel cuff on either side which held Rose's hands firmly in position against her body. Her legs were fettered too, with steel ankle cuffs and a short chain. She held a brass tray in front of her, her hands able to grasp it at each end. On the tray were dusters and a can of spray polish.

After a few long moments, Karen unfroze and muttered, 'Oh, I'm sorry,' then continued on past Lorna and her bizarre caddie. At Pauline's door, she hesitated and glanced back down the corridor. Lorna was opening the door to one of the apartments and was about to usher Rose inside. Karen turned back to the door set under its white arch, no different to the door to her own room on the floor above, yet this door was one she would rather pass by. She knocked sharply, just once, and without waiting for a response from within, entered.

Karen had never been inside Pauline's office before but had heard it described on the odd occasion by those who had. Even without foreknowledge, nothing within the room would have seemed out of place. Pauline, seated at her desk, regarded Karen coolly with her wide blue eyes and said, 'How nice of you to call in. Do sit down, won't you.'

'No,' answered Karen, holding her stare, 'just tell me what it is you need to see me about.'

Pauline smiled and looked her up and down, straightening her fingers and placing them together, prayer-like, under her chin. 'Well now, how do I put this without seeming indelicate?'

'Put what?' demanded Karen, folding her arms.

Pauline settled back into her chair. 'Your little escapade

with our handyman by the poolside a few evenings ago –'
Karen felt her blood chill. 'I'm afraid you were both observed.'

'Wh-what . . . what d'you mean?'

'Not just observed,' continued Pauline calmly, 'but recorded.' Karen felt as if her legs were about to give way
but remained silent, her eyes fixed upon Pauline's red lips.
'Fortunately for you, nobody has yet seen the tape.'

'Tape? What tape?' asked Karen hoarsely. 'How could
anybody make a tape? You're lying! You're making it up!'

Pauline's face remained cold and expressionless. 'We
both know perfectly well what happened, even if it was
dark. But that doesn't matter; it being dark that is. You
see James had set up a camera using an image intensifier.
It was just an experiment to see how well it worked. It's
amazing what science can achieve nowadays, isn't it? The
clarity of those pictures – just amazing.'

'And . . . and this tape,' said Karen, barely hearing herself speak, 'I take it you're . . . What are you intending to
do with it? Where is it?'

'To answer your second question first, it's in the cellar.
I have the key to the cellar door, of course. As to what I'm
going to do with it . . . well, that is up to you.'

'Up to me – I see. What d'you want? Me to get out, I
suppose!'

'When you're good and ready. But, meantime, I'm willing to offer you a deal. Look, do sit down. Over by the
window if you like – it will be so much easier.'

'No! Just tell me what you're after and I'll go. If necessary I'll talk to Sonia as soon as she gets back and that'll
be the end of both of us here!'

'No, I wouldn't do anything quite as drastic as that. We
can come to an arrangement quite easily. It is a simple
matter of establishing our roles in this house. We've all had
to do it, except you. And that is the problem. And as far
as going to Sonia is concerned, why should that worry me?
I'll say I was given the tape for safekeeping and would have
handed it to her anyway. After all, I'm not the one who's
performing on it, am I?'

'You still haven't said what you want!' voiced Karen angrily.

'Oh, I thought I . . . No, perhaps you're right. I haven't made myself clear enough.' Pauline stood up and placed her hands on the desktop. 'I said I'd offer you a bargain and I meant it. You shall have the tape – this evening if you want. But you'll have to come down for it and we'll sort out one or two little problems while we're there. Yes or no?'

'I haven't any choice, have I?' responded Karen. She eyed Pauline angrily and clenched her fists at her side. 'But I still don't know what you want! Why won't you say?'

'Oh, I'll make that clear to you later – if you show up that is.'

Karen bit on her lip and looked down at the carpet. 'When can I have it?'

'Tonight. Meet me at the back door and we'll go down and get it.'

'What time?'

'You can be there at 7.30. I'll wait no more than five minutes.'

Karen regarded her for a few seconds, then turned and left the room.

The remainder of the afternoon was not a happy time. Karen worked alone in the office until five o'clock, then returned to her room, showered and changed. She had a hair appointment at 5.30 and, with a few minutes to spare, arrived at the door of the beauty parlour wearing her saffron cotton blouse and white flared skirt.

When Valerie opened the door, Karen looked into her sparkling eyes and smiled. But Valerie was nothing if not perceptive, and although Karen affected a degree of normality she hoped was convincing, it proved at length not to be so. Some twenty minutes later, when Karen sat with her eyes closed and the brush plying her hair, Valerie asked, 'Want to tell me about it, deary?'

Karen opened her eyes. 'Tell you what?'

Valerie stopped her work with the brush and laid it aside by the sink. 'I can sense when something's the matter. I know everyone in this house better than most of them know each other. You're upset about something. Very upset, I'd say.'

'I'm not Val, really. I've had a bit of a headache most of the afternoon, nothing more.'

'Oh, is that what it is? Well, I'm almost finished now, so you go and lie down and rest. Come and find me later on and we'll go for a walk around the grounds, yes?'

'I'll see,' said Karen, smiling. But the smile was no more than a matter of facial geometry and Valerie knew that the person behind it was not smiling at all.

When Karen arrived at the bottom of the rear stairs there was nobody in sight. She looked at her watch. It was exactly 7.30. She walked past the end of the ground floor corridor but kept her eyes down, wishing to see no one and not wanting to be seen. In front of her was a short length of passage which ended at a storage room. To her right was the bolted door leading out on to the rear gardens and to her left the door to the cellar steps. She saw that this door was slightly ajar. A dim light showed from beyond it. She stepped closer and pulled the door open. The stairs were gloomy and the light was obviously coming from the room below. She looked about her. Still there was nobody. She waited and listened for a minute, hearing only distant voices from the main corridor.

'I suppose I'd better go along with this,' she breathed, and began cautiously to tread the stone steps.

At the bottom of the stairs was a dimly lit room. Against the wall to her left were set boxes and pieces of equipment, some of which she was familiar with from the secret room between the beauty parlour and Sonia's private suite. The chrome and black leather gleamed ominously in the yellow light of the single bulb. To her right was the entrance to another room – a room of forbidding darkness, but light shone through an arched doorway directly ahead. Beyond the arch she could make out a table upon which stood a number of small items, some of which were vaguely recognisable even at a distance. There was yet no sound, and no sign of Pauline, so Karen moved towards this next room. She began to regret having worn high-heel sandals, for the sound of her footsteps upon the stone floor was amplified and echoed about the walls mockingly. She stopped short of the archway. She could now see the dark wooden table beyond quite well, and see clearly what lay upon it. What she saw caused a stir of apprehension, but the main item of concern was the black video cassette, standing on its end in the middle of the table. She moved forward through the arch, pushing aside a bright steel chain which hung from the ceiling and ended at chest level, between her and the table.

The illumination came from two small lights on either side of the doorway through which she had just passed. She looked about the stone walls at the fittings and restraints. It was obviously a purpose-designed dungeon cell. She could see that there was nowhere anyone could be hiding. The cassette was little more than two metres away and there seemed no reason why she should not seize hold of it then retrace her steps back and out of this place.

She started forward and was reaching out when it happened. Her left arm was grasped from behind. Something cool and hard slipped quickly about her waist with a metallic rasp. Karen at once panicked and reached behind to pull the hands from her but this arm was also seized and in a moment her wrists were secured together by the steel handcuffs.

When she pulled away with a gasp and spun around, Pauline was smiling. But now the situation was quite different and Karen realised with alarm the nature of the trap she had fallen into. Pauline moved towards her quickly, and grabbing her manacled wrists, wrenched them up behind her, forcing her body forward and downwards.

'Let me go!' yelled the struggling Karen, to no avail.

Pauline held her for a moment and Karen felt cold metal pushed between her hands. When Pauline moved away from her and walked into full view, Karen realised that the cuffs were secured to the hanging chain.

'I do hope you're comfortable,' said Pauline.

Karen, knowing the futility of struggle, looked up at her

angrily from her stooping position. 'You don't imagine you're going to get away with this, do you?'

'Oh yes, I do. If you are to get away with your transgressions then why should I not get away with mine? If you tell Sonia, you will be the real loser. I think we know what I mean, don't we?'

Karen did not reply for she wondered, even in this situation, how much Pauline had guessed or found out regarding her own relationship with Sonia.

Her face was closer to the table and she regarded anew the things upon it. Near to the cassette was a short, black, braided leather whip, a pink vibrator in the shape of an amply proportioned penis, standing on its end, and a rubber ball gag. There, too, was a small tube, which meant little to her for the moment. Pauline had again moved behind her and Karen twisted about as fingers began to release the fastening on her skirt. Her attempts to resist were ignored and the skirt fell to the stone floor. She gasped but did not cry out as the fingers gripped the sides of her black briefs and pulled them down her legs as far as her knees, where they were ripped asunder and cast on to the floor in front of her.

Karen tottered as her right ankle was wrenched aside and enclosed by a steel cuff at the end of a short chain bolted to the flagstone. She knew what was to happen next but reasoned that it would not be in her interest to prolong the affair or to antagonise Pauline further. A moment later, she was held with her legs spread, fully exposed from the rear to the humiliating gaze of Pauline.

Pauline walked slowly around and stood before her. Karen saw how she was dressed from neck to toe in a smooth-fitting, black leather catsuit and short, high-heel black patent ankle boots. She reached about and took something from the table, holding it concealed in one hand behind her back. Karen tensed and attempted to turn around as Pauline moved to her side and said, 'We should have played this little game a long time ago. It would have avoided a few problems, I think.'

Karen could not twist around far enough to keep her in

view, but answered, 'Pauline, you've got to release me sooner or later so why go on with this?'

'It's going to be later!' came the voice from above and without warning, a black, latex gloved hand appeared before her face and pushed the large, red, rubber ball directly into her mouth. As the strap at the back of her head tightened, the ball became firm and immovable. There was a last tug and a metallic click as the padlock closed. Karen's eyes blazed in helpless anger as Pauline reappeared, bending before her with a satisfied smile.

'Well, well. Little Miss Prim and Proper under strict control at last! Whatever next?' She watched with horror as Pauline took the black whip from the table and circled her. 'All right, you little slut – now you'll see what it means to get on the wrong side of me!'

The first stroke fell with a burning sting. Karen jerked in the restraints and moaned. The second caused her to cry out louder through the rubber ball but there was nothing she could do to prevent the third, fourth and fifth strokes as they found their mark. Her stifled protests became louder and more urgent as the tears of pain and degradation flowed copiously down her cheeks.

After the sixth stroke, Pauline reappeared and placed the whip back upon the table, at the same time, picking up the tube and regarding the weeping prisoner with satisfaction as she slowly unscrewed the cap.

'If you don't know already, you're going to understand what total control really means. It means I can make you cry one minute and make you come the next. It's just the lesson you need, you snooty little cow!'

With a look of callous amusement, Pauline squeezed a centimetre of amber cream from the tube on to her middle finger. Karen's tearful eyes widened with apprehension as Pauline stepped behind and, reaching down through her legs, smeared the cream slowly between the lips of her sex. She recapped the tube and replaced it on the table, wiping the remains of the cream from her gloved fingers with a paper tissue. When she turned back to Karen, she had the vibrator in her hand.

166

'See?' she said, opening her fingers and lowering the object until it rested before Karen's face. Karen stared at it, transfixed. 'You're going to beg me to use this before long.' Karen stared in mute disbelief. 'But before that,' she continued, turning once more to the table, 'we have to take some more of our medicine.'

Karen squirmed in the restraints as the whip reappeared in Pauline's hand. She attempted a further protest but because of the bent position in which she was held, the ball gag had become tighter so that no more than a deadened murmur was possible.

Pauline resumed her earlier position and brought the whip down sharply across Karen's reddened behind, feeling the jerk of her body as the crack of leather against flesh rang about the room.

'I won't pretend that I find this in the least distasteful.' Another stroke fell. Karen began to sob loudly and uncontrollably. 'In fact, I'm rather enjoying myself.'

Despite the searing pain of the whip, Karen became aware of an insistent burning between her legs. She had realised at last the purpose of the amber cream and how it was beginning to irritate and inflame her.

Pauline continued her work with practised efficiency until Karen's behind displayed an abstract pattern of deep pink weals and her face had become a mask of sobbing misery, her hair wet and matted about the sides of her reddened face.

When Pauline, with a cold expression of satisfaction, laid the whip aside, one source of torment was finished and its place was quickly taken by another. The burning irritation about her sex intensified quickly and soon Karen, flexing her muscles in an ineffectual attempt to quell it, was moaning in piteous anguish with her eyes squeezed shut.

'Here's your salvation, Miss Prim!' came the voice into her world of despair. Karen half opened her eyes to see Pauline's boots directly in front of her, and the hands once more holding out the vibrator. At first she ignored it, telling herself that soon the torture must end. But it was not ending and she wanted to scream. 'Are we ready yet?' came the voice from above. Karen rocked her head from side to side in despair. 'I can leave you here and try again in half an hour if you prefer,' said Pauline. Karen opened her eyes wide and shook her head vigorously, sending out a desperate, muffled howl to say what she could not speak. 'Then I gather you would like a little attention?' Karen nodded her affirmative. There was no choice – the irritation was driving her insane. 'Are you begging me?'

Karen looked up at her expressionless face for a moment, nodded again and closed her eyes. As she did so, the vibrator began to hum. The touch of the cool, resonating head against the inflamed lips of her sex was like a cool spring in a fearful desert of torment. The instrument of lust was everything and it no longer mattered who held it or why. It murmured consolation about her clitoris and the voice from beyond said, 'I'm going to watch you come, just as I watch that other dirty little slut when she's had a good thrashing!'

Karen was determined that she would not let Pauline bring her to a climax, despite the overwhelming relief of the vibrator, which now began to enter her more deeply as it moved back and forth. But she wanted it to enter her fully, to assuage not just the irritation but the burning which had spread deeply through her loins from the effects of the whip. She would not admit to herself at first that she was losing control, but the fingers of lust were uncoiling and reaching out through her body, and soon she realised that she could no longer prevent them from taking hold of her completely as she stood invaded and helpless under the eyes of her captor.

Pauline saw her body stiffen though she could not see Karen's mouth draw back as her teeth bit hard on the rubber gag. But she could not fail to hear the stifled moans as the orgasm seized her in its grasp.

A few minutes later, she was released from her restraints.

At first she could not stand properly. The strain upon her limbs had been too great and Pauline eased her into one of the small wooden chairs.

168

'A few minutes, and you'll be able to walk,' said Pauline coolly as she placed the handcuffs on the table.

She took up a plastic bag from another chair and busied herself placing the things into it. Karen, attempting to release the strap which still remained secure about her neck, did not see what she was doing.

'By the way,' announced Pauline, turning to her with a smile, 'I forgot to bring down the key for the gag. That was silly of me, wasn't it?' Karen stopped her struggles for a moment and looked at her as she began to move away. 'Tell you what, I'll leave it on the carpet just outside your door. As soon as you're dressed you can go and get it. If you use the back stairs, and you're really lucky, nobody will see you wearing that. And, even if they do –' she smiled broadly '– you won't be able to tell them how you came by it, will you? And please don't forget to switch off the cellar lights!'

With that, she was gone and Karen was alone. She had not yet come to terms with what had happened, even as she pulled on her skirt. Her mind was in a state of turmoil, her behind a pulsing furnace, her body trembling uncontrollably. Her one thought was of getting to her room as quickly as possible and avoiding the further indignity of being seen wearing the ball gag. She reached up again and felt behind her head with her fingers in case Pauline had tricked her. But no, the padlock was there and quite secure. She looked at the table. The whip, the small tube and the vibrator were gone. And so was the video cassette.

She glanced under the table, then at the four wooden chairs around the room. Anger fought with shame and humiliation as she hurried through the two rooms and up the cellar steps, ignoring the light switch.

For a few long minutes, Karen stood shaking at the top of the steps with the door slightly ajar. From time to time there were voices but none of them came close. At last, with her heart beating hard, she made for the stairs.

She reached the second floor corridor with immense relief, a relief which was further reinforced by the sight of the small silver key lying inconspicuously by the skirting board

169

next to her door. She opened the door, stooped to pick up the key, then disappeared inside the room.

She did not attempt to remove the gag immediately, but walked to the bathroom and stood before the wall cabinet mirror, thinking that, perhaps the lock might be easier to undo if she could see it in the reflection. She regarded herself for a time, her face tear stained, her hair bedraggled and matted, the rubber ball fixed in her mouth and keeping her speechless. Even dressed, with her limbs free and in her own room, it remained locked in place and represented her domination by another. She lifted her fingers and stroked them over the red ball. What if Pauline had tricked her again? What if the key did not fit the small padlock? What if she had to go to Pauline's office and there was nobody in? Who could she turn to for help? There was only Valerie, and she might be anywhere, though most probably in the bar for it was now not far off nine o'clock.

The key did fit. She removed this last restraint and placed it, glistening with her own saliva, on the sink. Now she could close her mouth and her jaw ached. Furthermore, the mark of the strap impressed on her cheeks did nothing to improve her appearance. She returned to her bedroom and began, for the first time, to realise how much she had been compromised by what had happened. She could never face Pauline without shame and indignity, never conduct herself normally with the others if Pauline was present. And there was the tape. In spite of all that had been done to her, the fierce burning which still beset her flesh and the enforced degradation, she had gained nothing. Pauline held her as a sparrow in a net. She could be summoned at any time and would have to obey. Her relationship with Sonia would be finished if, or more likely, when, any of this was revealed. The more she considered the matter, the more fully she realised that there could no longer be any future for her at the house.

She threw herself down upon the bed and began to cry. She wept not just out of shame and humiliation, but with subdued anger at the stupidity which had handed over her happiness to Pauline on a plate.

There was a knock at the door. Karen remained still.

The knock was repeated and a voice outside called, 'Are you in?'

Karen got up and walked out of the bedroom, through the small lounge and up to the door. She placed her hand against it and asked, 'Who is it?'

'It's Val! Can I come in?'

'Oh Val, yes,' she sighed, pulling open the door and standing aside as the figure entered.

'I've been looking everywhere for –' Valerie stopped speaking for a moment and stood wide-eyed. She placed her hands upon Karen's arms. 'Lovey, what's happened? Just look at you – and your hair. What's been going on?'

'Val,' she answered tearfully, 'it's difficult to explain, but I'm going to leave. You might as well be the first to know.'

Valerie stared at her in silence for a few moments, then guided her over to an armchair. She sat down close by and said, 'Right, let's have it and then I'll get us a drink.'

When Karen had finished speaking, Valerie looked at her for a long time. Then she said, 'Just you stay here, I'll be back shortly!'

'Val, wait. Where are you going? Please don't say anything to her!'

Valerie turned before leaving the room. 'I'm going down to check on something – you can put the coffee on.'

'But Val –'

The door closed and she was alone again. But something had changed. She no longer felt tearful and dejected although she had no idea what Valerie was about to do. By the time Valerie returned, the light on the coffee percolator had blinked on red.

'Right, now just you listen,' said Valerie as Karen passed her a cup and saucer. 'I've called James from the beauty parlour . . . you're not supposed to know about my direct line either!' Valerie leaned towards her. 'He doesn't have a bloody image intensifier and he hasn't made any tapes outside since the party last year! She's told you a pack of lies!' Karen closed her eyes and leaned back in the chair. 'You're a silly girl for not checking it out,' continued Valerie, 'but that peroxide rinsed slag has nothing over you at all, you hear? Nothing!'

'Oh Val, I don't know what to say. Honest, you're a good friend.'

'So we won't have any more talk about leaving,' continued Valerie, 'or I'll put you into handcuffs myself!'

Karen smiled at her. 'God! I feel so stupid.'

'Well, never mind,' said Valerie, rising from her chair. 'I'm going to pay Auntie bloody Pauline a visit!'

'Val, no! You've done more than enough, really. It's my affair and I'll deal with her when the time comes.'

'There's something you ought to understand, deary,' said Valerie as she pulled open the door and swung around to face Karen with her gypsy eyes flashing. 'You're in a more vulnerable position than I am. That's number one. And number two –' Valerie pulled aside a strand of Karen's hair '– I did a good job on this earlier today and she's buggered it up completely! That is right out of order. You get yourself sorted out. I'll be back to collect you later and we'll have a snack at the bar. And I'll guarantee Pauline won't be there!'

'You look like you mean business,' remarked Jackie as Valerie closed the door of the beauty parlour behind her and stepped into the corridor clutching a black polythene bag.

'Oh I do, deary. Well, it's been one of those days, hasn't it?'

'Where are you –'

But Valerie carried on past her without further comment and continued purposefully up the main stairs. Jackie watched her, in her sleek black lycra catsuit with its long sleeves, wide red belt, and her soft, black, leather ankle boots.

'She into karate then?' came the voice from behind.

Jackie swung around to face Rose. 'Oh hi! You been down at the pool?'

'Yeah, been chatting to Angie and Kim. How about you?'

'I've been with a couple of the others in the bar. Are you going up now?'

Rose looked into her eyes for a moment. 'If you are Jackie, yeah. I wouldn't mind an early night.'

'No, me neither, Rosie,' she said, taking Rose's arm. 'But let's have a quickie in the bar first.'

There were three sharp taps at the door. Pauline, freshly showered and dressed in a black and gold kimono, lowered the magazine and looked up.

'Well!' she called. 'What is it?'

There was no reply. Pauline placed the magazine down upon the low table. Again, there were three taps, this time noticeably louder. Pauline arose from the green leather two-seater and walked over to the door. Pulling it open sharply, she found herself facing the hard, unblinking gaze of Valerie.

'Is this important?' she demanded.

'Very!' came the reply, and Valerie, pushing past, strode into the middle of the room and swung around to face her. Pauline regarded her with open-mouthed disbelief.

'And just what do you think this is all about? I did not invite you in here!'

'Close the door!' snapped Valerie.

'What? Get out of here now!'

Valerie lowered the bag to the floor then walked over to her. Pauline stepped back, hands on hips, expecting her to continue on by and out the way she had arrived, but Valerie did not. Instead, she stood before Pauline and each fixed their eyes hard upon the other.

'All right!' said Valerie. 'If you want everyone else in the house to hear this, it's OK by me!' She quickly lifted her hand and brought it with a sharp slap across Pauline's mouth. With an expression of startled rage, Pauline at once lashed back at her, but Valerie blocked the swing and pushed her hard, sending her reeling backwards towards her desk. Pauline recovered her balance and jerked the belt tightly about the kimono.

'It's that snotty nosed bitch that's latched on to Sonia – that's what this is all about, isn't it? Well, you might as well pack your belongings together with hers, because you're

173

both through! Do you hear? Bloody well through!' She surged back towards Valerie and flung her arm out towards the open door. 'Now get out!' she shouted. 'Out of my room and play fairy bloody godmother somewhere else!'

'Not really the best analogy, Pauline!' sneered Valerie. 'How about avenging angel?'

'Oh!' responded Pauline sarcastically. 'She's too weak-kneed to stand up for herself, is she? Like a little mouse behind that office desk!'

'No!' responded Valerie coldly. 'She's not weak, she's just innocent and trusting! She's not a nasty, scheming, petty-minded slag like you at all. That's her trouble – she's too honest! She thinks everyone else is as well! But in your case she's been wrong, and you've preyed on her like the vampire you are!' Valerie reached down and pulled up the end of the plastic bag, spilling its contents out on to the carpet. 'Now you're going to learn a bit of humility for once!'

Pauline stared in alarm at the gleaming metallic cluster on the floor and hurried immediately around to her desk. Valerie followed her warily as she pulled open a drawer and glared back.

'I'm going to whip the arse off you, you fucking upstart!'

The braided black whip uncoiled menacingly in Pauline's hands as she moved away from the desk. At once she raised her arm and swung the whip like a deadly snake at Valerie. It struck Valerie across the shoulder but she seized it and held it fast, yelling, 'That's all I need!' She lunged forward, knocking Pauline off balance against the desk and wrenching the whip from her grasp. Pauline screamed abuse at her but backed away, seeing now that Valerie was about to use the whip against her. But Valerie did not strike out. Instead she backed away and ordered, 'Out here – now!'

Pauline, trapped between the desk and the corner of the room, saw her chance. She made as if to obey, but once clear of the confines of the desk, threw herself upon Valerie, who cast the whip back towards the window where it smacked against the green leather two-seater. For a few seconds, they pushed and pulled at each other, each trying to swing the other off balance, Pauline attempting without success to take hold of Valerie's hair. Then, seeing the opportunity, Valerie swung her leg behind Pauline's and heaved her to one side, causing her to lose her balance and sprawl headlong on to the floor. Valerie did not hesitate and in a split second was astride her, holding Pauline face downwards and unable to rise.

Ignoring the oaths of abuse, she wrenched away the kimono, pulling it part way down her body and trapping her arms in the sleeves. This brief respite gave Valerie the opportunity to reach over and take up that which lay nearby with the plastic bag. Pauline began to heave and struggle in desperation but Valerie remained cool and methodical. She wrenched the kimono down further until one of Pauline's arms was free of it. But the arm was not to be free for long, for the smooth steel cuff closed upon it and snapped shut in a cool, final embrace. The other wrist soon joined it in enforced and close proximity.

Valerie stood up and dragged the kimono from the writhing but now subdued Pauline.

'You'll not get away with this!' Pauline hissed. 'I swear you won't!'

'I don't give a bugger,' breathed Valerie.

The cuffs were joined only by a short, rigid link, making them more restrictive than they might have been. From that link ran a short steel chain of some twenty centimetres which ended in a pair of slightly larger cuffs, joined like the others. With Valerie sitting astride her, for Pauline continued to resist the inevitable, these were soon snapped about her ankles. When Valerie moved away, Pauline lay on the carpet of her own office – hog-tied, naked and helpless. The verbal abuse had stopped.

'It'll give you a chance to ponder for a while, won't it, deary?' mocked Valerie, bending close to her ear. But Pauline's restraint was not yet complete, for one other item remained close by, still awaiting use. Valerie picked the harness up and again stood astride Pauline. 'This could be easy or it could be difficult. Either way,' she breathed, 'it's going on.'

The buckles rasped and the leather straps tightened about Pauline's head, forcing the black latex ball into her mouth and the soft rubber pads over her eyes. With the harness firmly secured, Valerie moved aside and regarded the helpless form. Her eyes turned to the whip, lying across the leather seat as if about to slither along the green cushions of his own accord. She took it up and stepped back over to Pauline, placing a foot on either side of her and grasping with her other hand the short length of chain connecting the wrists and ankles. A murmur of protest ensued as Valerie braced herself.

'Are you ready for this, deary? Your little friend is about to turn on its nasty old mistress.'

Pauline jerked as the first stroke fell across her flesh with a resounding crack. There followed many more, hard and in rapid succession, each interspersed by a groan of muffled outrage, growing ever louder from the squirming figure beneath. At length Valerie released her hold and stood back to admire the criss-cross assemblage of blurred and angry pink weals covering much of Pauline's backside.

'Well now,' she breathed, 'I rather enjoyed that, didn't you? After all, it is one of your favourite occupations, isn't it?' Pauline remained still, though Valerie could hear her breath rasping hard around the gag. She coiled up the whip and placed it on the coffee table. 'Right, I'm off to enjoy myself while you consider the error of your ways. I can't really say how long I'll be gone, but don't worry, I'll close the door in case anyone comes in and tries to undo you!'

A stifled groan of anger followed Valerie to the door. She glanced back briefly before closing it. As she turned towards the stairs, two figures approached, their arms linked. their conversation punctuated with laughter.

'Hi again!' Jackie said, grinning.

'Wotcher!' added Rose.

'I hope you two aren't going to make a lot of noise,' said Valerie, pressing an index finger to her mouth.

'What's up?' asked Jackie in a hushed voice.

'Oh, your Auntie Pauline's not feeling too well and mustn't be disturbed.'

'Nothing too serious, is it?' sniggered Rose.

'Only a temporary inconvenience,' answered Valerie, continuing on her way with a smile of satisfaction.

'We'd better try and be quiet then,' giggled Rose as they entered Jackie's room.

'I don't give a sod what she hears,' grinned Jackie as the door closed. 'I've got another little toy. Want to see it?'

'Yeah, all right.'

Jackie crossed the room and pulled open a drawer. Rose followed close behind.

'Ooh-er!' said Rose, wide-eyed, as Jackie held the object out in her hands.

The large, flesh-coloured penis was realistically modelled, as was its lesser companion, protruding out parallel beneath it with unmistakable purpose. From this double implement of lust hung a pink nylon harness which the smiling Jackie tugged with her other hand.

'What d'you reckon?'

'Well,' answered Rose with a mischievous giggle, 'I've never seen one that goes up both . . .' She reached out and squeezed the soft head of first the larger and then the smaller organ. 'Yeah, all right then.'

They crossed the bedroom and entered without switching on the light. Jackie placed the dildo on the bed and turned to Rose, taking her hand and kissing her. Rose held her waist and returned her kisses. Each breathed warmly about the ear and neck of the other and both trembled.

Pauline listened intently. Still lying on the carpet, hogtied in enforced silence and darkness, she twisted her head around, a thin trickle of saliva glistening on the rubber ball. In the distance there were sounds, sounds that would normally have passed unnoticed. But her hearing had become a little more acute and her attention concentrated, despite the still angry burning around her buttocks. She heard the laughter and the long, moaning cries, and she knew where they were coming from.

Through her mind ran the words she could not physically speak.

'Bloody sluts, all of them. I'll sort the lot of them out once I get started. They'll find out what discipline really is!'

9

Escapade

'It seems I should have been paying more attention to what was going on under my own nose.' Karen, avoiding eye contact with Sonia, did not reply. 'This sort of thing cannot continue, of course. Apart from other considerations, it isn't good for business. I will not have people in conflict here – obviously it has to be ended or kept within strict limits now and for good!'

Karen looked up at Sonia's dark eyes. Her expression was not one of anger but of determination. Her manner was quite impersonal in a way Karen had not experienced since her early days at the house.

'Sonia, whatever you think of me, there's something I have to ask you.'

'Well?'

'It's Valerie. I don't think that ...' Karen sighed and looked at the trees, bathed in sunlight outside the office window. 'What I'm trying to say is, I don't think that she should suffer because of me. She's been a good friend all the time I've been here and she would never let you down.' Karen looked at the silver locket lying where she had placed it on the coffee table between them and clenched her fists. 'Look, none of this would have happened if I hadn't gone out that night with Mike! You've had all the juicy details, haven't you? It's my damn fault! I don't suppose I can blame Pauline for being there but she didn't have to do what she did. That's why Val tried to help me.'

'Well,' breathed Sonia, rising up from the green leather chair, 'Valerie is going to Tuscany for a few days. She was due for a break anyway.' Karen rose too and faced her, a

179

feeling of nausea stirring inside. 'As for Pauline,' Sonia continued, 'it's a much more delicate situation than you realise. There are, I'm afraid, obligations on both sides. She is from now on to direct her attentions to those in her sphere of influence rather than to the more, shall we say, self-motivated girls. That, hopefully, will mean no further difficulties. Is there anything else you wish to say?'

Karen stared at her for a time, then, with a quiet 'No', turned and walked towards the door. Since the beginning of this interview with Sonia, she had felt herself moving into bleak and hostile waters. Now, at the end of it, she was cast upon a lifeless, grey shore. She held the door handle and twisted it, feeling physically cold, expecting the door to open into a day of despair as she got her belongings together in readiness for departure.

'Where are you going?' The voice behind her expressed itself in a tone drained of emotion, with almost a lack of interest in the question.

Karen, pulling the door ajar, half turned. 'What?'

'I just wondered, that's all.'

'You know where I'm going.'

Sonia folded her arms across her black leather biker jacket and held Karen's gaze. 'You seem to have forgotten something – or do you no longer consider it important?' Karen continued to regard her with incomprehension. Sonia gestured down at the silver locket. 'This.'

Karen let her hand slip from the door handle and glanced at the object lying abandoned on the coffee table. 'I-I don't understand ... I thought ...'

'What did you think?'

'I assumed that I was no longer required.'

Sonia's dark eyes held her. 'Did I say you were to leave?'

'No ... no, you didn't. But I can't see how –'

'Oh for God's sake, girl,' cut in Sonia, 'come and sit down and I'll get us a drink. You've got a face like a wet Sunday!' Karen closed the door and moved back to the armchair in front of the coffee table. She watched Sonia take two glasses from the cupboard. She did not sit down. 'Do you mind a splash of amontillado?' asked Sonia.

'No, that's fine,' replied Karen weakly.

Sonia returned and placed the two glasses, filled with clear, pale amber, by the locket. They sat once again facing each other. Karen watched and waited for her to speak. A faint smile passed across Sonia's face for the first time that day.

'I suppose these little things are sent to try us,' she said, raising her glass.

Karen sighed and picked up her glass. She stared at it for a moment then said, 'I'm sorry, I just took it for granted you'd want me out. If I'd been in your place I would have been furious.'

'I doubt if you would, my dear, not if you know people as I do. Despite being away from here so often, I had a fair idea what was happening, which is why I had no objection to Mike being allowed into some of our little theatricals. He's like most men would be in his situation so I considered it better to let him express his needs on our terms rather than his. As for Pauline, well, she shouldn't have overstepped the mark, but you do have to understand one thing if you don't already –' Sonia drank a little more of the sherry '– and that is that her actions are not as unpalatable to some people as they are to others.'

'Yes,' replied Karen, recalling her role acting and intimacies with Sonia. 'I'm perfectly aware of that and we all know what she does to Jackie. But there's a difference between . . . well, never mind. Look, I'll try to forget it for your sake, but I don't think I could speak to her again, ever.'

'I don't think you spoke to each other much anyway,' said Sonia, smiling, 'so I can't see it making any difference.'

Karen herself now smiled for the first time. 'I don't know what I would have done if I'd had to go, I really don't. You're very understanding.'

'But that is what it's all about,' responded Sonia. 'How could I be angry with you for showing a little human weakness when my whole business is built upon it? I am above all a realist, Karen. I do not pretend people are other than what they are. In fact, I depend on recognising it.'

'You had me weighed up,' remarked Karen softly.

Sonia looked at her with concern. 'Please, my dear, you must not think that. It wasn't ... it isn't like that at all, certainly not now. You're being very unfair to me if you think that.'

'No, please,' said Karen, 'it wasn't meant ... Look, I wouldn't be here now if it wasn't for –'

'Yes, I know, but I am a little sensitive about our relationship. We must both gain from it. I've always been concerned about that.'

Karen leaned towards her and smiled. 'Sonia, I'm all right about it, I really am.'

Sonia leaned forward and reached out to take her hand. 'Look, I've got a little treat for you if you'd like it.'

Karen looked at her in anticipation. 'Go on,' she said softly.

'How would you like a few days in Paris?'

'That sounds nice.'

'It would allow the dust to settle a bit here, and if you don't mind you could take some master tapes and discs to Armand for me. You remember Armand and Josephine? He told me they chatted to you at the party last year.'

Karen recalled her encounter with Armand and Josephine very well indeed. She felt her throat go dry as she answered, 'Oh, er, yes, the publisher, I remember.'

'Well,' continued Sonia, 'I'll have them show you around the city. Josephine can put you up above our shop near the Bastille Opera House. How does that sound?'

'It sounds wonderful,' replied Karen, 'especially after all this upset!'

'Well, you can forget about that for a few days and I'll look after things here until you get back. Kim can help me out when necessary.'

Karen placed the empty glass on the table and regarded the silver locket. She reached out towards it, then looked up at Sonia. 'You wanted me to keep this before.'

'I still do, as long as you wish to have it.' Karen picked it up and slipped it into the pocket of her blue skirt. 'How do you feel about a bite to eat?'

'Yes, OK.'

They stood up and moved close to each other. Sonia took Karen's arms and squeezed them gently, before kissing her on the lips. Karen took Sonia, holding her by the waist and pulling her close so that they remained cheek to cheek for a few seconds. Sonia slipped her arms around Karen's shoulders and felt the other's tears, warm upon her own cheeks.

A few minutes later, as they approached the entrance to the bar, two figures emerged and pulled up short before them.

'Oh! Er . . . hello!' said Jackie, with a look of surprise.

Rose said nothing, but stood aside and waited.

'What are you looking guilty about?' asked Sonia.

'Nothing,' replied Jackie, 'I just didn't see you. We're off out in a few minutes.'

'Yes,' added Rose, 'we're going for a walk.'

'Does Pauline know you're going out?'

'She's not in,' responded Jackie.

'Ah, no,' said Sonia, 'she's out shopping for the day, isn't she? I forgot about that. Well, make the most of it!' The two girls disappeared up the main stairs in silence. 'I don't know what they're up to,' said Sonia as she and Karen entered the bar, 'but they'll be for it again if they're caught.'

'All part of the game though, isn't it?' breathed Karen.

'But of course it is,' replied Sonia. 'All part of the game.'

'I hope you haven't changed your mind!' said Rose, emerging from the bathroom in a white bathrobe.

'No, I suppose not,' answered Jackie. 'What are you going to wear?'

'Jeans and T-shirt. What about you?'

'Oh, the same. Look, how are you going to do this and how long will it take?'

'Don't you worry, precious,' said Rose, grinning, 'just a little hairpin and five or ten seconds. I'll be done and back in here by the time you're out of the bathroom.'

When Jackie appeared in the small lounge, Rose sat in

an armchair reading a magazine. Jackie looked at her. 'Well?'

'Yeah, done,' answered Rose. 'It was dead easy!'

'I hope nobody saw you.'

'Course not,' said Rose, 'I've never done one so quick. Come on!'

The girls walked quickly across the three metres of daylit corridor and slipped into the darkened room. The door closed behind them with a soft, reassuring click. Jackie soon located the light switch and the room flooded with a warm pink glow from the hidden lights above the cornice.

'Rose, this is stupid,' whispered Jackie. 'You'll see all this in a week or two anyway, if you haven't cleared off.'

'Yeah, I know, but it'll be when we're on duty and we won't be able to muck about, will we? Anyway, what makes you think I'm going to clear off?'

'I don't know. There are things you might not like – I mean things they make you wear and do –'

'It doesn't bother you any so why should it bother me?' asked Rose as they trod the luxurious maroon carpet and stopped at the group of chrome and black leather seats arranged about the coffee table in the centre of the room. Rose inhaled the rich aroma of the leather and ran her hand over its cool opulence.

'Blimey, how some people live,' she muttered.

'Sit down Rosie. I'll get something to drink.'

'There's loads of wine,' grinned Rose as she eased herself into the sighing leather.

'Really! How d'you know?'

'I didn't just open the door, love,' said Rose, obviously pleased with herself, leaning back with her hands clasped behind her head. 'I went and took a quick peep around the place too.'

Jackie smiled to herself and carried on to the small kitchen. Rose listened to the chink of glasses and heard the soft pop of the cork. A minute later, Jackie emerged from the small room and joined her.

'It's a dry white. I hope it's OK.'

'Bound to be!' laughed Rose, eyeing the slim green bottle

which already glistened with condensation. 'That Karen,' said Rose, watching Jackie pour the wine, 'and Sonia, what do they do for blokes? Are they a bit, you know?'

'What does it matter?' responded Jackie.

'Well, I suppose it doesn't really. But what we've been doing, it's good fun, a good laugh, right? But we like fellas as well. I've seen the way those two look at each other –'

'Rosie!' cut in Jackie. 'Forget it, please! Everyone's OK here, whatever they do.'

'What, even her over the other side of the corridor?'

Jackie did not answer her but drained her wine glass and rose from the armchair. 'Look, how much did you see in here?'

'Er, well, I popped my head into the kitchen, as you know. I had a quick peep into the shower room and went to take a look through there.'

Rose gestured towards the archway at the far side of the room with the heavy black curtain suspended behind it.

'Oh, you know what's in there?'

'No,' answered Rose, 'I couldn't find the switch so I came back to our room.'

'OK,' continued Jackie, refilling the glasses, 'bring your wine and we'll have a guided tour.'

'Mind if I join you?' asked Annette.

Angela looked up from her book and smiled. 'No, of course I don't.'

'I need to be near the window to watch out for our visitors.'

'What visitors?' asked Angela.

'Oh, they're not the usual sort. These are from a publishers in Berlin – they want to see our set-up and plan the photography for a new magazine Sonia is involved with.'

'Oh, something different or just the usual?'

'It's supposed to be different,' replied Annette, glancing through the conservatory window. 'The idea is to publish several collections containing artistic studies of fetish and bondage scenes – no blatant sex.'

'I see – more upmarket. Respectable even.'

185

'Something like that. She hopes it might even be allowed in the UK.'

'God, whatever next?' mused Angela.

'Well, the demand is there all right, mainly because their censorship laws fuel it.'

'Are we all going to be in it?' asked Angela. 'If so, I'll warn my family back in England!'

'They'll never see it.'

'I wouldn't bet on that, knowing my father!'

Annette looked at her watch. 'I've to phone Pauline as soon as they show up. She's in on it as well.'

'Is she going to dress up for them? Gestapo perhaps?'

'You're very cynical today, dear. What's up?'

'I suppose I'm bored,' replied Angela. 'Karen and Val are away, Kim's stuck in the beauty parlour, Jackie and her pal have vanished, Mike's doing something with the bloody drains at the back of the house and the rest went off this morning to Carcassonne for a day of culture.'

'Oh, that was the mini bus, was it?'

'Yes. I'd have gone myself but Sonia wanted me to run the bar. You didn't want a drink, did you?'

'Not yet, thanks. But as soon as these four show up we'll all want a bite to eat and a few drinks.'

'Pauline too?' asked Angela, her blue-grey eyes opening wide.

'Yes, I'm afraid so.'

'Damn, we're out of arsenic!'

'Never mind, dear, we both know she's immune don't we? Ah!' They turned their heads towards the window. A blue Mercedes oozed along the driveway towards the house, the sun flaring intermittently from its windows and chrome. 'You'll have something to do now,' laughed Annette, rising from the table.

'How do I look?' asked Rose, twirling herself about before the section of mirrored wall.

'Fantastic!' answered Jackie with a giggle.

Rose regarded her image in its shimmering, skin-tight lurex dress with long sleeves, low scooped neck and short

186

skirt. Her legs gleamed dully in their sheer, black nylon and she stood with her feet poised in gold vinyl, stiletto heel sandals of impractical height.

'Do wonders for your legs, don't they?' she added.

Around them, in the warm pink ambience, lay the sinister contrivances and furniture of restraint in their purposeful leather, chrome and bright steel. The doors of the large walk-in cupboards stood gaping open to reveal their racks of clothes and garments. It was the third dress Rose had tried on and various items were arrayed across a nearby leather bench.

Jackie wore her small, gossamer black briefs. Above her waist she was naked. On her legs she had carefully adjusted a pair of garter-top stockings in fine black net with seams at the back, and on her feet, open sandals of a similar, precarious height to Rose's but in black patent leather.

'I don't think you'd want to walk too far in these, especially after all that wine,' she said to Rose's image in the mirror.

Rose grinned, walked unsteadily to the open cupboard and began once more to rummage among the contents. Jackie joined her and placed an arm about her waist. Rose kissed her on the lips and they both chuckled.

'Oh look!' gasped Rose. 'Here's one of them things they had on me when I first came here.' She pulled the limp black sheath from the rack. Its numerous straps swung freely about and its brass buckles gleamed in the soft light. 'Do they make you wear them as well?' she chuckled, swinging it from side to side.

'If I've been a bad girl,' answered Jackie.

'Oh look!' came Rose's voice as she peered deeper into the cupboard. 'Isn't it pervy? There's more stuff down here.'

'You'll get used to it, Rosie,' laughed Jackie, 'especially if you go on the way you are!'

'Here's my favourite colour,' came Rose's voice as she pulled out a garment in metallic silver vinyl. 'I've seen one of these as well, haven't I? In your room that time when Valerie and Cheryl came for me.'

'Well, it's similar,' said Jackie, 'except it fits on you the other way around and fastens down the front and it's got a soft lining to make it cosy.'

Rose let the garment fall to her side and slipped an arm around Jackie's neck. Jackie closed her eyes and felt the warmth of Rose's breath on her ear. 'What say we have one of our little games in here, with this?'

Jackie kissed her and they both laughed softly. 'I don't mind,' said Jackie, 'but be careful while we're feeling pissed.'

'Go on!' responded Rose. 'I used to drink more than this when I was still at school. Let's see what this is like on you, since you've seen me in one.'

She kissed Jackie again and their lips remained together longer still.

'All right then,' giggled Jackie.

Rose had no difficulty in easing Jackie's arms into the sleeve, despite them being behind her back. She pulled the two halves of the garment over Jackie's shoulders until it almost encircled her.

'God, it's tight,' she muttered as she attempted to join the heavy duty zip fastener at the waist. Eventually, with squeals of amusement from them both, she succeeded in engaging the zipper and moving it a short way up. 'God!' Rose tittered. 'It wouldn't do to be overweight, would it?'

'It's made for slim people,' laughed Jackie. 'Everyone is slim here except some of the visitors!'

Rose tugged harder, almost pulling Jackie over, both of them spluttering with amusement.

'It's going! It's going!' cooed Rose. Suddenly the zipper moved up to the neck with a soft purr. 'Done it!' she giggled. 'Oh, there's a dinky little lock on it. I hope there's a key.'

Her remark was followed by a sharp click, after which she released Jackie and stepped back.

'Blimey! It looks really tight on you.'

'It stretches a bit,' responded Jackie, standing helpless, encased from neck to waist in the sleek, metallic vinyl, her arms folded tightly across her back within its restraining grip.

'I think I'll bugger off now and go for a swim,' announced Rose with a grave expression.

Jackie's mouth dropped open.

'Hey – no!'

Rose spluttered into laughter. Jackie's face broke into a broad grin. Rose moved forward and kissed her. Jackie responded with no little ardour.

'Just imagine,' said Rose, 'if we were both wearing one of these. What would we do?'

'That's a silly question,' answered Jackie, 'we couldn't do anything, could we? Anyway, you couldn't put it on to yourself, could you?'

'No,' answered Rose, 'but there's another way. I'll show you in a minute, but first . . .'

She kissed Jackie once more. This time, their lips remained together and Rose's fingers slipped down the front of her briefs. Jackie stiffened with a sudden intake of breath as the fingers invaded the folds of her sex and found the focus of her sensuality. She closed her eyes, sensed Rose moving downwards then felt a hand pushing the elasticated briefs until they were about her ankles. Even as she freed herself of them, the fingers continued their devilish work within her and she parted her legs as much as she could until Rose's lips rejoined hers. Each had learned, during their short acquaintance, how low the threshold of sensuality was for the other.

Rose had slid her other hand about Jackie's waist to hold her more tightly, for she began to twist and writhe in ecstasy as she felt the crisis approaching. Rose felt the heat of her body and the turmoil of excitement rising quickly within her. When it burst forth, Rose gripped her as Jackie's head fell back with eyes closed and mouth agape, crying out as though in pained anguish, quivering in her arms.

At last, she sighed and opened her eyes. Rose released her and stood back a little. 'Doesn't take you long, does it?'

'You're an expert, Rosie, that's why!' breathed Jackie. Rose looked about the room, reached behind her back and started to release the zipper on her own dress. Soon the lurex dress was off her and draped over a nearby chair. Rose stood naked except for the open body tights and high-heel sandals. 'Come on,' offered Jackie, 'undo me and we can change places.'

'Not yet,' answered Rose, 'I've got another idea.'

Jackie watched in silence as she walked a short way across the room. She stopped and reached upwards to where a pair of steel manacles hung from a chain above her head. From these, she withdrew the key and, grinning, held it up for Jackie to see. Either side of her were steel cuffs, each connected by a short chain to bolts in the floor.

'Rose, for heaven's sake, what are you up to? Come and get me out of this!'

Rose ignored her request and walked away, pushing through the black curtain and disappearing from sight. Moments later she returned empty handed, her face bearing a mischievous grin, and went back to the spot from where she had obtained the key.

'Rose!' hissed Jackie, approaching her with an expression of anxiety. 'What are you up to?'

Rose did not answer, but bent down and undid the ankle straps to release her own sandals, placing both by the chair where the dress lay. She positioned herself under the hanging manacles and spread her legs apart. Jackie watched, helpless, as Rose, with little difficulty, snapped first one and then the other cuff about each of her ankles. Jackie started forward in alarm as she reached up, stretching her arms above her head, taking hold of the suspended handcuffs.

'No, Rosie! Don't!' But it was too late. The cuffs closed with a terminal click and Jackie stood wide-eyed before the now helpless and immobile Rose. 'Rose!' she said in disbelief. 'You're crazy! We've had it now!'

'No, we haven't,' Rose said to her. 'The key is on one of the armchairs out there. If you want to be undone you have to go and get it and bring it to me so I can get loose first. Simple!'

'But . . . but why?'

'I just dared myself, that's all. I wanted to see what it

was like with the two of us. All you've got to do is shove that seat over, stand on it with the key in your teeth and give it to me.'

Jackie regarded her for a few seconds then grinned. 'Oh well, in that case there's no rush.' She approached Rose until the two were face to face and looking into each other's eyes. After a moment, they resumed kissing. 'You're good fun, Rosie,' Jackie whispered, brushing her lips about Rose's soft neck.

From there it was but a short way to her breasts, with their reddened and prominent nipples displaying an enthusiasm for what Rose knew Jackie would do. Jackie took her time, for time had become of little importance. For the time being the domain of pleasure was theirs to roam at will.

Jackie teased and sucked the nipples but soon found leaning down further to be awkward, with her arms held so rigidly behind her and the exaggerated heels of her sandals. So she fell to her knees on the soft carpet before the stretched out figure. There she felt the heat of Rose's stomach on her cheek and beheld her sex, smooth and naked.

Rose, because of what she had done in rendering both of them so helpless, found her excitement heightened and felt the currents of anticipation running through her body in a way she had not experienced before. The electric tingle of Jackie's lips and tongue about her most intimate place caused her to stiffen and tug against the manacles. The futility of attempting to pull free only reinforced the growing intensity of her lust.

Jackie teased and licked her clitoris, finding Rose moist and inflamed with passion, pushing out her loins to make the invading tongue go deeper. Jackie heard her first cry of 'Aaah!' and worked with greater vigour as more cries followed. Each cry was louder and longer than the one before it, until Rose's body heaved and stiffened. Jackie tasted her climax as the loudest and longest cry rang through the room.

Rose hung gasping in the chains. Jackie kissed her stomach and struggled up on to her feet. Rose at last opened her eyes to find Jackie close to her.

'God!' she breathed. 'I thought that'd never end.'

Jackie looked at her for a moment then said, 'I'd better find the key and we can get ourselves out of this.'

She walked with poised deliberation towards the heavy curtain and pushed her way through edgeways at one side of the arch. Rose, stretched out in the manacles, watched the curtain sway back and forth. Now alone, she felt impatient and vulnerable.

Jackie approached the group of chairs and spotted the small silver key at once, lying on one of the leather seats. She moved close, regarded it for a moment, then bent forward. It was obvious that she was not going to reach it with her mouth while standing upright. She got down awkwardly on to her knees in front of the chair, pushing it back slightly, but now finding herself only a short distance from the key. Leaning down so that her nose and mouth were pressed against the leather, she was able to take the key between her teeth and adjust it into a comfortable position with her tongue and lips. She raised her head and, using the chair as a prop, began to lever herself back on to her feet, wishing as she did so that she had the use of her arms. But as she leaned hard against it, the chair slipped back and she pitched forward with a sharp cry, letting the key fall from her mouth. The key slipped to the rear of the seat where the leather dipped down against the back. Jackie eyed it with consternation. She shuffled forward on to the seat until she was again close to where the key lay in the cleft. Squeezing her face into the engulfing leather she was but a tongue touch from her goal when, because her action was pushing open the gap in the upholstery, the key slipped down and vanished.

Jackie pulled back and gasped in open mouthed disbelief.

'Oh, it can't,' she muttered, 'it can't!'

She remained for some time, looking at the place where the key had lain, her mind in turmoil, thinking at one point to use her foot in an attempt to retrieve it but realising that she could not undo the straps which held on the sandals. She twisted from side to side in the straitjacket, but that felt tighter and more secure than ever. She struggled up to her feet and, with a sideways glance at the empty chair, hurried back towards the black draped archway.

'Rose!' she gasped. 'The bloody key's fallen inside the chair – I can't reach it!'

'What? You're joking!'

'I'm not joking, Rose. It's gone!'

'Oh, Christ!' responded Rose, looking up and grasping the chain above her to which the manacles were attached. 'There's no way I can get out of these – you've got to do something or we've had it!'

Jackie looked about her in desperation.

'There must be another key around somewhere. Most of the locks are the same!' Jackie walked erratically about the room, scrutinising the equipment and restraints. None held a key. The silence was broken only by the creaking of the chains as Rose twisted about in despair. 'There's nothing,' she said at last.

'They must keep them somewhere, Jackie. You've got to keep looking! What about the cupboards?'

'Rose!' cried Jackie in exasperation. 'How can I do anything while I'm wearing a bloody straitjacket? We should have taken turns as I wanted, then this never would have happened!'

Rose sighed loudly. 'Sorry Jackie, it looks like I got us both in the shit. You'll have to try and –'

'Shhh!' hissed Jackie. 'I can hear someone.'

Both of them turned their heads towards the archway. There were voices, several voices, on the other side of the curtain. And they were getting closer.

'All of these rooms are ideal for studio sets, of course,' came Annette's voice as the curtain swung aside, 'and almost anything can be moved around to suit the –'

Annette regarded the two girls with a bemused gaze. Behind her entered four middle-aged men in casual attire and behind them, Pauline. They gazed at Rose and Jackie in silent wonder, except for Pauline, whose expression remained one of indifference as she eyed them both coolly.

Annette turned to the four males with a broad smile and

said, 'Oh, I almost forgot, we set up a couple of the girls in situ, just for you to have an idea of how it looks in use.'

The men looked at each other then at Annette. One of them broke into a grin and said, '*Ja*, that is very good!'

'*Ja*! Very good!' they all agreed.

Pauline smiled and turned to Annette. 'Perhaps you'll continue on with our guests while I see to the girls.'

'Of course. This way, gentlemen,' said Annette, ushering the small party back through the curtained archway.

The voices diminished, but not as quickly as Pauline's smile. She stood with arms folded, her cold, round features contrasting with the long black gown with its gold braided high collar and long sleeves.

'Well,' she said at last, 'you're almost doing my job for me, aren't you? You obviously enjoy being together like that so I don't see why we shouldn't go a little further, do you?'

'It wasn't her fault!' protested Rose. 'It's me who's to blame – I got her in it!'

Pauline regarded her as an entomologist might view a mounted specimen. 'I think you have both got yourselves "in it", haven't you? And your speech! I really am disappointed after all the encouragment you have been given. Very disappointed indeed!'

'Ever so sorry,' muttered Rose.

'Ever so sorry,' mocked Pauline.

'And me,' added Jackie, knowing as she spoke that it would make no difference to Pauline's intentions.

'Oh, "and me" too? Just the terrible twins, aren't we? Well, let's see what else we can do together, shall we?' She walked briskly over to a wall cupboard, pulled open the door and reached into it. Moments later, she was at Rose's side. 'You'll wear this,' she said, pulling the leather harness over Rose's head, 'until you've done as you're told!'

The harness was pulled tightly around Rose's face, head and neck, cutting off her vision with its padded leather triangular shapes and firmly plugging her mouth with its black rubber ball. Once secure, Pauline snapped on the small brass locks to prevent its removal.

'That's better. Now, I'm going to unlock your wrists and ankles and sit you down for a few minutes. You needn't bother to try and get that off either. It will come off when I'm good and ready and not before!' Once the manacles were undone, she guided Rose to a nearby stool and pushed her down on to it. Rose remained still with her head slightly bowed and her hands on her lap, while Pauline turned her attentions to the now trembling Jackie. 'You can stay just as you are for a while. I shall be back shortly.'

Pauline turned and swished out through the black curtain. Jackie walked over to Rose and bent towards her.

'Sorry sweetie,' she breathed into Rose's ear, and placed a soft kiss on her neck.

In the beauty parlour the phone rang.

'Yes?' answered Kim. She listened to the voice on the other end, then replied, 'No, nobody else today . . . I don't know if I'm allowed to . . . yes, I know Valerie is away but . . . yes, all right I'll leave it unlocked as long as I don't get into trouble . . . yes, I did hear what you said and I'm not trying to be awkward, it's just that I'm supposed to be responsible for . . . all right, I'll be gone by then!'

She replaced the phone on its wall socket and muttered, 'Domineering old cow.'

When, fifteen minutes later, Pauline returned, Jackie was in no way reassured by the sight of her. She had discarded the black gown in favour of a white satin blouse, fawn jodhpurs and tight-fitting dark brown knee boots. In her belt was positioned, ready to hand, the short, black, braided whip, which even Jackie was loath to encounter.

'Now,' announced Pauline, with hands on hips, 'you are each going to be released in turn to shower and use the toilet. You will then return to me. The main door is locked so you will not be leaving until we are all ready!' She moved over to the subdued Rose and pulled a small silver key from her blouse pocket. In a few moments, Rose was free of the head harness, passing her hand over her mouth and blinking. 'You had better go first,' said Pauline, standing over her. 'And I'll tell you once and once only. If either of you disobeys me, you will both –' she patted the whip and glanced at the still helpless Jackie '– and I do mean both, regret it!' She pulled the coiled whip from her belt and prodded Rose on the shoulder with it. 'Go now and make sure you do everything – I mean everything! And if you don't, I'll do it for you!'

Rose folded her arms across her chest and walked with a slight stoop towards the curtain. Once she was through, Pauline turned to Jackie. 'You'll continue wearing that and wait until I'm finished with her!'

Pauline made her way through the curtain and Jackie was alone, wondering what was to befall herself and Rose.

In the private intimacy of the shower room, Rose carried out the instructions virtually in the manner of a routine. The layout of this room might not be identical to that located in Pauline's suite, its lights might not be as glaring, but the fittings and functions were the same. She understood perfectly the procedure with the rubber bottle, soap solution and plastic pipe with its smooth pink nozzle and small valve. At least she was free to carry out the operation for herself and not suffer the humiliation of Pauline obliging her while under restraint. She had begun to admit to herself some time ago that it was a far from unpleasant experience and suspected that Jackie found it more acceptable still.

After showering and drying herself, Rose stood in hesitation near the door. Was there any point in trying to hide her nakedness with a towel? She opened the door to the outer room slowly. At once she met Pauline's gaze.

'What are you waiting for?' came the voice from near the cluster of chairs.

'Oh, er, nothing. What shall I do now?'

'You can start by coming over here!'

Rose walked slowly towards her, making no effort to cover her nakedness. She felt her body trembling and told herself that it was because the room was cool after the hot shower. On the chair nearest to Pauline lay something which looked half familiar but, because of its colour, not familiar at all. Her nose was telling her more than her eyes, for the strong and yet subtle odour of latex suffused the air and all but vanquished the aroma of the black leather chairs.

'All right,' ordered Pauline, reaching down to pick up what had caught Rose's attention, 'turn around and stand still!'

Rose stepped back and ventured, 'What's that? What are you up to?'

Pauline immediately dropped the item back on to the chair and pulled loose the whip, shouting, 'You will do as you're told!'

'Hey! No!' shrieked Rose, cowering away from her. 'Don't hit me!'

But the braided thongs swished and caught her an angry, biting sting across her thighs. She fell to the carpet and raised her arms defensively.

'Now, say once more what you just said and say it politely!'

'I . . . I . . .' Rose stuttered. 'Please don't hit me.'

Pauline watched her eyes moisten with tears then ordered, 'Now get up and stand still or I promise you you'll get more!'

Rose, her eyes fixed on the hand holding the instrument of persuasion, clambered to her feet and stood silent.

'Let's try again,' said Pauline.

Rose wiped her fingers over her eyes and waited. Pauline laid down the whip and moved behind her to the chair. Rose knew what Pauline was about to put on to her but made no protest and no attempt to resist.

The first part of the procedure took little time at all. Rose pushed her arms past each other across her middle and inside the cool, powdered embrace of the thick, rubber sleeve. The heavy latex garment was then pulled quickly about her body and over her shoulders to enclose her from neck to waist. The second stage took longer, for Pauline reached back to the chair and picked up a long length of white cord. Starting at the collar, she threaded the lace to and fro through the metal eyelets, working down and tightening the straitjacket about Rose's slim form as she went. With each tug, it constricted further, almost overbalancing her so that Pauline ordered her to lean forward to counteract the pulling. By the time Pauline had finished and tied the knot just above her behind, Rose's arms were squeezed immobile across her abdomen by the thick latex. From behind, she heard a breath of satisfaction.

There were other items heaped by the side of the chair. Pauline turned her attentions to these. Rose saw that they were long boots in the same colour and material as the restraint which held her. Pauline kept her standing but positioned her against the back of one of the chairs in order to put them on her. Even so, Rose found the proceedings difficult. The boots fastened with long zippers from heel to thigh, and each was fitted with a rubber strap around the top to secure it firmly about the leg.

'Don't move until I tell you,' came the order.

Rose remained, propped against the chair, her feet poised on heels of a height to which she had not yet become accustomed.

She next heard the sound of rustling paper but dared not turn around. Pauline soon reappeared and Rose caught her breath when she saw what was held in the fingers.

'Close your mouth tightly!' came the inevitable order.

Rose obeyed. Moments later, her mouth was sealed shut by the strip of white plastic tape, the pressure of Pauline's thumbs ensuring that adhesion was complete.

'Now go and wait in there while I deal with the other one.'

Pauline indicated the direction of the small kitchen and gave Rose an initial push to start her on her way. She walked with caution for not only were the heels at first a little precarious, but the long, tight boots did not allow her to flex her legs properly. As she moved across the room Rose caught a glimpse of herself in one of the large wall mirrors. The restraint, like the boots, was all but invisible, for it was translucent pink and blended closely with the colour of her own skin.

Jackie had heard the cry and the crack of the whip from

the other side of the curtained arch. She knew that Pauline would eventually call for her and wished that the waiting was not so prolonged. When Pauline did appear, it was almost a relief and she went in subdued obedience.

As Pauline unzipped and removed the vinyl restraint, Jackie glanced about the room. Rose was not to be seen, but she knew that it was not a good time to ask about where she was. For Jackie, the course of events was the same, and after the brief episode of freedom in the bathroom, she found herself once more inside a restraining cocoon, albeit a variation of the previous one, as her arms were now folded in front of her.

With Jackie silenced in the same manner, Pauline summoned Rose back into the room and each contemplated the plight of the other. Jackie saw the inflamed track across Rose's thigh where the whip had caught her. Each wondered what fate held in store and if they were to be left as they were or if Pauline's plans went beyond what they had so far endured. Part of the answer still lay upon the chair, white and folded neatly against the black leather. Rose and Jackie were each bedecked in cotton gowns, pulled about them and done up with tapes at the back. This told them one thing at least – that they were to be taken elsewhere in the house other than just across the corridor.

Pauline walked over to the main door and pulled it open. Rose and Jackie looked at her questioningly even though their restraints and nakedness were covered up.

'Move, will you?' she addressed them. They stepped to the doorway. 'We're going down to the beauty parlour via the back stairs. I doubt if anyone will see you both, for what that is worth. Most of them are away, in case you didn't know.'

They followed her with difficulty because of the boots, having no alternative other than to face her anger and its consequences, until they reached the blue door halfway along the ground floor passage. Jackie was surprised that Pauline should have access to the parlour in this manner. She wondered if Sonia knew and what Valerie would have to say if she found out.

When they entered through the unlocked door, the lights were already on. Jackie almost expected to find Kim inside, but she was not to be seen. Instead, they encountered the soft pink lights and luxurious emptiness of what was Valerie's domain, now entered by an intruder who Jackie knew had no right to be there. The beauty parlour should have been a welcoming and friendly place, as it always had been, but with Pauline here it had lost its soul and became a place of indifference.

She pulled around the two swivel chairs in front of the sinks and the long wall mirror.

'Sit down!' she ordered.

They sat.

Pauline walked to the large cupboard at the far end of the room and pulled open the doors. They saw her reflection in the mirror as she returned, with an array of black leather straps hanging over one arm. She at once, beginning with Jackie, secured the two girls on the chairs with straps buckled about their ankles, thighs, chests and necks. Both sat looking in helpless wonderment at what she might be about to do, expecially Jackie, who even after some considerable experience of life under Pauline, had not yet encountered this train of events. Pauline's next moves caused them both a surge of alarm.

She pulled open two of the drawers but not finding what she sought, closed them. Then from a third, she extracted a roll of the white adhesive tape which they were only too familiar with, and a pair of scissors. Having cut from the roll four lengths of some eight or nine centimetres, she turned first to Jackie and said, 'Close your eyes.' Jackie let out a muffled protest and twisted her head away. Pauline moved closer. 'It goes on whether they're closed or not but it will be better if they are. Make your mind up quickly!'

Jackie hesitated for a moment, but seeing the tape move closer still, did as she was told. Pauline applied the tape deftly, sealing shut first her left eye and then the right. Rose watched with incomprehension, knowing that her turn was imminent. She closed her eyes without being ordered and waited. The sensation was very odd, for though only three small pieces of adhesive material had been applied to her face, Rose was deprived completely of speech and vision. With the other things they had put on her, she expected such limitations, for that was what they were designed for – so why do it this way? And what was Jackie thinking? Did she have the answer?

'You have both continued to defy me,' came the voice. 'I have told you not to do it! I have warned you time and time again!'

There were sounds which, for the time being, meant nothing; drawers opening and closing, objects being placed upon the work surface; something, a litter bin perhaps, being placed by Jackie's chair.

'Now,' continued Pauline, 'I am going to make sure you do take notice. Things are going to be different after today!'

The first either of them knew of her intentions was when Jackie felt her hair being pulled back. The snap of scissors close to her ear made her start and utter a long, 'Mmmm!'

She knew the futility of struggle but tried all the same, tensing against the straitjacket and the straps as the scissors continued their work, letting out stifled protests until it became obvious that they were as pointless as her endeavours to get free.

The snipping became more rapid and seemed closer still to her ears. Her scalp felt oddly cool. When the scissors stopped, the clippers took over, and before long, Jackie felt their cool touch upon her scalp. Rose knew the meaning of the sounds and she too tensed her body against the restraints, imagining that the rubber straitjacket tightened further as she tried to move her arms inside its stubborn hold. And for Jackie, after the clippers came the electric shaver to do its final work.

Rose waited, her heart beating strongly, as the hands took hold of her. She uttered no protest, nor did she attempt to move again, but allowed herself to relax and accept what she had no means of avoiding.

A few minutes later, Jackie instinctively pulled her head around as unseen fingers touched the side of her face.

'If you do that again,' came the voice, 'I'll leave the tapes on!'

Jackie stayed still and the fingers returned. The smell of methylated spirits assailed her nostrils and her skin instantly chilled as the liquid soaked under the edge of the adhesive tape. First one eye and then the other was uncovered, and though she could have opened them immediately, she did not. She was afraid. When she summoned enough courage to look, she would have gasped in astonishment had she been able to use her mouth. She glanced sideways at Rose, who regarded her too for a moment. Gone was her own golden brown hair and gone was Rose's straw blonde too. Jackie began to wonder if soon she would wake up in bed next to Rose and find that it had all been an unpleasant dream, and the hairless features which stared back at her were only a memory.

That possibility was dispelled as Pauline began to undo the straps which held them both to the chairs. After they were released and able to stand, Pauline moved to the end of the work surface and took up something which had lain so far unnoticed by Rose and Jackie.

'You're both going to need these,' she said, holding up the two wigs. One of these she fitted over Jackie's shaven head, the other over Rose's. Jackie looked at their reflection in the long mirror. The glossy, silver-blonde hair was shot with strawberry pink. It hung down her back and over her shoulders and its fringe part way down to her eyes. The two girls saw themselves transformed.

'Come on, we're going back up!' announced Pauline after she had fixed the white cotton surgical gowns around them both.

She conducted them out of the parlour and into the short passageway to the main door, switching out the lights behind her. Soon they were ascending the rear stairs to the first floor, Pauline leading them like a priestess with two weird acolytes. They were comparatively relieved upon reaching the corridor not to have been observed, though it could be doubted they would have been easily recognised.

Jackie expected that they would be taken to Pauline's

room but they were not. Instead, they stopped outside Jackie's own apartment and Pauline opened the door to usher them in. When they entered, the door closed behind them and they both waited for Pauline's next move. There was only silence. After a time, Rose and Jackie slowly turned around. Pauline was not with them. They looked at each other and moved their heads and eyes questioningly. For the lack of anything else to do, they walked into the middle of the room and waited in enforced silence. They could not have said how long it was before Pauline returned, though it was probably not as long as it had seemed. She swung open the door and stood by it, waiting.

'Come along both of you, quickly!' There was no question of disobedience. 'I've had a few things to get ready,' remarked Pauline as they passed along the corridor towards the front of the house.

It was at the last door on their left that they were brought to a halt, Rose looking at Jackie with apprehension. Jackie recalled that this was the room where Pauline had held the mock school class. She and the other girls who did domestic duties knew it was not replete with the furnishings and fittings to be found in the other rooms for it was intended to be adaptable – it had even been used for private parties, as Jackie was aware from her own involvement.

They passed through the ante room and into the curtained-off area. Pauline moved ahead and pulled aside a section of the curtain on its ceiling track, allowing the afternoon sun to flood across the carpet and pointing the way through for Rose and Jackie.

The room was largely empty. A low, black leather bench stood along the wall to their right. Jackie regarded it for a moment with mixed feelings. Directly in front of the window stood two upright, high backed chairs finished in heavy pine and black leather. The chairs faced each other less than a metre apart and the straps hanging at various points from them rendered their purpose unambiguous.

'Over here,' ordered Pauline, stepping across the room to the chairs. 'Now, sit down.' The girls hesitated. 'Sit!'

They sat, facing each other. Pauline at once set to work with the straps, securing both of them to the chairs at ankles, knees, thighs, waist and chest, the metallic rasp of the buckles speaking the language of complete restraint. Pauline tugged the wig from each of them, leaving their heads startlingly naked in the bright light. Finally, she attached the neck straps so that, apart from limited movement of their heads, Rose and Jackie were utterly immobile.

'Good,' breathed Pauline, picking up the two wigs. 'I don't expect either of you will get up to anything for the time being. Now, you had better listen to me carefully. You are going to be under my direct jurisdiction for the foreseeable future. It's going to be weeks before you get enough of your hair back to go out, and if either of you do anything stupid, it will be shaved off again so you have to start anew. They watched her cold blue eyes intently, as well as listening to her deceptively calm voice as she continued, unblinking. 'You will both do increased domestic duties on this and the second floor. At such times, provided you behave, you will wear these –' she held up the wigs '– otherwise people will see you as you are. Daytime meals will be taken in your room. Before you take exercise outside the house, or when you take an evening meal downstairs, you will again have to come to me –' she turned to Jackie '– as you will when your services are required by our visitors, though I dare say a few of them might prefer you as you are now! You will be accountable to me every minute of the day and night, and if one of you fails to be where you should be at any time, both will be punished. You will find yourselves more often under restraint, so you had better get used to it. It won't, however, be entirely wasted time. We already doubtless have some interesting photo studies in the can from today's little frolics and I'm sure there will be opportunity for plenty more.' She turned to go, then hesitated. 'Oh, and in case it isn't already obvious why I put you in here, it may become so during what is left of the afternoon. You will at any rate have the next three hours to consider it.'

Three hours! Jackie had seldom spent half that time under such strict restraint. What, she wondered, must it be like for Rose? Rose, not considering yet how heavily time might lay upon them, wondered how Jackie would behave towards her as a result of their folly, undertaken at her instigation. She wished she could speak to tell Jackie that she would somehow make up for it. Jackie too, frustrated by her own enforced silence, wanted to talk to Rose, to reassure her that she was not to be blamed in any way and that things would not be spoiled between them.

They turned their faces to the net curtains and felt the warmth of the afternoon sun through the glass. Close to the poolside stood Mike, and behind him on the pathway, a parked wheelbarrow with a spade propped against it. He was talking to Lorna and Kim, both of them circling about in the clear, shimmering water under the mellow blue sky. On the other side of the pool, where the tables, chairs and coloured sunshades were, Annette sat with the four male guests. Angela, in her short, blue, satin halterneck dress appeared bearing a tray of drinks and joined them at the table. Jackie realised that this was to be denied to her and Rose for a long time to come.

10

Adventures in Paris

It was late afternoon when Karen disembarked from the high speed train. Never having visited Paris before, let alone a Paris railway station, *La Gare de Lyon* proved moderately intimidating. Nevertheless, with one hand over her shoulder bag and the other clutching a small fawn suitcase, she soon found her way to the main ticket hall and located the bureau de change where Sonia had said she should wait for Armand.

She had barely lowered her case to the floor when a voice called, '*Mademoiselle* Karen!'

She turned to see the round, smiling face and brown eyes heading towards her.

'Armand,' she said as he squeezed her arms and kissed her on the lips. 'I've just arrived, I –'

'Yes, I saw you. I went to buy some cigarettes and I watched you crossing the concourse. How are you?'

'I'm fine, thank you. And thanks for coming to meet me.'

'Oh, but that is the least I can do,' he replied, taking hold of her case and taking her arm. 'I would not have any lady from Sonia's house arrive alone in Paris, but you are even more special and you have never before visited *la belle cité*.'

They stepped out into the bright afternoon and Armand said, 'I did not bring a car. It is easier to walk but if you prefer, we can take a taxi as long as you are not frightened of our traffic!'

'No,' she answered, 'I wouldn't mind stretching my legs if that's OK with you.'

'Certainly,' he said. 'It is a little way to the shop from here. We must first cross the Boulevard Diderot then we go along Rue Abel for some distance.' Away from the station, they strolled and talked in the warm air. 'Over to our left,' gestured Armand, 'is our new *Opéra de la Bastille*. Tomorrow you will tell me all the places in Paris you wish to go, so that I will take you there.'

'I leave it up to you Armand,' she said, tucking her arm into his. 'You and Josephine shall be my guides as long as you have the time.'

'Nothing will give us greater pleasure, *Mademoiselle*. Nothing.'

The shop, with its small double front, lay in a busy, colourful street a little way north of the Rue du Faubourg. In ornate art nouveau letters in gold on maroon above the door, it bore the name 'Sybaris'. About the street were boutiques, bars and cafés, some of them with their tables and chairs spilling out on to the pavement.

'Gosh, just about everything seems to be going on around here,' remarked Karen as they entered the shop.

Barely were they inside when a voice rang out, 'Ah, Karen, you are here, this is wonderful!'

The figure approached them from where two customers stood by a display of shining black garments on a rack. She was, as Karen remembered her from the night of the party at the house, a little younger than Sonia, with softer features and long dark hair. She wore her black leather catsuit with its accoutrements of small silver chains and zip fasteners. She held Karen and pressed her mouth upon hers. Karen squeezed her arms, tasted her warm, perfumed breath and felt the tingling of her own body as her heartbeat quickened. There was a time, not so long ago, when she would have tried to deny herself the pleasure of a kiss like that. But as Josephine looked into her eyes, she caught her breath and both read the unspoken message.

Josephine released her and frowned. 'I saw you through the window a few minutes ago. You did not come by taxi! Surely this terrible man has not made you walk all the way from *La Gare de Lyon*?'

'Oh no, of course he didn't,' responded Karen, seeing Armand's look of injured innocence. 'I wanted to walk and see a few of the shops.'

'But I hope you made him carry your *valise*!'

'*Mon Dieu!*' breathed Armand.

'Of course he did!' laughed Karen. 'Like a true gentleman.'

'Then,' continued Josephine, 'make sure he remains a gentleman and carries it upstairs to your room.' She glanced at the young couple occupied in subdued conversation by the clothes rack. 'I must attend to these people now,' she said, lowering her voice and rolling her eyes. 'I thing they wish to buy something very naughty and I have to give advice.' She regarded Armand with mock seriousness for a moment, then turned again to Karen. 'Do not let this man into your room if you value your honour.'

She returned with a smile to her customers and the bemused Armand took up the suitcase saying, 'Ah, so often I fall the victim to her tongue.'

Smiling to herself, Karen followed Armand up the narrow stairs, reflecting upon the shop. It bore Sonia's stamp, as did the boutique in Béziers, though that sold mainly clothes. Here, the now familiar odours from the secret rooms of the house were evident, and equally familiar were many of the items on display in the shop.

The first floor landing was somewhat dim, being lit at one end from only a single, small window, though with its thick and brightly coloured carpet and the Matisse prints upon the walls, it was far from cheerless. Armand pushed open the pine panelled door and stepped back for Karen to enter. She did so and was greeted by the visual warmth of pine furnishings and oriental rugs. She liked the room instantly. She felt that the room in its turn welcomed her. A shaft of sunlight illuminated one wall and the small chest of drawers standing against it.

'That is OK for you?' asked Armand, 'If you prefer a hotel –'

'Oh no, Armand, this is perfect, it really is.'

Armand's sun-bronzed face broke into a wide grin and

he lifted her suitcase on to the bed. He turned to her, brushing with his hand a wisp of black hair which had fallen across his forehead.

'I think you will wish to have a rest now,' he said, smiling, 'and I must return to my apartment. Josephine will close the shop in one hour and then she will talk to you.' He walked to the door and turned to her before leaving the room. 'Each night you are with us, we will go out to dinner, yes?'

'Sounds wonderful.'

'OK,' he smiled, 'so tonight I have a table for us at a place where we can relax. I will call for you both at eight o'clock, unless you prefer later. Often we eat much later.'

'Armand,' she said, walking over to him, 'any time is all right, and I look forward to it very much.' She placed a hand on his shoulder and kissed him softly. 'And thanks again for meeting me.'

'My pleasure, *ma chérie*,' he said, grinning, then made his way back down the stairs.

Karen opened her case and removed a few items before making her way around the bed to look out of the window. Below was a small courtyard with potted plants set about on the flagstones, and beyond it the elegant old houses and streets with their mixture of smart new shops and more venerable businesses from a different age. It was no surprise to her that the shower room reflected, on a smaller scale, those at the house. Why the consistency? she wondered. Perhaps it was intended that, wherever you went in Sonia's little empire, you would always feel at home. It was not a concept Karen disliked in the least and she wondered for a while if any of the others had spent time here, as she felt they must have. She unpacked the remainder of her things, wondering what she might wear for the evening. Karen had told her not to worry about taking along too many clothes as Josephine would be able to provide whatever she needed.

She closed the small suitcase and placed it against the wall, then sat down on the bed to remove her shoes. After thinking of nothing much for a minute or so, she lay down to watch the sunlight slowly vanish from the wall. A little later, she was asleep.

There was a distant knocking and from beyond the darkness, a voice called her name. Karen opened her eyes and looked about her, blinking. For a moment, she had forgotten where she was. It was still light outside but the illumination in the room was subdued now that the sun had dipped below the rooftops.

'Karen!' came the voice again.

'Come in!' she called, easing herself from the bed.

The door opened. The dark eyes and smiling face of Josephine appeared. 'Hello. I have brought you a cup of coffee.'

'God, what time is it?'

'It is almost seven o'clock,' said Josephine gently, offering Karen the cup and saucer.

Karen looked her up and down. Josephine had changed for the evening. The catsuit was gone and she now wore a bronze vinyl jacket with black felt collar and cuffs, matching vinyl mini-skirt, black stockings and ochre, high-heel sandals in textured leather. Under the open jacket was a gossamer sheer, black nylon blouse with a small red bow at the neck. From her ears hung two pendant earrings in the form of ancient Greek coins.

'Oh, you look wonderful,' said Karen, sipping the coffee. 'I wish I had brought a few more things now.'

'But you don't need,' said Josephine. 'Everything is here at the shop for you to choose.'

'I'd better make a move and get showered and changed, hadn't I? Is where we're going very far?'

'No, not far – just around the corner. Less than five minutes to walk.' Josephine turned to go. 'When you are ready, put on the gown from the bathroom and come down to the back of the shop. Everything you will need is there.'

Twenty minutes later, Karen was in the shop. 'Well, I just don't know,' declared Karen, eyeing the racks of clothing. 'There's so much here I'm lost for choice!'

'You want to be chic?' asked Josephine. 'You want to be

elegant? Or do you want to be, er, courageous? No this is not the word . . . audacious, that is it. Do you want to be audacious?'

'Mmm, not too audacious, but –'

'Do you like this?' asked Josephine, pulling a vivid red dress from the rack and handing it to her.

Karen held the dress up and scrutinised it thoughtfully. It was ruffled, frothy and full about the skirt, with shoe-string straps at the shoulders and very low cut.

'No,' said Karen after some consideration, 'it's too bright - too frivolous.' She pushed through more of the clothes. 'Ah – now this looks more like it!' She lifted out a dress in cobalt blue lurex and turned to Josephine. 'Well, what do you think?'

'You must try it on,' she replied. 'Come, I will help with the zip.'

Karen turned her back on Josephine and undid the soft blue gown, slipping it from her body and draping it over the clothes rack. She pulled the dress over her head, assisted by Josephine, who let her hands run over Karen's slim body as she helped with it. Karen allowed the hands to pass over her breasts and down her stomach without, or rather, taking care not to show, any sign of objection.

'It is perfect!' declared Josephine when Karen turned around to face her and pushed her hair back over her shoulders.

The dress was sleeveless and held up by thin straps, scooped low over her breasts and close fitting above the waist. Below the waist it was looser and flared slightly, ending well above the knee without being conspicuously short.

Karen walked over to the nearest full length mirror and spun around in front of it. 'Yes, definitely. If it's OK with you, I'll wear this one.'

'Of course!' responded Josephine. 'And now, to go with the dress we will have –' she stooped down and ran her finger back and forth above a selection of shoes '– ah, these I think.' She lifted up a pair of dark blue leather open sandals with medium-high stiletto heels.

Karen regarded them for a moment. 'Yes, I agree, they look fine.'

'And to complete the ensemble,' laughed Josephine, picking up a small flat packet, 'these!'

Karen reached out and took the transparent packet from her. 'Josephine, I did manage to bring a few pairs of tights!'

'No, no,' put in Josephine, 'those are better to wear, you will see.'

'I needn't have brought anything at all,' laughed Karen, 'except underwear!'

'Not tonight!'

'What?'

'Not tonight – do not wear anything beneath!'

Karen stared at her with amused surprise. 'I can't .... I mean, I've never been out like that ... I don't think I –'

'But you must!' insisted Josephine. 'Be daring – nobody will know except you and I.'

'Yes, but ...'

Josephine slipped an arm about her waist and smiled into her eyes. 'You must be naughty this evening, *ma chérie*.'

In the closed intimacy of the shop and with the urging and compelling Josephine, Karen laughed and said, 'Yes, what does it matter, I will.'

Back in her room, Karen opened the packet and pulled out the tights. She had removed the dress and stood perfumed and naked before the long mirror on the wardrobe door, slipping her fingers down the heat of her stomach and over the smooth skin about her sex. The small clock on the chest of drawers told her that Armand would arrive in only ten minutes. She wanted him to find her as she was. And not only Armand, but Josephine too, for something had happened to her since she had arrived in Paris, or certainly, since she had arrived at the shop. What it was she could not be sure. The atmosphere of the street and the shop? Armand and Josephine? Her own long years of sexual repression which Sonia had first released? She did not know. Nor did she care.

212

She began to dress, pulling on the tights, finding them completely open and cut away from front to back, sheer and seamed. The blue lurex dress might have been made for her, the way it flattered her breasts and defined the smooth curves of her body. The gossamer nylon on her legs reflected the light of the bedroom in a soft sheen. The blue leather sandals enclosed her feet with a comforting intimacy which seemed entirely natural. About her neck hung the silver locket but something was still missing. Josephine knocked on the door and called her name.

'Ah, *magnifique*!' pronounced Josephine as Karen opened the door and revealed herself. 'I think you look wonderful also!' Karen reached up to where her light brown hair fell in loosely ordered abundance about her bare shoulders and touched her ear.

'I'm going to scrounge some earrings off you as well, I'm afraid. Yours look so much nicer than the ones I brought.'

'Oh, these!' replied Josephine. 'You know these are genuine. They are coins I bought a long time ago from a dealer in Italy. They come from Sybaris. You have heard of this town? Its people – they have a life of pleasure and luxury until they are destroyed. But the image remains – that cannot be destroyed and so I name this shop after it.' She reached up and began to detach one of the earrings. 'You shall wear these tonight and I will –'

'No! No, Josephine!' cut in Karen. 'I've taken too much already today! I'll borrow something from the shop but I won't take those from you!'

Josephine lowered her arm and smiled. 'Very well, *ma chérie*, but you have taken nothing, for it has all been offered to you first, and Sonia says you must have everything.' Josephine slipped her arms about Karen's shoulders and the two drew closer until their lips were almost touching. Each breathed in the perfumed warmth of the other until their lips met with electric fire and Josephine said, 'There is plenty of time for us yet, *Mademoiselle* Karen.'

They walked down the stairs and back into the shop. Josephine led her to a display case inside which were arrayed a selection of gold and silver earrings. She lifted up the glass lid and reached inside.

'Do you like these?'

Karen examined the earrings in the artificial light of the shop, for now, outside it was dusk. They were in the form of small Renaissance sun disks, with full lipped imperious faces radiating silver flames.

'*Le Roi Soleil!*' laughed Josephine.

'Yes,' enthused Karen, 'I love these. I must pay you for them and take them with me when I go back.'

'Go back?' said Josephine. 'Do not think of that yet. This is your first evening and you have seen nothing of Paris!'

They left the intimacy of the shop and stepped out into the bustling street. In the warm air and half light, everything was becoming alive.

'We have only a short walk,' said Armand, who had now joined them, 'to the end of this block and left. Then we are almost there.'

Armand did not exaggerate, for in no more than five minutes they were at the doors of Le Coq d'Or and he was confirming his reservation with the receptionist.

The restaurant was not large but warm and intimate and irregular in shape. Its ten or so tables, mainly occupied, were scattered about in apparent randomness, some near the centre of the room, some within the odd shaped alcoves which gave the place its unplanned character. The soft, diffused lights illuminated pastel-coloured walls upon which, where space allowed, were hung oriental prints depicting scenes from the Arabian Nights. The ceiling was painted dark blue with a myriad of gold stars and a crescent moon upon it, and from here hung at odd places multi-coloured bead curtains, some to pass across other openings to the room, others to lend a hint of privacy to the alcoves.

It was to one of the alcoves that they were led by the waiter, who pulled aside the bead curtain and gestured for them to pass through. The table inside was, like the other tables, circular with a heavy, white damask tablecloth reaching down almost to the dark brown, polished wooden

214

tiles of the floor. Karen saw that within this alcove were three niches. Inside one stood an ornate metal jug of indeterminate eastern origin, and in the other two, small oriental style metal and glass lamps whose squat candles were each topped by a small waving yellow flame. Karen moved around to the back of the alcove.

Josephine removed the vinyl jacket and placed it, carefully folded, upon the spare fourth chair. Karen could not help but look at her breasts, of average size but well formed and perfectly visible with the prominent nipples pushing out at the front of the chiffon blouse. She realised that Armand, the tips of his fingers resting against his lips, was watching her in turn. She shifted her gaze to the bead curtain and out into the restaurant to the other diners, then back to her own hands.

'Well, what do you think?' asked Armand, smiling into Karen's eyes. 'Do you like this restaurant?'

'Yes, it's gorgeous,' replied Karen, feeling the contours of the red brocade seat through the thin material of the dress, remembering that she had nothing on beneath except the open body tights. 'I'd like to read all of the Thousand and One Nights. I know only a few of them from school; the ones they allowed us to see.'

'Ah, well,' said Armand, 'Le Coq d'Or was not one of them. He was an invention of the Russians! Perhaps the people who opened this restaurant did not know it!'

'But who cares?' added Josephine. 'So long as the food is good.'

As if on cue, the waitress pushed through the bead curtains. She, like all the restaurant staff Karen had seen, wore oriental style loose-fitting trousers in deep blue silk and pale blue top in similar material but adorned with gold swirls and scrolls. They ordered their food and wine, Karen at last able to utilise her knowledge of French properly for the first time since her return.

Soft music played from concealed speakers as they talked, ate, drank and laughed together through the evening, losing all sense of time. After a third bottle of champagne appeared on the table, Josephine asked, 'Do you know, will there be another party in the fall?'

Karen glanced from one to the other, remembering what had happened between the three of them at the party last year, hoping her reddening cheeks were not obvious.

'A party? Er, no, not this time. I think Sonia has something else planned.'

'Ah, yes,' put in Armand, 'she talked of a fashion show in the house. That I think will be very different, no?'

'God, yes,' replied Karen as Armand poured more champagne, 'I daresay it will.'

'And you will take part in this?' asked Josephine.

Karen looked at her, wide-eyed. 'Me? Er . . . oh, no, I don't think so.'

'But you should!' said Armand. 'You are as beautiful as any of *Mademoiselle* Sonia's girls. You are, how do you say – second to none?'

'*Absolument*!' agreed Josephine.

'Well, I don't know,' laughed Karen. 'It's not really me, and I don't think Sonia would ask me anyway.'

'Oh, such a pity,' said Armand in a tone of deep concern as he reached across and squeezed her hand.

'Still the *étrangere*,' said Josephine, smiling and searching into her eyes.

Karen looked down at her glass and said, 'I don't know really. Maybe not as much as you think.'

Josephine looked down at the floor, leaning to one side and reaching down to pull aside the tablecloth as though she had dropped something. Armand appeared not to notice. She straightened up and, glancing over her shoulder, slipped from the chair and down on to her knees next to the table. Karen watched and looked at Armand questioningly as she pulled up the tablecloth and disappeared from view. Armand continued to ignore her but moved his chair back a short way. Karen sipped more champagne then began to say, 'Has she lost –' but got no further. She started, took a deep breath and glanced down wide-eyed as something pushed between her knees and forced apart her legs. Armand smiled at her and reached for her hand.

'No! Wait!' she gasped, as two arms pushed under her thighs and lifted them so that her feet lost contact with the

216

floor. Armand squeezed her right hand but she thrust her left under the table as she felt herself slip forward in the chair and her legs being forced apart even wider. 'No!' she gulped. 'No . . . Josephine! No!'

A mild electric current passed through her as something moise and very warm invaded her exposed sex and found the clitoris as an arrow finds its target. Her eyes darted about her but Armand affected a pose of benign indifference to what was happening. Only the bead curtain separated them from the rest of the people in the busy restaurant and anyone walking casually by could easily see into the alcove where Karen would be facing directly towards them.

But the tongue went about its outrageous mission and explored deeper into her. Her body began to respond to its dancing upon the stage of her sensuality even though her mind kept on saying it must stop. The loose-fitting skirt of her dress was by now pushed up high on her thighs. She could not wriggle her legs free, for they were too close to the underside of the table and pushing against a table leg at each side. The burning was spreading throughout her and becoming unquenchable. She dragged the tablecloth up over her waist to ensure that nobody could see what was happening but this only served to remove the final obstruction from Josephine's voluptuous progress. Lips as well as tongue fastened upon her and she felt herself wet, inflamed and losing control.

At that point the waitress, a girl of not more than twenty, entered, swishing aside the bead curtain and carrying a tray with three small cups of coffee perched upon it.

Karen, her face flushed, looked at her in dismay and attempted to lean forward, putting her elbows on the table top and letting her head drop forward to hide her expression. But Josephine was not going to stop and Karen was beyond self-control, breathing hard and knowing that she was about to come in full view of the waitress.

Armand took the tray and smiled at the girl. '*C'est moi qui sers.*'

Josephine's tongue coursed unrelentingly about the jewel

of her pleasure, arcing blue fire throughout her body until she felt herself dissolving into burning lust.

The waitress turned without another glance and departed, leaving the beads to sway back and forth. Karen, her eyes shut tight and mouth agape, fell back, with elbows pushed hard against the chair, her body convulsing with gasps and a long, subdued moan.

It took some time for her to compose herself. Josephine was sitting back at the table nonchalantly, sipping the remains of her champagne. Armand, doing likewise, took Karen's hand again and squeezed it.

Karen looked ahead through the bead curtains and swallowed hard. 'Look you two . . . it's not . . . you shouldn't have . . .'

'More champagne?' asked Armand, picking up the bottle.

Had she been at the house, Karen would have risen an hour and a half earlier than she did at Josephine's. But she was not at the house and in this room, the window faced west and so did not receive the morning sun. Also, the previous evening had been a long one and she did not recall the time, in the early hours of the morning, when they had returned to the shop and Armand had left them. The busy little onyx clock ticking away on the bedside table with its twinkling pendulum, told her it was almost 9.30. She got up.

When she emerged from the bathroom, there was a tapping on the door. She tightened the belt about her gown and walked across the room. Outside the door stood a smiling Josephine, in a purple and gold kimono, her black hair spread down across her shoulders.

'Good morning,' she greeted, holding out a small brass tray upon which rested two steaming cups of coffee. 'Did you sleep well?'

'Y-yes,' replied Karen with a degree of unease, recalling the events in Le Coq d'Or. 'Come in.'

Josephine entered and placed the tray upon the small circular table, then pulled back a chair to sit down. Karen joined her. They sat and remained silent for a time, drinking their coffees.

'Today,' announced Josephine at last, 'I think you should see a little of Paris. If you like to go on the river, we can take a boat and see many famous sights from there. Then,' she continued, 'we will take lunch on the Left Bank and we can explore the Latin Quarter. It is not too much to walk so you will not be tired.'

'What about the shop?' asked Karen.

'Oh, I will not worry about the shop today,' answered Josephine with a wave of her hand. '*Mademoiselle* Sonia says we must take care of you and you must be happy here with us. You know,' she continued, 'Sonia is very fond of you and wishes always you should be happy.'

'You're all one big family, aren't you?' commented Karen.

'Of course, and she says you are one of us, and I say so too.'

Josephine stood up, leaned over and kissed her. Karen returned her kiss with the warmth in which it was given. Josephine gathered up the cups and said, 'We should get ready to go now.'

Karen looked into her eyes for a moment and perceived an expression which told her that Josephine's thoughts were on things other than their sightseeing tour.

'And I think,' she continued, 'we should be a little glamorous today, yes?'

Some time later, they left the shop arm in arm and breathed the warm, mid-morning air, Josephine wearing a long-sleeved top in thin black ribbed cotton, a high-waisted, slightly flared mini-skirt in purple satin and tightly laced, black leather knee boots with stiletto heels. Karen had opted for a short sleeveless dress in blue-grey stretch velvet which moulded to every curve of her body, and white stiletto heel sandals with criss-crossing ankle straps. Their legs were sheathed in alluring, sheer black nylon with a silken sheen.

Karen felt good as they walked down the busy street and knew that desirous eyes were upon them both. Even so, her mind turned for a moment to the house and she wondered how events were faring after the recent upset.

For some, circumstances were not altogether as they might have wished. Jackie and Rose could not leave their room and go downstairs for fear of being seen. Their breakfast and drinks had been brought up, on Pauline's orders, by Angela, who had tapped on the door and placed the tray down in front of it. In the middle of the morning, Jackie's phone rang and the two were ordered to Pauline's suite, next door.

They stood before her in their housecoats, sullen and unspeaking. Pauline looked at their denuded scalps, smiled and said, 'I don't expect any problems from now on with either of you. You'll find your uniforms laid out in the bathroom. Make sure they are adequately powdered before putting them on. As soon as that is done, you will both be given a wig to wear and you will stay on domestic duties up here until 2.30. Provided everything in my rooms and the others to which have access is done to my satisfaction, you will be allowed to keep the wigs until six o'clock. You will be able to go down to the bar for a late lunch and take some exercise in the gardens. Depending upon how well you both comply, your free time could be extended in due course. Any problems and you will simply face more restrictions.' She leaned back in her chair and regarded them for a moment. 'Do I make myself absolutely clear?' Jackie and Rose nodded then looked down at the floor. Pauline thrust back her chair and stood up with a glint of anger in her eye. 'Your answer, please! I want to hear your answer! And look at me when you speak!'

The girls looked up at her staring eyes, Jackie feeling her lips quiver, Rose biting hers.

'Yes,' they said in unison.

'Good,' stated Pauline. 'And there is one more small thing for you to remember. From this moment on, neither of you will address me as anything other than "Miss Pauline". Is that also understood?'

'Y-yes, Miss Pauline,' answered Jackie blandly.

'Yes, Miss Pauline,' repeated Rose.

'Good! Now go and get changed!' Pauline watched them disappear through the entrance to the bathroom, picked up the telephone and keyed in three numbers. 'Hello James . . . yes, it is me. There may be a few interesting studies for you to get on tape over the next three hours . . . no, up here in some of the first floor rooms . . . no, nothing spectacular, just fetish magazine stuff . . . fine.' She replaced the phone.

In the blue tiled bathroom, Jackie and Rose dressed in silence, each glancing at the other, neither daring to say a word in case the ever alert Pauline should overhear. For a time, they were both quite naked, each seeing the body of the other, smooth and hairless from head to toe.

Each pulled on a pair of sheer, black, open body tights with back seams, the gossamer nylon swishing softly against their skin. Next came the shoes and both sat to put these on, for the black patent sandals, with their long stiletto heels were fixed about their ankles with slim leather straps and small brass buckles. When Jackie and Rose stood, they appeared as tall and elegant mannequins. Each helped the other with the dresses, for the subtly shining black latex needed to be handled with care and the back zips were almost impossible for one person to manage. The dresses, with their short flounced sleeves and low scooped necks, both edged with white lace, were skin-tight and daringly short. Neither was provided with anything to wear beneath. Rose had already conceded to herself that she found the bizarre outfits and the restraints disturbingly erotic though she was sure that neither of them could allow it to repress the anguish and humiliation they felt at the forced removal of their hair and the severe limitations that had been imposed upon them. If Rose had any intention of discussing the matter further with Jackie once they were working alone, that intention was soon to be thwarted.

The two of them walked, arms by their sides, with careful, measured steps towards the waiting Pauline. Both noticed the long, blonde wigs draped over the two-seater, as they also saw the small assemblage of articles lying in wait on Pauline's desk.

'Stand here!' she ordered, indicating an area of carpet near the desk. Jackie saw, as she had expected to see, the steel cuffs. The other two items she regarded with a little more misgiving. 'We'll have these on first,' announced Pauline, stepping around the desk. In a moment, Jackie, followed by Rose, found her wrists enclosed by bright metal bands, joined by their ten centimetres of chain. Their ankles too were fettered, though with a little more chain between the cuffs, to enable them to carry out their tasks. 'Most of these will be covered by the wigs,' muttered Pauline as she moved behind them.

Jackie was first to have the flesh-coloured rubber ball pushed into her mouth. The latex strap, also flesh coloured, contained a steel band which, where it ends were exposed at the back of her head, formed a ratchet lock. The gag tightened with repeated clicks until Pauline was satisfied that it was perfectly secure and effective. Rose glanced sideways with a look of expectancy but dared not speak. Moments later, that facility was denied her too, with a final metallic click. They remained motionless while Pauline crossed over the room and returned with the wigs. The wigs were fitted snugly over their heads and draped over their shoulders, the glossy blonde tresses contrasting starkly with the black sheen of the latex. Hanging down Jackie's and Rose's cheeks as they did, they concealed most of the band which held the ball gags in place, as Pauline had predicted, so that at first glance it might not have been obvious that such restrainst were being worn at all.

Pauline looked into Jackie's eyes. 'You know quite well be now what a thorough job is required. I hope,' she continued, glancing at Rose, 'that this one does too!' She stepped over to the main door and pulled it open. 'Come on, both of you! Get moving!'

The two girls turned and made their way with measured steps until they were in the corridor.

'Don't forget,' came the voice from behind as Jackie reached for the handle on the broom cupboard. 'I'll be checking up from time to time!'

* * *

It was 5.30 when Karen and Josephine returned along the busy street and approached the shop. Their walk was less sprightly now, their tread a little weary, for not only had the day been hot, but both had spent a good deal of time in conversation over lunch and consumed more white wine than was their daytime habit.

'I hope you haven't missed any good customers,' said Karen as Josephine unlocked the door to Sybaris.

'Oh no,' answered Josephine, 'we sell much by the post. Much more than we sell in the shop.' The door closed like a sigh of relief against the people and the traffic outside and Karen at once felt the intimacy of the shop closing in upon her with its sensual odours and its merchandise, all devoted to the pursuit of carnal pleasures. 'Take your shower now if you wish,' offered Josephine, 'and I shall take mine, and then you can choose what you will wear for this evening. Armand will arrive at 8.30 for us.'

Half an hour later, Karen, warm and refreshed, tightened the belt about the blue gown, pushed her feet into fur lined slippers and left the room to find Josephine. Josephine, wearing her kimono and with her long hair let down over her shoulders, was already in the shop. A few of the small spotlights were switched on and the deep-red blinds were closed against the outside world.

'Ah! Here you are!' exclaimed Josephine. 'Look, I have taken out a bottle of champagne; it is very cold. We can enjoy it and we will choose what to wear. We have lots of time!'

Karen eyed the bottle of champagne, glistening with condensation, standing with two glasses upon the counter. She still felt under the influence of the wine from earlier on in the day but Josephine was good fun, the shop was an Aladdin's Cave to be further explored and the prospect of being a little further divorced from reality did not seem a bad idea.

Josephine poured the champagne and handed a fizzing glass to Karen. She kissed her and said, 'I was very naughtly last night, but Armand said I would never dare to do anything like that in public and now he is wrong. But I

223

must not do that again because you were embarrassed.'
Karen, in the face of her matter-of-fact attitude towards
such a blatant act of intimacy was at a loss for a response
and so did not reply. Both drank their first glass of champagne and Josephine poured out a second before speaking.
'I have decided. Tonight I will wear something plain and
red – not too short. We are going, I think, to a Japanese
restaurant.'

Karen wondered what, if any, was the connection, but
decided she would wear something a little more conserva-
tive too. She could not imagine many of the dresses in the
shop complying with that description. As if reading her
mind, Josephine said, 'There is more to choose in the storeroom at the back; things we have in our catalogues.'

'You have catalogues?' said Karen.

'Ah, *oui*, some for ordinary clothes, some for what you
see in here and some for special goods people may not wish
to buy in a shop. When we finish this glass, I will show
you.' When they had each finished their second glass,
Josephine poured again, this time emptying the bottle. 'We
can take these,' she said, and moved, with Karen following, through a pair of louvre doors set in a white archway
at the rear of the shop and set back from the stairs.
Josephine switched on the light.

Although the room was not particularly small, the inside
was cramped, for all around were racks, shelves and more
racks. The aroma of leather and latex was almost consum-
ing, though most of the clothing in front of Karen
appeared to be made of more commonplace materials.
Karen and Josephine, sipping their champagne, plied
through the racks until Josephine said, 'Ah, *bien*! This I
will have!' and pulled free a high-neck, long-sleeved dress
in plain red satin. 'And you, *ma cherie*, have you seen a
dress you would like?'

'Two or three actually,' answered Karen, continuing on
to the end of the room.

She downed the last of the champagne and placed the
empty glass on the seat of a small stool, feeling markedly
unsteady as she bent forward. Her eye at the same time

caught sight of various items hanging on a lower rack. She pushed them aside to take a closer look, seeing the heavy vinyl in several shades and feeling its cool softness before it dawned on her what they were. A hand caressed her cheek and the voice behind her said, 'Ah, *ma cherie*, I do not think you could go out to the restaurant in one of those.'

The hand reached past her and pulled one of the garments free of its hanger with a swish and a metallic tinkle. Karen bent up unsteadily, resting her arm against the edge of a shelf.

'Oh God,' she laughed, 'I didn't realise . . . I mean . . . all those colours and trimmings, it just didn't look like –'

'Never mind,' said Josephine. 'You choose your dress and take it up. I will clear away the glasses.' Karen returned to the dress racks and pulled out a sleeveless dress in deep mauve crêpe nylon, with an ankle length skirt split up to the thigh. 'You like that colour I see,' remarked Josephine as Karen left the storeroom. It was very nearly the same colour as the vinyl straitjacket Josephine still held in her hand.

Karen went back to her room and was zipping up the top of the dress when Josephine knocked and entered.

'You must try it on in my room; there is a bigger mirror.'

Karen turned. 'Yes, OK.' She followed Josephine along the narrow landing.

Josephine's room was more spacious but contained much the same furniture, though there was a larger pine wardrobe with a correspondingly larger mirror on one of its doors. Karen stood before the mirror and turned about slowly, seeing how well the top of the dress fitted her slim body and defined her breasts and waist. The long skirt with its split side revealed most of her thigh as she turned.

'*C'est magnifique!*' declared Josephine.

Karen smiled at her in the mirror then opened her mouth in surprise when she saw what lay on the bed behind Josephine. 'Oh! What's that doing –'

'Just a little joke!' laughed Josephine, picking the garment up. 'It is very chic, no?' Karen turned and regarded it. The vinyl looked soft and supple. It's glossy, deep mauve was edged at the collar and waist with a contrasting deep brown trim and, as Josephine turned it around in her hands, Karen saw that the inside was lined with short black fur. 'These are designed to be fashionable as well as to ... to ... well –' she smiled at Karen '– you know what they do.' Karen stood silent. 'Now,' continued Josephine, 'we must hang this dress up until we are ready to go.'

She helped Karen unzip the dress from the neck to the base of her spine, and then to slip it off down her legs. Karen, wearing only her sheer black bikini briefs, watched as Josephine placed the dress carefully over the back of a pine chair. Too late she realised that she had left the blue gown in her room. Josephine turned to her with a smile and a hint of mischief in her brown eyes. 'Now perhaps we will try this other little thing.'

Karen looked at her wide-eyed as she reached to the bed where 'this other little thing' lay and picked it up.

'Josephine, no!' protested Karen, backing away and covering her naked breasts with her crossed arms. 'You're not putting that on me!'

'Ah! *Mon Dieu*!' responded Josephine with a look of injured reproach. 'Do you think I would hurt you? I am your friend. Just to see for a moment how this fits you is all I want. It is a new line. Never before have I seen it in use.'

Karen relaxed and said, 'For a minute – that's all.'

Josephine smiled. 'But of course.' She walked up to Karen with her eyes fixed on hers. The effects of the drink played no small part in Karen's acquiescence. She swayed a little as she slipped her arms through either end of the internal sleeve and past each other until they were folded inside its snug embrace. The fur lining caressed her as Josephine pulled the garment about her upper body and moved around the back to tighten it. To the rasp of the buckles at its rear, the jacket constricted about her until it fitted as a smooth, sleek membrane from neck to waist. She found the sensation of the fur pressed about her body quite strange. It was comfortable, even comforting, and as she well knew, totally secure. 'Oh, I knew you would look good in this,' said Josephine, moving back to admire Karen's reflection in the mirror. 'It is perfect. It fits you like a glove, I think.' She moved around to face Karen and placed her hands on the sides of her face. 'Armand will not be here for a long time yet. There is no need to hurry.'

'Josephine, you said only a minute! I only agreed –'

The sentence was not finished, for Josephine's lips met hers in sensual warmth. Karen felt a tingling up her spine and a murmuring in the pit of her stomach.

Josephine's lips brushed with fire across her cheek and to her ear.

'I am famous for little white lies,' she breathed. 'Did you know?' Karen did not reply and their lips met again. She was aware of Josephine's intentions, or thought she was, and made no attempt to pull back as the cool fingers slid deftly under the elastic of her briefs and over the hairless skin of her vulva. 'I think now I will seek the little pearl in this shell of love,' breathed Josephine. Karen caught her breath and closed her eyes as the intruding fingers found their goal.

As the currents stirred within her loins, a question lurked at the back of her mind. Why was Josephine so anxious to satisfy her sexually? There were normally two sides to a deal. Where was the other side to this?

But for the time, the question was to sink beneath the waves of pleasure which were lapping over the threshold of her self-control. Josephine tugged the little briefs down and soon had them removed from her. Then as if in answer to Karen's stillborn question, Josephine slipped off her kimono so that she revealed herself naked for the first time. But Karen caught only a momentary glance of her slim body and its dark triangle of pubic hair before they were pressed together and they sucked and nibbled at each other's ears and lips as Josephine's fingers played their dialogue of lust with her. Slowly, they manoeuvred towards the bed until they were almost on it. With one hand, Josephine wrenched away the coloured bedspread and threw it over a nearby chair, revealing what had previously been hidden beneath. As Josephine pushed her down on to the bed, Karen glimpsed the double ended dildo, pink and purposeful against the black bed sheets. Josephine picked it up and Karen rolled on to her back, twisting against the vinyl restraint.

'Look, it's getting awkward,' she gulped. 'I think I'm going to need the bathroom!'

'Oh!' laughed Josephine, leaning over her. 'Me too! It is all that wine we have!'

Josephine stroked again at the source of Karen's pleasure, inflaming her further, despite the growing discomfort elsewhere. Soon, she felt the cool, pink rubber head of the dildo caressing her and, resting on the pillow, closed her eyes, hoping that the fulfilment she so desired would arrive before her other need became an emergency. She did not see Josephine slip the other end of the ample organ into herself but was aware of a slight break in the attention she had been receiving from it. In a moment, it pushed hard against the inflamed lips of Karen's sex and she spread her legs wider to allow it to enter fully. Josephine, reaching above her, began to work it expertly inside them both with a laugh and a sigh of 'Oh la-lah!'

Karen wanted to take it deeper into her and pushed her pelvis against the motion of Josephine's so that each squeezed against the heat of the other's stomach. This act fuelled their voluptuous urges and Josephine began to increase the speed of her rhythm, gasping as she moved. They swayed and lurched upon the bed in carnal abandon, Josephine letting out repeated, high pitch cries with each thrust, Karen gasping in unison. The boiling tide of sensuality overwhelmed them together, Karen moaning loudly, arching her back and twisting from side to side against the confines of the straitjacket, Josephine bucking wildly and crying out as though in desperation, both consumed in a golden frenzy of lust. They each let out a sigh and relaxed. Karen remained with eyes closed as Josephine withdrew the glistening instrument of delight from them and dropped it on to the disarrayed bedding. Karen squirmed about and attempted to get upright, saying, 'For God's sake, undo me before it's too late!'

Josephine fell upon her with a mischievous laugh, pushed an arm under her and kissed her with undiminished ardour. They struggled up on to their knees together until they were face to face, Josephine still laughing and cooing, Karen with an expression of pained anguish.

'Now I think we will come again!' chuckled Josephine, kissing her repeatedly and holding her with her arms around her neck.

Karen, with mouth agape, tried to pull away and jerked her imprisoned arms uselessly against the restraining vinyl. She looked with wide-eyed desperation into Josephine's smiling face.

'I can't hold it, Josephine! I can't any longer! Christ. I'm going to –'

'Me too!' laughed Josephine. 'Me too!'

She held Karen, with their lips sealed together, as the floodgates opened and both released a drenching cascade into the bedsheets, Josephine letting out repeated gasps of pleasure, Karen moaning loudly with exquisite relief as their fountains continued in copious flow.

Josephine began to laugh again and Karen, aware of the sodden bedsheets under her knees, was speechless for long impossible seconds.

'Now I will undo you,' said Josephine, shuffling around behind her.

'Oh God, what an awful mess,' groaned Karen. 'Everything's bloody saturated – ruined!'

'No, no,' laughed Josephine, 'it is OK. All goes into the machine for washing. I will do it when you have your shower, then I will take mine.'

'But the mattress!' exclaimed Karen, pulling her arms free.

'That is dry. It has a plastic sheet.'

'A plastic sheet! You . . . you mean you do this sort of thing . . .?'

Josephine regarded her with amusement. 'I do it just this once. I think it is very naughty but I always like to try this!'

Karen stepped off the bed, avoiding the soaked sheets with her feet. She looked at the bed for a moment then back at the grinning Josephine. 'Another few days of this and I'll be bloody well exhausted. I'll need to get back to work for a rest!'

11

Retribution Falls

It had been Jackie's idea originally that they should have
a picnic lunch one Sunday but, ironically, when they set off
from the house late on that morning, Jackie was the one
who was absent. Everyone knew why she and Rose ventured outside so infrequently during the day and why,
when they appeared for evening meals, it was always together. When they were free to converse with others,
nothing was mentioned about the wigs nor were their prolonged absences alluded to. Cheryl had gone back to
London during the week and Sonia had left for Luxem-
bourg the day after. Valerie had returned from Italy the
previous day and Karen was expected back that afternoon.
Pauline was, of course, in residence but no visitors were
due until Wednesday when a business conference was to be
held at the house with guests from Switzerland and the
United States.

The house itself had taken on an air of pensive quietness
so that, carrying between them an ice box and three plastic
bags, Valerie, Annette, Angela and Kim set out along the
path feeling that life revolved around them for the present.
Beyond the house, two of the girls could be seen in the tennis court and by the pool, Lorna and a companion sat
reading under a sunshade in the still, warm air.

'It's going to be a scorcher today,' remarked Angela as
they left the gravel path and made their way over the
grass.

'It's a pity Mike couldn't come along,' said Valerie.

'I did ask him,' commented Annette. 'He could have carried most of this stuff for us if he had.'

231

'You're cruel,' laughed Angela. 'He probably realised you only wanted to make use of him.'

'More likely,' responded Annette, 'because we're only wearing summer dresses and not going out in black seamed stockings and mega-high-heel shoes.'

'Poor dear's only human,' said Valerie.

'You're right, Val,' added Kim, 'he is human. I can tell.'

'What are you on about?' asked Valerie, eyeing her with deliberate coolness.

'I'm just saying, he's definitely human – look.' They followed the direction of her gaze and saw the subject of their conversation approaching from the right, pushing a wheelbarrow. 'See,' offered Kim, 'only a human could do that!'

'I'm going to give you to Pauline later,' muttered Valerie. 'She needs another victim.'

'Hi!' said Mike. 'You're not off picnicking are you?'

'No,' replied Annette blandly, 'we're catching Concorde.'

'Take no notice,' said Angela as he stopped beside them. 'They're being sarcastic today. It must be the heat.'

Mike looked up into the hazy sky. 'I wouldn't go out too far,' he said, 'I reckon we're in for some rain.'

'It does feel a bit close to me,' observed Annette.

'The barometer was down this morning,' he added. 'How far were you going?'

'Along the valley,' answered Kim. 'About halfway to the old bridge.'

'Hmm,' he said, 'rather you than me.'

'Why couldn't you come with us?' asked Kim.

'Orders,' he replied. 'Jobs to be finished.'

'But Sonia's away,' said Angela.

'I know.' He smiled. 'But the creature from the black lagoon isn't – and anyway, like I said, it's going to rain.'

'Oh well,' said Valerie, 'perhaps we'll not go so far.'

'I could always come out and rescue you in those clinging wet dresses of course,' he said, grinning.

'Randy sod!' commented Annette as he lifted the wheelbarrow and made to leave.

After finding a spot, the girls had been sitting on the

grass for less than three quarters of an hour when Valerie shielded her eyes and looked towards the distant sea. 'I think Mike's right, you know. It's looking dark out there and the breeze is picking up.'

'I don't fancy the idea of running back with this lot,' commented Annette.

'Why don't we go over by the summer house?' suggested Angela. 'If the worst comes to the worst, we can always shelter in there.'

'A good idea,' they all agreed, and after collecting up their things, set off.

They were only a half minute away from the summer house when the first drops of rain began to fall; large heavy drops splashing on the leaves as they passed by the trees.

'Oh Christ!' exclaimed Valerie, looking up at the ominous, darkening sky. 'I think this is it!'

Kim reached the door first, flinging it wide to allow them in as the skies opened and the torrent began. They stood inside the little octagonal building, looking about them as the rain thundered like a cavalry charge upon the wooden roof and the surrounding trees became obscured by the drifting curtains of water.

'Oh well, it's only once in a while,' mused Annette, 'but I'd rather it was on a working day.'

'Let's finish off the goodies,' said Angela, lowering her bag on to the wooden floor.

'What are you up to?' asked Valerie, eyeing Kim.

Kim was reaching up to where the wooden ribs of the roof converged and met at the top of the central iron post. 'Someone's pushed a note in here,' replied Kim. They watched as Kim unfolded the paper. It appeared to have been torn from a spiral bound notebook and was ruled with feint blue lines. It bore the message, 'Teusday – 22.00. F.'

'Somebody can't spell,' observed Angela on reading the black felt-tip message.

'Wonder how long it's been here', said Annette.

'Not all that long,' answered Valerie, 'Mike painted the place only recently.'

233

'I can't think of anyone who's name begins with "F",' said Angela. 'Can any of you?'

'There's no one at the house,' answered Valerie. 'I think this is from someone outside.'

'Who to?' asked Kim. 'It wouldn't be any of us – would it?'

Each regarded the others for a few moments.

'Sonia will throw a bloody fit if any of us have been bringing a bloke in at night!' said Annette.

'Who's it most likely to be?' asked Angela.

'Well,' answered Valerie, 'we all know that, don't we? Except that Pauline won't allow her or Rose out after dinner, so that seems to let Jackie off the hook.'

'Somebody will have to hide in the trees and watch,' said Kim.

'I know,' grinned Annette, 'if James's cameras were switched on around eleven o'clock on Tuesday, we'd see who goes in and out of the house, won't we?'

'Only Sonia can authorise that, I would have thought,' said Angela, 'and she's not back until next weekend.'

'Karen could,' put in Valerie.

'Yes,' said Kim, 'but what if it's her who's . . .'

'No,' responded Angela, 'it's not Karen. I'm sure it isn't.'

'I agree,' added Valerie, 'and even it was, just our knowing would put a stop to it.'

'It's not Mike either,' said Angela. 'If he was meeting someone, he's got his own place to do it.'

'OK,' said Annette, 'Val can talk to Karen when she's back and we'll all know the answer on Wednesday.'

'You'd better put that note back exactly where you found it,' said Valerie to Kim. 'Whoever it's for will be coming to get it during the next day or two!'

James tapped at the door lightly; so lightly that Karen, working at her word processor, did not hear. Eventually he pushed open the door and called her name.

'Oh! James!' she said as the gaunt, white-haired figure approached her across the office. They met halfway and she stared hard at the large brown envelope he held out to her. She took it carefully and looked up at the pale blue eyes, regarding her with their magnified stare through the heavy spectacles.

'I take it,' she began, 'that you managed to . . . that there was someone –'

'It's all on there,' he said softly. 'Everything you could possibly want – all inside this house.'

'Er, I see . . . so it is one of us?'

Karen waited for a while in silence, wondering if he was about to reveal the name.

'You may be in for a shock,' he said gently. 'Sonia must be informed about this as soon as she gets back. You'll see why.'

'Of course,' answered Karen, squeezing his arm. 'And thanks for staying so late last night, James.'

'Well,' he replied, turning towards the door. 'I hope we've done the right thing here. Do keep me informed, won't you?'

The door closed and Karen ran her fingers over the envelope, feeling within it the hard form of the video cassette. She picked up the telephone and keyed in the beauty parlour code.

'Val, it's me . . . yes, I've got it . . . no, he didn't say . . . no, I don't mind – my room at 5.30. I can't wait until after dinner either . . . yes, I'll tell Annette, I think she's, er, entertaining our guests with two of the others at the moment . . . yes, see you later!'

'I'd better pour us all a drink first,' said Karen, pulling the black cassette from its envelope. 'Oh, there's something else in with it.'

A small white envelope fell out on to the coffee table. Across the front of the envelope was written 'STILLS'.

'Oh, he's done print-outs as well,' said Valerie. 'We could look at those now.'

'I'd think I'd rather watch the tape first,' voiced Angela.

'Me too,' added Kim, 'I love the movies.'

With the main light out, they huddled around the television

set as the screen glowed into speckled life. Karen poured each girl a glass of red wine.

'Karen!' hissed Annette. 'Press the bloody button before we all have a seizure!'

The screen cleared to show the first floor corridor from the direction of the main stairs.

'I didn't know he had cameras there,' said Karen. 'I hope they're not on our floor too.'

'Definitely not,' answered Valerie, 'but they're all over the place on the first and he could record anyone going by up the stairs at the front or –'

Her eyes widened and all four leaned forward.

'Bloody hell!' breathed Annette.

Two figures had appeared from the direction of the back stairs; one male, one female. They hurried along the corridor and stopped at the door of the first guest room. Pauline, in black catsuit and high-heel knee boots, unlocked the door and ushered her visitor iniside without hesitation.

'You know who he is, don't you?' asked Karen, looking at the three intent and illuminated faces close to hers.

'I think we all do,' replied Angela. 'It's Inspector Gautier of the *gendarmerie*.'

'F for François,' added Valerie.

'F for frantic,' added Annette, 'because that's what Sonia's going to be. We do have an arrangement with Gautier and some of his pals but I don't think –'

'Look!' cut in Angela.

The scene changed to the inner sanctum of the guest room, the area behind the curtained-off archway. Pauline had changed her attire and had on a short-sleeved, white chiffon, open neck blouse, transparent enough to show her ample breasts clearly through the material, naked but held up and emphasised by a black sling bra which cupped them beneath. Around her neck was a black patent leather choker with a ruby red stone set into a gold cameo at the front. Her arms were encased in shoulder-length black latex gloves, sleek and skin tight, catching the glow of the spotlights which were switched on above. Equally sleek and moulding to her figure was the latex mini-skirt with high waist and glittering metal ring at the front where the zip began. The subtle sheen of gossamer black nylon on her long legs was complemented by the crisp sharpness of the black, patent leather open sandals with their cross-over ankle straps and exaggeratedly high stiletto heels. Karen freeze-framed the picture.

'Doesn't she just look the part,' breathed Annette.

'I'm impressed,' added Valerie. 'She obviously means business!'

Karen said, 'Well, James seems to have taken the time to edit the thing so I guess we'll only have the juicy bits.'

'Yes, he's such a helpful soul,' commented Valerie as Karen released the picture hold.

Inspector Gautier was stocky, bordering on stout, and aged about 40. His suntanned, rounded face was topped by short, curly hair which receded at the front and grew thin on top. The diminishing hair above was more than adequately compensated for by the ample growth about his chest and other places which were clearly visible due to his nakedness. As the scene cut from one angle to another, it became obvious that Gautier's hands were manacled behind his back. As Pauline, braided whip in hand, walked slowly around the standing figure, his arousal was equally apparent. She stopped in front of him, looked him up and down and, appearing to berate him, pointed with the coiled whip at his erection.

'It's a pity we don't have the sound,' remarked Annette.

The scene moved into close up, the compliant Gautier riveted to the spot with his eyes fixed on the strutting dominatrix before him. She appeared to shout louder, then, in a sudden movement, brought the coiled whip smartly down against his rampant penis, causing him to jerk involuntarily and screw up his face in anguish. His erection at once wilted and Pauline began to circle again, moving around him three times before stopping behind. She uncoiled the black whip and, taking half a step backwards, brought it down sharply across his behind. Though his eyes remained closed, his mouth flew open in what must have been a loud cry. The whip fell again, Pauline mouth-ing silent abuse at her victim as her hand was raised for a third and a fourth time. The effects of the whipping were evidently not all detrimental as Gautier once more devel-oped a prominent erection. Pauline moved around to his side to observe it, pointing at it with her left hand. She ap-plied the whip again and again, her mouth all the time dispensing silent vehemence, her face a mask of ridicule. Nevertheless, Gautier did not move and despite the con-tinued application of the whip, or perhaps because of it, maintained his erection firmly, to the apparent disgust of Pauline who wielded the instrument of persecution even harder.

The angle changed once more and the immobile Gautier could be seen from the side.

'Oh God!' exclaimed Karen. 'Just look at those marks on him – he's red raw!'

Annette leaned towards her and whispered, 'Are you all right, dear? Would you like a glass of water?'

'What . . . me . . . I –'

'Of course she's all right!' cut in Valerie.

Angela smiled to herself and Kim winked at Karen.

The scene cut and they saw Gautier down on his knees in front of a gesturing Pauline. She applied the whip several times across his back then stood before him, pointing at the metal ring on her skirt waist and then down at her shoes. Backing away momentarily, she pulled over an upright chair and sat down, crossing and re-crossing her legs pro-vocatively in front of his attentive eyes. After a short time, she thrust a foot out under his nose and at once, Gautier began to kiss and lick her shoe. The scene appeared in close up for ten or fifteen seconds before changing.

Now Pauline was standing, with the inspector still man-acled and on his knees in front of her. This time he was occupied in attempting to pull down the metal ring of her skirt zipper with his teeth, encouraged by the occasional flick of the whip across his inflamed behind.

'He's obviously had plenty of practice,' remarked Valerie as they watched the zip open and the tight latex stretch

238

away at either side. The zip fastener ended over the firm flesh above her sex and Gautier released the ring, Pauline, with her pelvis close to his face, peeled the rubber skirt down slowly to reveal the open body tights and nakedness of her sex with its fine brown hair.

'What did I say about peroxide?' muttererd Annette.

Pauline sat down and spread her legs wide to give Gautier a full view of her most intimate place. He did not move, as though under orders to remain still. The command was given when Pauline tapped the coiled whip against her knee. Without hesitation, he shuffled forward, his erection bouncing up and down in time with the movement of his knees. Pauline shook the whip out as he pushed between her parted thighs, his face showing the look of a little boy having been given free access to a candy stall. He lowered his head and at once his tongue found the goal of his desires. He pressed home eagerly and she spread herself wider still, watching him intently, her left hand gripping the edge of the chair, her right slowly raising the whip. When she judged the time right, down it came across his already streaked behind as if to drive him on to greater effort. It fell repeatedly, with less force than before, though upon much abused and tender flesh. It appeared to work, for Gautier was like a starving man fallen upon an unexpected feast, his tongue darting and playing inside her until she threw down the whip and gripped both sides of the chair, pulling up her legs and wrapping them tightly around the back of his head, almost levering herself up against him as the climax overtook her.

The screen went dead. Nobody spoke for a moment.

'Now I've seen everything!' said Kim at last.

'Sonia can't know about this, can she?' said Valerie, looking from one to the other.

'I wouldn't have thought so,' answered Karen, 'otherwise Gautier wouldn't have been leaving notes, would he?'

'And I don't suppose Pauline's doing it for nothing either,' added Annette.

'Right,' put in Valerie, 'so that means she's freelancing. He's paying her directly if he's paying at all.'

'D'you think we've got her?' asked Angela.

'Too bloody right I do!' replied Valerie. 'And I say we sort her out before Sonia gets back!'

'Let's have a look at those stills,' said Annette.

Karen pulled open the envelope and shook three colour prints out on to the table.

'Yes, all the best bits!' said Valerie, looking at each in turn by the light of the TV screen.

'You know what I think?' said Karen. There was a silence.

'Well?' prompted Annette.

'I think we should put her on trial.'

Valerie smiled and said, 'Now that sounds worth consideration. Let's find ourselves a little corner in the village café and work it out over dinner.'

Pauline sat in her jodhpurs, blouse and knee boots, over a half-finished lunch in the conservatory, a newspaper propped against the table. Annette entered from the direction of the bar, smiled at Lorna and Rachel, then walked casually over to Pauline's table.

'How are we today, dear?' asked Annette, placing a white envelope down in front of her.

Pauline regarded Annette for a moment with expressionless blue eyes then looked down at the envelope. 'What's this for?' she asked coolly.

'Why not take a little peep?' said Annette mischievously. Pauline watched her walk back through the bar room before picking up the envelope. She examined it casually then slowly eased open the flap and extracted the contents, seeing first the note which read, 'There are more pinned up in the beauty parlour if you care to see them.'

She looked at the photograph.

'What's got into her?' remarked Rachel as the figure hustled by, knocking aside a chair and disappearing out into the main corridor.

'Looks like she's seen a ghost!' answered Lorna.

'Somebody's in for it,' added Rachel.

Pauline hurried along the ground floor corridor, reached

the blue door of the beauty parlour and hesitated. With a shaking hand, she reached out to the brass handle and pushed. The door opened. The light was on in the small passage but the inner door was closed and she could hear no sound beyond. She released the outer door and, walking cautiously forward, heard it click shut softly behind her.

She stood before the inner door. Still there was silence.

With an expression of cool determination she gripped the handle, pushed open the door and strode in.

She met the gaze of three figures, seated on stools at the near end of the long wall mirror. Annette, Valerie and Kim each wore shimmering black catsuits in stretch vinyl with wide, red, vinyl belts and red leather high-heel sandals.

'Do come inside, deary,' said Valerie. 'We're all waiting.'

Pauline stepped forward, clutching the white envelope, and waved it before them.

'I'll take the rest of these now!' she demanded in the glare of the spotlights, for the room was brightly lit throughout.

'You'll take nothing!' came the voice from behind her.

She swung around to see Karen, dressed exactly as the others, pushing shut the inner door and leaning back against it with arms folded.

'Oh!' declared Pauline, starting towards her. 'So Miss Prim and Proper's in on it as well, is she?'

'Yes,' answered Karen in a low voice, 'and I assure you I'm not lying my mouth off about having a video tape, because that's what the stills are taken from.'

'Well,' responded Pauline, turning to face the other three, 'hand it all over to me and nothing more will be said. If you don't, you're all finished.' She swung to face Karen again. 'Including this bloody little dyke who I suppose is behind it all!'

Karen, with eyes blazing, stepped quickly forward and at once slapped her hard across the mouth. Pauline lurched back, her face a mask of outrage.

Valerie and Annette caught hold of her before she could respond in kind.

'I don't damn well care what I am!' Karen shouted. 'But

241

at least I'm with people who understand! And I don't have to spit venom or take it out on others to make myself feel important!'

'She speaks for all of us!' added Valerie.

'Yes,' said Annette, 'all of us tarts and floozies, Pauline! One big happy family you don't belong to at all!'

'You're all bloody well mad!' shouted Pauline. 'You'll all be out on your arses before the end of this week and I'll see to it!'

'We'll see!' responded Valerie, nodding to Annette and Kim.

Valerie and Annette seized her arms and Karen, stepping forward, took hold of her blouse and ripped it asunder from neck to waist, exposing the black lace brassiere which held her full and firm breasts in place. Pauline looked at each in horror as the blouse was pulled from her arms, the fastening at the back of the brassiere released and fingers pulled at the belt about her waist.

'Damn you!' she screamed and began to struggle and kick out.

Valerie struck her across the mouth twice in rapid succession.

'You'll do as you're told and keep calm!' declared Valerie. 'Or you'll get this!'

She reached down, picked up the black, braided whip and held it coiled under Pauline's nose. Pauline took a deep breath.

'You ought to recognise that,' said Karen. They continued to hold her as Kim appeared in her field of vision, holding something dark and ominous in her hands. The aroma of latex at once became evident and Pauline, naked above the waist, resumed her struggle. 'If you keep this up,' announced Karen, 'I'm going out to the bar and I'm going to pin the rest of the photographs up where everyone can see them!'

'Yes,' said Annette, 'then they'll all know, Pauline, and you'll never look anyone in the face again.'

'And if Sonia finds out who you've been at it with,' continued Valerie, 'and how he's been getting into the house at night, you'll wish you'd never been born.'

242

'So let's do it the easy way, shall we?' said Karen, stepping back to allow Kim to move forward.

'You mean you won't show those to Sonia?' Pauline glowered as first one arm and then the other was pushed into the embrace of the heavy rubber sleeve until her arms were folded together across her chest.

'We're going to come to an arrangement with you,' said Valerie as they drew the straitjacket over her shoulders and around her upper body.

Kim moved behind Pauline while Valerie and Annette held her still and Karen stood with eyes fixed upon her. The swish of laces being threaded through brass eyelets was all that could be heard for a minute or so as the heavy latex began its inexorable tightening. Valerie joined Kim for the final adjustments as the two edges of the garment were drawn together. Annette held Pauline steady at the front until the tugging ceased and the laces were knotted securely at the back of her waist.

Pauline stood enveloped in the darkly gleaming rubber, her arms enclosed within its secure grasp looking at her captors.

'Well, that wasn't as difficult as it might have been,' remarked Valerie as she and Annette loosened and eased off Pauline's knee boots.

'It's a pity Angie had to go out this afternoon,' said Karen.

'Perhaps it's as well,' replied Annette, 'she's far too forgiving.'

When they began to undo the buttons of her jodhpurs, Pauline once more became animated, pulling back and saying, 'No, I won't have this! Do what you bloody well like with the tapes and the photographs – undo me now! This minute!'

'Too late for that, deary,' replied Valerie, 'but you can leave here any time you like just as you are.'

Pauline looked agape at her, tensing visibly against the restraint, only now beginning to realise how the situation was developing. Kim appeared behind, holding something up in her hand for Valerie to see over Pauline's shoulder.

Valerie glanced at Kim and nodded. That was enough. And though Pauline should have known what was coming, for she had often carried out the action herself, her face showed startled disbelief as the rubber harness was pulled over her head and the black latex plug implanted between her open lips, stifling the shriek of protest which had barely stirred in her throat. Annette and Valerie held her firmly as the web was stretched and buckled like a heavy elastic cage, the soft rubber ring on the inside of the mouth cover sealing her lips against the plug.

She twisted about with a muffled 'Mmmm!' Her eyes darted from Valerie to Karen then to Annette.

'Oooh! If looks could kill!' remarked Valerie.

'Well, they can't,' followed up Annette, 'and neither can her mouth now.'

'Sit on here!' ordered Valerie, propelling their prisoner back towards one of the chairs before the long mirror. The others gathered about her. 'All right,' began Valerie, 'we've all got reasons for wanting you here, some more than others, so you may as well hear mine first. You've manipulated me several times in the past; worst of all when Karen arrived last year and you tricked us both. I know you keep notes on me and I know you try and find out from others what I do when I go out on my own in the evening.'

'And me,' put in Annette. 'You've had tabs on me ever since I arrived and I know how much you've delved into my past when it's none of your bloody business!'

'And Kim,' continued Valerie, 'despite the fact that she is my assistant, you've taken it out on her when Sonia's been away, knowing she would keep quiet because she didn't want any upset, and causing me problems in the bargain!'

Karen moved forward to face her. 'You've had it in for me since the day I arrived. You've resented me for no good reason I can see other than the fact that I'm close to Sonia. Well, it isn't something I've done to annoy you. It isn't anything to do with you and it never was! Everybody else understands and accepts me except you. You've always been resentful because you couldn't take it out on me the way you do on Angela and the others. And you should

244

never had done what you did to Jackie and Rose, let alone to me! It's ironic, isn't it? You're the one who is supposed to keep order here and make sure the rules aren't broken yet you are the worst transgressor of all! Sonia wouldn't have been put out too much by anthing we've done. But you! Bringing in the police inspector by the back door!'

'And how much was he paying you on the side, dear?' asked Annette.

'Yes,' added Valerie, 'you had better have a good answer for that one in a day or two!'

They regarded Pauline for a time. Her expression of defiance was gone. In its place was a countenance of resignation and she no longer looked any of them in the eye.

Kim, who had been absent for a number of minutes, reappeared and announced, 'Everything is ready!'

They pulled Pauline to her feet and walked her along the soft carpet of the parlour. For the first time, she looked about her. At the other end of the range of sinks and the long wall mirror stood the sinister chair with its hanging leather straps and its leg supports springing out at each side. She saw the electric shaver ready and waiting, and the permanent depilator, already plugged into its socket. She knew that there were cameras hidden all around the room as well as behind the mirrors. She knew they would be switched on and waiting, for the chair was well illuminated by spotlights.

They went on past the standing hairdryers, waiting like hooded figures in their corner, then up to the bathroom door.

Pauline stopped suddenly, framed in the doorway of the brightly lit room. There, lit up in gleaming porcelain splendour, stood the low bowl with its padded back rest and array of leather restraints. And above it, bulging with its contents and suspended from its bracket some two metres above the floor, the bright pink rubber bottle, its clear plastic tube coiling downwards to the pink nozzle which lay resting inside the bowl. Three pairs of hands told Pauline exactly where she was headed.

'You're going to be a star at last!' sang Annette.

Valerie turned to Karen, who stood close behind. 'Look deary, I don't suppose this is your scene. Why don't you go and find out what she's done with Jackie and Rose? If you need keys to release them, you'll find them all in her desk – top right-hand drawer.'

'It's important one of us goes,' added Kim. 'They might be in an awkward situation.'

'Yes, all right,' replied Karen.

They half lifted, half pushed the reluctant Pauline on to the waiting bowl and held her while Valerie worked quickly with the straps. Soon, she was spread wide and immobile, watching helplessly as Valerie pulled on a pair of skin-tight, transparent pink latex gloves. Kim's face was set in a faint smile. Annette placed a hand under Pauline's chin and pushed back her head.

'This will be a new experience for you, dear. Who knows, you may even get to like it!'

Karen hurried up the main stairs, meeting nobody on the way. On the first floor corridor she stopped at the door of Jackie's room and tried the handle. The door was unlocked and opened inward quietly. The small lounge was dimly lit from a lamp standing in one corner.

There were sounds, incomprehensible sounds, coming from beyond the bedroom doorway which stood ajar on the other side of the room. Karen hesitated, then moved forward quietly. It was obvious, as she reached the bedroom door, that the room was adequately though not brightly lit. The noises coming from within were not those of conversation but could have been sounds of pain or pleasure. In the background, there was music playing from Jackie's radio.

The door was just wide enough for Karen to look inside.

Rose and Jackie each had their arms folded behind their backs within a tight, sleek cocoon of metallic grey vinyl, enclosing them from neck to waist. Otherwise, they were naked, their heads as free of hair as were their pubic areas. Rose lay back in a small armchair with her legs spread

246

wide apart and hanging over either side. Her eyes were closed and her mouth hung open, moans and gasps passing from it as her head moved rhythmically from side to side.

Jackie knelt before her, head down between her thighs, her lips fastened upon the reddened sex of her partner, her tongue darting about and stoking the flames of Rose's sensuality. Even in secure bondage they were willing and able to feed each other's lust, and perhaps, thought Karen as she watched in silence, because of it.

Rose became further agitated, jerking against the restraint and moaning loudly. After a moment her body heaved repeatedly and she cried out so loudly that Karen moved back from the door. As the cries died down she turned away and tip-toed back across the lounge, thinking that to return in another half hour might be more appropriate.

Epilogue

'I get the impression everyone knows that Pauline is leaving,' said Sonia. Karen, sitting opposite her in the green leather office chair, did not reply but lifted up her coffee cup. 'I don't expect anyone is about to tell me in full what has happened,' she continued, 'but considering what occurred earlier, this seems a not altogether unwelcome development.'

'I don't think anyone will disagree with you on that,' answered Karen.

'No, I imagine they wouldn't.'

'Where is she going?' asked Karen.

'Well, it has worked out rather conveniently from my point of view. She asked if she could go and work in London. She is to change places with Cheryl.'

'You mean Pauline will be running Cheryl's operation?'

'Yes. I have a feeling some of our establishment clients might take quite well to her more aggressive approach. I don't think she's ever been entirely happy here – she's more of a city girl. As for Cheryl, I find her more adaptable. She isn't quite as ready to inflict pain as Pauline but her methods are just as effective in their own way. She is generally liked as well.'

'Sonia,' said Karen, looking down at her empty cup. 'I don't want you to think anyone had been underhand or deceitful. Val, Annette, Kim, Angela and me – we'll all be frank and open with you.'

'No,' answered Sonia, reaching out and holding her hand. 'It's time for me to be honest with you.' Karen looked into her dark eyes and Sonia continued. 'I know what has led up to this, but there is another dimension you know nothing about. People have wondered why I let her get away with so much. Well, you might as well be told. She has knowledge of my business affairs and some of my contacts which would, if disclosed, prove rather embarrassing to me. I have always had to take that into account when dealing with Pauline. So you see, my dear, what you and the others have done has redressed the balance. She would dread the idea of anyone outside seeing those photographs –'

'You know about those!' interrupted Karen.

'Yes, I do,' said Sonia. 'James is a loyal employee and a good friend –'

'Sonia!' cut in Karen. 'That's not fair! We all are. None of the girls would ever –'

'Karen dear! I didn't mean it that way. I don't doubt you at all.' She placed her other hand on Karen's and they drew closer. 'What's happened is of benefit to all of us and I'm glad because you will be happier here now, I hope.'

'Yes,' said Karen, leaning forward until their faces were very close. 'Of course I will.'

They were silent for a time. Sonia lifted her arms and placed her hands upon Karen's cheeks.

'Perhaps you would like to join me this evening for a drink.'

Their lips moved closer, the electric arc of sensuality passing between them even before they touched.

'Yes,' answered Karen softly. 'This evening. I'll be here with you again.'

NEW BOOKS

Coming up from Nexus and Black Lace

House of Intrigue by Yvonne Strickland
January 1996   Price: £4.99   ISBN: 0 352 33055 4
Karen cannot resist the lure of the depravity which surrounds Sonia's house but the ruthless disciplinarian Pauline has a score to settle with Karen, and an endless array of instruments with which to settle it. The effect of the punishment only serves to increase Sonia's disobedience, and the naughtiness intensifies.

Slave-Mistress of Vixania by Morgana Baron
January 1996   Price: £4.99   ISBN: 0 352 33054 6
Queen Vixia, now free to indulge her sadistic desires, focuses upon the virginal Lady Laylanda as her next victim. But Laylanda's resistance only increases the humiliating punishments inflicted on her. On the other hand, Brod must gain power by arousing as many orgasms in women as possible, and he has no problems finding willing candidates.

Bound to Obey by Amanda Ware
February 1996   Price: £4.99   ISBN: 0 352 33058 9
As the newly appointed servant, Caroline has more discipline in store for her than she expected, and a far less substantial uniform. As she learns more about her kinky employers she discovers she can be witness to even more deviant antics than she ever imagined possible.

The Island of Maldona by Yolanda Celbridge
February 1996   Price £4.99   ISBN: 0 352 33028 7
The women of Maldona are an ancient order devoted to physical perfection, Sapphic love and strict discipline. Their leader, Jana, and her slaves set out on a quest and recreate their passionate rituals of punishment and reward on a deserted island. But the goddess Aphrodite threatens their harmony and the rivalry comes to a head in their naked physical battle.

White Rose Ensnared by Juliet Hastings
January 1996   Price £4.99   ISBN: 0 352 33052 X
Against the backdrop of the Wars of the Roses, another battle is
taking place. Rosamund, now recently widowed, finds herself at
the mercy of Sir Ralph Aycliffe, a powerful knight who will stop
at nothing to humiliate her and enslave her beyond redemption.
Only a young squire will risk everything and battle over her body.

A Sense of Entitlement by Cheryl Mildenhall
January 1996   Price £4.99   ISBN: 0 352 33053 8
Angelique inherits a half share in a Buckinghamshire hotel, but
this is a hotel with a difference. In it the clients behave strangely
and the labyrinth of hidden passages reveals a secret room where
the weirdest and wildest erotic fantasies can be acted out.

The Mistress by Vivienne LaFay
February 1996   Price £4.99   ISBN: 0 352 33057 0
Emma Longmore is very much enjoying her role as mistress to
Daniel Forbes, and her salacious means of passing the time in-
volves initiating the daughters of local dignitaries in the arts of
lovemaking. But when it seems Daniel is tiring of this lifestyle and
diverting attention onto the household staff, Emma becomes
drawn to the flaunted libidos of Paris.

Aria Appassionata by Juliet Hastings
February 1996   Price £4.99   ISBN: 0 352 33056 2
The inexperienced Tess is about to play one of opera's most no-
torious roles, Carmen, in a production that promises to be as
raunchy and explicit as it is intelligent. Tony Varguez takes on
the task of educating her, setting the stage for unbridled erotic
exploration and painstaking research. But like the character she
is to play, Tess soon finds herself torn between two equally be-
guiling lovers.